A Climate for Death

© Copyright 2020 R.T. Lund

ISBN 978-1-64663-193-3

This is a work of fiction. The characters are both actual and fictitious. With the exception of verified historical events and persons, all incidents, descriptions, dialogue and opinions expressed are the products of the author's imagination and are not to be construed as real.

REVIEW COPY: This is an advanced printing subject to corrections and revisions.

Published by

◤ köehlerbooks™

3705 Shore Drive
Virginia Beach, VA 23455
800−435−4811
www.koehlerbooks.com

A CLIMATE FOR DEATH

R.T. LUND

VIRGINIA BEACH
CAPE CHARLES

Canada
Eagle MT.
Grand Port
Ely
Grand Marais
Tofte
Beaver Bay
Shovel Point
Minnesota
Split Rock Lighthouse
Two Harbors
Duluth
Wisconsin
Twin Cities

"A sad tale's best for winter . . ."
William Shakespeare

This book is for Christina.

CHAPTER 1

February 1, 2020
Near Two Harbors, Minnesota

COREY DALBEC WAS LOST in a hibernating sleep under the warmth of a flannel comforter. Married to Rachel for less than a month and starting a new job, he wasn't prepared for what was to come. He didn't stir when flashes of red and white light shot through crooked blinds covering the bedroom window and danced on the headboard. The screeching, metallic cry that followed jarred him awake.

"Oh my God, what was that!" Rachel screamed as she bolted upright and then squeezed Corey's left bicep with both hands. Clad only in plaid boxers, Corey sprang out of bed and strode across a cold hardwood floor to the double-pane window facing the lake. Rachel followed. He yanked the frayed cord so hard the wooden blinds detached from their mounting bracket and landed on his feet.

"Jesus fucking Christ, that hurts!" he cried while Rachel peered through the frosty second-story window.

Ignoring her husband's injury, she cupped his elbow with her right hand and pointed outside with her left.

"Corey, that looks like part of a plane. It must have hit the lighthouse. We're lucky it didn't crash into our bedroom!"

About a foot taller than his wife, Corey could see the wing of a prop plane in the snow a few feet from the lighthouse. Several competing thoughts rattled his brain. Intelligent and resilient, Rachel looked up at Corey bewildered, hoping for a response from the lighthouse caretaker. With forced composure, he looked in her eyes while gently laying his outsize hands on her narrow shoulders. He observed something he'd never seen before on her soft, pretty features—a mixture of fear and terror.

"We'll be fine," he said. "I'll get dressed and look for survivors. You call 911 and tell them to bring all the fire and rescue personnel they've got."

"All right, but please, please be careful. It's nasty out there, and you're not trained for this."

• • • • • • • • • • • • • • • •

Corey Dalbec thought he was prepared for winter on the North Shore. After all, he'd grown up in White Bear Lake, a tony suburb of St Paul. But he'd spent the last twelve of his thirty-one years in California, earning a degree in recreation and tourism management at San Diego State and working as a park ranger for San Joaquin County northeast of San Francisco, where the temperature rarely dipped below freezing.

He dressed in his warmest winter outfit: blue jeans, a cotton sweatshirt, fur-lined parka, cowhide work gloves and Sorel winter boots. While not horrible, this attire was no match for an air temperature of twenty-five below and a northeast wind off the lake gusting over thirty miles per hour. Fortunately, adrenaline would help him ignore how cold he was.

Stuffing his cellphone and high-powered flashlight in his jeans and grabbing a first-aid kit and portable fire extinguisher from the storage pantry in the kitchen, Dalbec unlocked the back storm door and carefully descended icy wooden steps that led to a unique backyard. Forty-five degrees and about a hundred feet to his left stood Split Rock Lighthouse.

Security flood lamps illuminating the lighthouse helped him assess the scene, though his view was hampered by blowing snow that pelted his eyes and stung his cheeks and forehead like hundreds of biting flies. It appeared the black metal cap atop the lighthouse, the section encasing a thousand-watt beacon with a twenty-two-mile reach, was undamaged. Dalbec wondered if the crash would have occurred had the powerful lantern, decommissioned in 1969, still been lit. He would examine the rest of the brick structure later. He trudged through waist-deep snow to reach the smoldering fuselage, which must have bounced and slid over fifty yards in the ice and snow before ramming into a grouping of spruce, birch and aspen shielding Split Rock's visitor center.

Expecting a fiery wreckage and burn victims, he encountered something very different. The square fuselage was mostly intact, including the plane's port wing with a bent propeller and most of its tail. The notable exception was the horizontal stabilizer. It must have been sheared off by the lighthouse and likely plummeted over a hundred feet to the frozen lake below. A steady trail of smoke or steam rose from the plane's midsection, but it seemed benign compared to the ferocity of the winter storm.

Dalbec dug the flashlight out of his jeans and scanned the outside of the plane. A name had been painted in red on its tail, *CP Eagle*, just to the right of the make and model painted in gray—*King Air 250*. He recalled that CopperPlus—*CP*—was the name of a controversial company that was trying to mine copper and nickel in northern Minnesota. He didn't know much about small aircraft, or any aircraft for that matter, but he'd been a passenger in a Cessna four-seater, and this plane was much bigger. Except for some lights on the instrument panel in the cockpit, the inside of the plane was dark. Missing most of its starboard wing, the King Air was tilted to the right, which made its windows more accessible. He shined the light in one of the oval windows and was shocked by what he didn't see. There were six or seven tan leather seats and a few tray tables, along with broken plates, beer bottles, napkins, plastic cups and food scattered about, but no passengers. Not only were there no passengers in the cabin, but the cabin door on the port side was open.

"What the fuck?" Dalbec muttered while slogging through the snow to the other side of the plane. All that was left of the plane door were severed steel cables and an opening about five feet by three feet. He tossed the flashlight, fire extinguisher and first aid kit into the cabin and then hoisted himself through the opening. Though Dalbec was impressed with the King Air's fancy interior, at six feet, five inches tall, he wasn't impressed with its five-foot ceiling. Retrieving the flashlight, he inspected the cabin in a crouched position and observed a briefcase on a collapsed tray table and a couple of open laptop computers on the floor. Among the food and drink items strewn about was a broken wine bottle and what appeared to be red wine splattered everywhere. Upon closer inspection, Dalbec was certain the substance was redder and thicker than wine; it was blood.

Moving toward the cockpit, he did a double-take at the sight of a human form. He focused the LED beam on the back of a man he assumed was the pilot. He was wearing a white shirt and some type of headset, and was slumped forward on his knees between the two pilot seats, his forehead resting on the instrument panel. Dalbec removed his right glove and applied pressure with his index and middle fingers on the man's neck over the carotid artery. He couldn't feel a pulse, but he saw blood on the man's collar and down the front of his shirt. Then he shuddered at the sight of a bullet hole just below his left temple.

Hearing sirens from multiple emergency vehicles approaching on Lighthouse Road, Dalbec exited the plane to meet with law enforcement and rescue personnel. As he turned to leave the cockpit, his head down to avoid hitting the ceiling, he saw a handgun on the floor under the pilot's seat. His training as a park ranger kept him from picking it up.

He jumped down from the open door and back into the blizzard, shaking his head and wondering, *What the hell happened on that plane?*

CHAPTER 2

A WELL-STOCKED WET BAR separated the sitting area from two spacious bedrooms in Suite 2102 at the Four Seasons Inner Harbor. Jenny Pierce had just made herself a bourbon and water on the rocks when she heard the electronic lock release. She turned to see her boss, best friend and imaginary lover enter the room.

"Where were you? I was so worried when you didn't come back and didn't answer my calls and texts."

"I'm so sorry, Jenny. Dinner with Alex went later than I thought, and I didn't have a chance to contact you."

"It's two in the morning, Liz. I ordered a bottle of your favorite chardonnay and some cheesecake four hours ago. I was sure you'd be back by ten."

"Hey, I said I was sorry. This guy is the one, Jenny. I'm telling you, he's the one."

Not sure what that meant, Jenny got defensive. "And that means you have to fuck him?"

"If that's what it takes, you bet it does." Thinking that was harsher than necessary, Liz softened her approach. "I really do appreciate the wine and dessert, Jen. How about I open a bottle and we talk about this on the couch."

"Okay," said Jenny, not wanting to fight and hungry for information.

Elizabeth Vandenburg was a firebrand, passionate about protecting planet Earth, especially the future of the northern wilderness she loved. Her mother, Joy McFadden Vandenburg, was the great-granddaughter of an ambitious Scottish lumberman who'd made millions in the late nineteenth century harvesting forests of balsam fir, white pine and birch in Canada and northern Minnesota to make every kind of paper product imaginable. Different from more recognizable family dynasties like the Hills, Congdons and McMillans, the McFaddens kept vast wealth hidden from the scrutiny of the media and, in turn, the public. The family wisely exited all forest-related businesses in the mid-twentieth century, but not before amassing a fortune.

Like Liz, her mother was an only child, whose doting grandfather established a trust that paid her over a million dollars a year. Sadly, Joy and her parents died within three years of each other in the late 1990s. A seemingly healthy forty-five-year-old freelance travel writer, Joy complained of a crushing headache after an early-morning ski on the groomed Nordic trails of Lester Park. Liz was a sophomore at Macalester College in St. Paul when her father called with shocking news—her mother had suffered a fatal brain aneurysm.

On her thirty-fifth birthday, Liz had inherited the corpus of the McFadden family fortune, over $500 million. And while she loved and admired her mother, Liz adored and worshipped her father.

Bill Vandenberg grew up in Ely, Minnesota. Neither of his parents went to college; his dad was a fishing guide on Lake Vermillion, and his mother cleaned rooms for two local motels. Bill studied forestry and history at Bemidji State and worked part time as a law clerk for Southern Minnesota Legal Assistance while attending night law school in St. Paul. Two weeks after he was admitted to the bar in the late 1970s, he opened a solo law practice in a small office above a family-owned drugstore in the Lakeside neighborhood of East Duluth. Over forty years later, the law office of William Vandenberg had a new sign, some updated office furniture, and a couple of iMacs, but otherwise hadn't changed much. A lawyer, a paralegal, and an office manager devoted half their practice as counsel for nonprofit environmental groups like the local chapters of the Nature Conservatory, the Sierra Club, and Honor the Earth, and the other half to individual litigants who couldn't afford to pay them.

Bill Vandenberg and Joy McFadden had met in 1976 at a campaign rally for Jimmy Carter and Minnesota favorite son Walter Mondale in Leif Ericson Park. Joy had just graduated from a small liberal arts college in Wisconsin with degrees in American studies and English and was working as an assistant textbook editor for the short-lived Duluth office of Harcourt Brace Jovanovich. Nearly six feet tall, with dark-ginger hair down to her shoulders and a Pepsodent smile, Joy towered over the lean, blue-eyed man who usually tied his long, prematurely white hair in a ponytail. Bill was quick with a self-deprecating story and a smile and slow to anger. They made love in Bill's apartment the first night they met. During twenty-two years together, the intensity of their physical attraction was only exceeded by the sincerity of their mutual respect.

They were a perfect match in other ways as well. Bill's law office would have collapsed without Joy's money, and Joy's lingering guilt over how her family made its fortune might have consumed her without the altruistic outlet that Bill's firm provided.

Liz knew exactly what to do with the family wealth. She quit her job as communications director for the Minnesota Environmental Partnership and worked with her dad to establish the Vandenberg Family Foundation, a 501(c)(3) dedicated to promoting, protecting and preserving clean air, clean water and clean energy everywhere.

With initial funding of $200 million, the Foundation distributed over twenty-five million to environmental causes in its first three years. At the same time, Liz became one of the most generous contributors to environmentally friendly Democrat and Green Party candidates in the Upper Midwest.

Liz hired Jenny Pierce as the foundation's first executive director in 2018. Jenny grew up in Thief River Falls in northwestern Minnesota, the youngest of eight children. Her only sister, Mary, was the oldest, with six mayhem-creating, hockey-playing boys in between. Her father, Bernie, a devout Catholic who toiled on an assembly line for forty years building snowmobiles, coached baseball in the summer, hockey in the winter and football in the fall.

Jenny and her mother, Carolyn, a homemaker and part-time nurse's assistant at a care facility, were best friends until Jenny came home for Christmas after her first semester at St. Catherine's and confided in her best friend that she was a lesbian. Carolyn's mother grew up on the White Earth Indian Reservation in rural Mahnomen County, and Carolyn was a proud member of the White Earth Band of Ojibwe. The Ojibwe were not very accepting of "two-spirited" people. Carolyn was also a practicing Catholic, so Jenny was disappointed but not surprised when her mother wiped away tears and walked away, saying she wasn't ready to discuss the issue. Eventually, she softened her stance, but still didn't want to talk about it.

Her mother was pleased, however, that Jenny embraced her Native American heritage. She majored in American Indian studies and wrote her senior honors paper on Winona LaDuke, the celebrated Ojibwe activist and environmentalist. Jenny sent LaDuke a copy of her paper and in return received an offer to interview for a job at Honor the Earth, an environmental advocacy group.

Jenny was living in Detroit Lakes and writing grant proposals from Honor the Earth's modest office in tiny Callaway, Minnesota, when she met Liz Vandenberg in 2017 at one of the last organized protests over the Dakota Access Pipeline. The controversial site was near the Standing Rock Indian Reservation on the banks of the Missouri River in central North Dakota. Liz was immediately impressed with Jenny's enthusiasm and intelligence. She gave her a newly minted Vandenburg Foundation business card and urged her to submit a resume.

Jenny was smitten with Liz, who was dynamic, beautiful and unattached, the latter by choice. Jenny had just broken up with a yoga instructor from Alexandria, but not by choice. She was exceptionally bright, well read in politics and literature, and a great conversationalist. A tall, striking woman with broad, expressive facial features, long, sinewy limbs and ample breasts, Jenny kept her dark-brown hair ultra-short to facilitate an active lifestyle filled with tennis, softball and hockey. She had no trouble attracting partners, but her possessive, controlling nature sometimes pushed them away. And, being one of eight children, she had an unhealthy need to please and impress those she loved.

Liz was aware of this when she hired twenty-seven-year-old Jenny to lead her foundation. She sensed early on that the ambitious, energetic executive director was attracted to her and selfishly did nothing to deter it, believing that an unattainable relationship might motivate Jenny to produce superlative results for the foundation.

• • • • • • • • • • • • • • • •

Wearing black jeans and a white silk blouse, Liz slipped off her penny loafers and folded her legs beneath her on the white leather couch. She'd uncorked the bottle of chardonnay and poured herself a full glass, even though she'd already overindulged with Alex. Jenny handed her a dessert plate with the smaller of the two slices of cheesecake before plopping down next to Liz. Struggling to stay awake, she refused to let the Sandman keep her from learning more about the first person Liz had pursued romantically since Jenny had known her.

"You just met this Alex yesterday, right?" Jenny asked.

"I've known who he was for a few years," said Liz. "He's lived in Duluth since 2013 but was named CEO of Generosity Energy in 2016. I'm skeptical of most alternative and renewable energy companies. As you know, most are just in it to make a quick buck using tax breaks and subsidies."

"And the Drummond administration has been trying to get rid of them," Jenny interrupted, trying to impress her boss.

"Don't get me wrong, Jen, we desperately need the good operators. And let's not get started on that asshole Drummond; it's too late and I've had too much to drink. Anyway, I've been impressed with what Alex has done at Generosity so far. They started as a solar play, mostly for utilities and municipalities, and now Alex has invested in wind farm operations. He's even acquired a turbine manufacturing company. Yesterday, he participated on a panel on accelerating renewable energy adoption. He claims the US has the technology and ability to replace all fossil fuels with renewables, including minimal nuclear, by 2030 without hurting, and in fact improving, our economy."

"What's in it for him?" Jenny asked. "A million-dollar salary and stock options when the company goes public?"

"Far from it. Generosity was originally incorporated by a California billionaire who grew up in Duluth. He was one of the original guys behind the private Impeach Drummond movement. It's a Minnesota public benefit corporation; one hundred percent of its voting stock is owned by his foundation, and all profits are either reinvested in renewable energy R & D or distributed to environmental causes. Alex is paid two hundred thousand a year, and no bonus, no incentives, no stock options."

"So why is this guy so committed to the cause?" Jenny probed.

"I still don't know that much about him. He doesn't like talking about his past, although tonight after dinner he opened up a bit. He grew up in the Twin Cities and, you'll like this, I guess he was a decent hockey player. He played for Brown University, where he majored in physics. His dream back then was to become an astronaut. A few weeks before graduation he got a call from his mom; his dad was killed in Iraq. That changed everything."

"His dad was in the military?" Jenny asked.

"No. He was a mercenary for KBR. He was driving to a jobsite and got ambushed by Sunni rebels who were trying to commandeer an oil field. He died from his wounds in a German hospital. He and Alex were very tight even though he'd been divorced from Alex's mom for years. Alex went straight from graduation to some Army officer school in Georgia. That was in 2004. He left the service six years later. Said his experiences in Iraq and Afghanistan made him see clearly that our military and foreign policy involvement in Islamic countries, especially Afghanistan, has been a total failure. That's not a fair description of what he said, but I'm too tired to explain it better."

"How'd he end up working for Generosity?"

"His dad's involvement in the oil business got him killed. But that's not all. He lost a couple of close friends when a bomb exploded in Afghanistan. He can barely talk about it, even today. The bottom line is he got a master's degree in environmental policy at the U of M and is as committed as anyone I've met to saving the planet. Plus, he's super articulate and charismatic."

Jenny looked away to hide her scowl. In the two years she'd known Liz, she'd never shown any romantic interest in men. Quickly turning back, she asked, "So what exactly did you mean when you said he's the one?"

"He's the one to win back the eighth congressional seat for our side and to make a difference in Washington. He can help us stop CopperPlus, Polymet, Line 3, and a host of other bad shit."

Relieved, Jenny paused for a couple minutes and then said, "Maybe so. I thought you meant you were in love with him."

Liz didn't respond. She was snoring softly.

CHAPTER 3

February 1, 2020
Isle Royale National Park

IF KELLY ANN KINNEAR had a weakness as a park ranger, it might have been her fondness for frequent and diverse sexual encounters, mostly with older men. A varsity lacrosse player in high school, she spent her free time in college and graduate school smoking pot, drinking vodka and club soda, and engaging a select group of administration and faculty members in intellectual and other forms of intercourse. She'd had standards, however—never sleeping with one of her teachers and never dating married men. After graduating with honors, she landed her dream job with the Park Service.

At twenty-nine, Kinnear wasn't interested in a long-term, monogamous relationship. Like Chaucer's Wife of Bath, she had a small but curiously attractive gap between her two front teeth and an insatiable appetite for adventure. Her cotton twill uniform, including a variety of embroidered brown ranger caps, didn't do much to enhance her natural beauty, but her playful grin, tight blonde curls, and twinkling wintergreen eyes overcame the uniform's limitations in most cases. And in most cases, the uniform was on the floor when it mattered.

"Carl, hey, Carl, wake up," Kinnear whispered as she shook the well-muscled shoulder of the naked man who was taking up more than his share of a double bed and two wool blankets.

"What the fuck, Kelly!" Carl protested, rotating to face her. "It's only five o'clock, and I didn't get to sleep till at least two."

"Sorry for keeping you up, Doc," she teased while gently stroking his tired cock. "Seriously, Carl, I haven't slept at all. I know I heard Pack II howling out near Sargent Lake. It sounded like they were going berserk over a kill, but that shouldn't happen at two in the morning during a blizzard. Something very weird is going on."

"So, what do you want to do, go out there now, in this weather? With the wind chill, it must be forty below."

Carl Gruber was a large-animal veterinarian from Hayward, Wisconsin. A divorced, forty-something father of two adult children, Gruber embraced the outdoors and was actively involved with the National Parks of Lake Superior Foundation and Friends of Isle Royale. Though he'd hiked and camped on the island many times, this was his first winter experience at the park, and the study team was excited to have a veterinarian. He'd known Kinnear for less than a week.

"C'mon," Kinnear prodded as she sprang out of bed and slipped into a layer of thermal underwear. "I'll make a pot of coffee and get our backpacks ready with some energy snacks and water. You grab the gaiters and put fresh batteries in a couple of headlamps; it'll probably be dark until we get there."

Even though Gruber thought snowshoeing in these conditions was foolhardy, Kinnear's enthusiasm was infectious enough, and her current spell over him strong enough, that he gave up trying to resist.

"At least I'll be able to use my new altimeter," he said. "How much new snow fell overnight?"

"The forecast was for six to eight, but it's so damn cold I'd be surprised if we got more than three. Meet me in the kitchen when you're ready."

• • • • • • • • • • • • • • •

Kinnear had joined the NPS in 2013 after earning her master's in forest science and wildlife ecology at the University of Wisconsin. A biology major in college, Kinnear grew up on a busy farm near Clarion, Iowa, and fell in love with animals of all shapes and species while birthing, nurturing and feeding hogs and calves with her dad. Big John and Annie Kinnear beamed when their only child was runner-up to Betty-Lou Baisel in the 2006 Pork Queen contest at the Wright County Fair. Kelly Ann was relieved she hadn't won.

From April through November, Kinnear led hiking expeditions and presented lectures on a variety of topics from grizzly bear mating to sustainable camping at Denali National Park and Preserve in Alaska. But her favorite time of year was the dead of winter—real winter—when she'd proven on multiple occasions to be a valued member of the annual wolf study in Isle Royale National Park. It was her dream job in a perilous and remote environment.

Isle Royale attracted about as many tourists in a year as the Grand Canyon in a day. Designated a national park in 1940, the remote island was only accessible by ferry, private watercraft or seaplane. It sat at the northwest corner of Lake Superior and was often referred to as the *wolf's eye*, with the twin ports of Duluth and Superior serving as the nostrils and the Keweenah Peninsula of Upper Michigan the gaping jaws.

With no paved roads but hundreds of miles of trails, over forty inland lakes, and thirty-some campgrounds, the park lured hikers and nature lovers. Minnesotans often wondered why the island was part of Michigan, since its western edge sat but twenty miles from Grand Portage, Minnesota, whereas Copper Harbor, the closest Michigan shore, was over fifty miles away. Sometimes ownership had more to do with opportunity than proximity. Michigan became a state in 1836 and claimed Isle Royale as part of its Upper Peninsula over a decade before Minnesota became part of the Union.

The island was settled by copper miners, lumberjacks, fishermen and Ojibwe, but they'd all been gone for close to a hundred years. The park closed from November through mid-April every year, mostly because of extreme weather conditions and a lack of affordable, reliable winter transportation to and from the island. The dense boreal forest rising above the coldest, cleanest, clearest and deepest of the Great Lakes hosted a limited number of wildlife species, species able to reach the island in the first place and then able to survive. There were no deer, bear, raccoons, or wildcats. There were red fox, beavers, otters, snowshoe hares and squirrels as well as eagles, loons, woodpeckers and ducks. And, of course, moose and wolves.

Moose settled onto Isle Royale around 1900 and thrived without a natural predator. News of their abundance must have reached Ontario because a handful of Canadian wolves made the daring trek to the island across an ice bridge in the late 1940s.

In 1958 researchers began studying the relationship between the island's wolves and moose, initiating the longest-running predator-prey study in the world. During the mid-twentieth century, wolves were driven to extinction in many parts of North America where they'd previously thrived. The study was intended to dispel longstanding myths about wolves—that they kill for sport, decimate livestock and threaten humans.

The population of both species fluctuated considerably over the past sixty years. The wolf population ranged from the mid-teens to high twenties, whereas the moose numbered between 700 and 1,500. Until recently. After several years of inbreeding and disease, the wolf population plummeted to only two animals. A string of warmer winters didn't help, as ice bridges between the island and mainland didn't form, stopping the wolves' winter migration to Isle Royale.

In 2018 the National Park Service approved a plan to restore the predator-prey balance by relocating twenty to thirty wolves from Minnesota, Wisconsin, and Canada to the island. Ironically, the 2018–2019 winter was unusually cold, enabling one of four wolves the Park Service brought to Isle Royale in the fall of 2018 to escape her new home and return to Canada.

The 2020 wolf-moose study began January 21, the day after the MLK Jr. holiday, and was scheduled to continue until mid-March. Led by biologists and research scientists from Michigan Tech, with the assistance of park rangers and committed volunteers, the teams would observe and monitor the fifteen wolves that had been introduced to the island in early 2018 and fit thirty to forty moose out of a population that had swelled to two thousand with radio tracking collars.

Study participants bunked in rustic cabins near Rock Harbor on the southeastern edge of the island and, weather permitting, would traverse the lakes and trails on skis and snowshoes and often spend a night or two camping out in tents. They also made observations and performed animal counts from low-flying aircraft rented from a float plane operator out of Two Harbors. January of 2019 was one of the ten coldest months on the island over the past hundred years. January 2020 turned out to be the coldest.

• • • • • • • • • • • • • • •

By the time Gruber and Kinnear reached Greenstone Ridge, the sun ached to be visible on the eastern horizon. If its heat were ever needed, it was on this Saturday morning. As the duo clomped through the forest, the nascent dawn sky cleared, but the wind had shifted to the northwest, plummeting temperatures to depths neither had ever experienced. Kinnear, who was struggling with numbing toes and fingers, had reservations about leaving the protection of the dense woods to venture onto one of the largest inland lakes on the island, completely exposed to the open air.

Wearing ski goggles and Ergodyne fleece masks, they barely spoke to minimize moisture that would freeze on their faces almost instantaneously. Kinnear noticed her partner was limping slightly; she worried about frostbite and muscle cramps.

"How are you doing, Carl?" she asked. Even though Sargent Lake was now in sight, she was about to suggest that they turn back and return to the relative comfort of their rustic cabin when Gruber removed his mask and goggles and stuffed them in a pocket.

"Did you bring binoculars?" he asked with urgency.

She unzipped a side pocket in her backpack and removed one of her prized possessions, a pair of Steiner BluHorizon binoculars. She handed them to Gruber.

"What is it? What do you see, Carl?"

"Look over at the far east side of the lake," he said, adjusting the focus on the binoculars. "Oh my God, Kelly! Oh my God!"

"It looks like a dead animal of some kind surrounded by blood," said Kinnear, squinting to focus a few hundred yards down a steep hill and across the snow-covered lake.

"It's a dead animal all right," said a shaken Gruber, handing the binoculars to Kinnear. "A bloody, dead human animal."

Suddenly, the wind died down, and Gruber and Kinnear covered the distance from their perch on the north side of Greenstone Ridge to the east side of the lake so fast they both started to sweat inside their thermals.

"This makes no sense," said Gruber. "Wolves don't attack humans, especially up here where the moose are so plentiful."

"Just hold on a minute, Carl. Let's not make any conclusions about what happened until we take a closer look. I'm more surprised that someone would be out here in this weather. Where did they come from? I'm sure we're the only fools from the study out here this early."

Gruber was right. Wolves generally wanted nothing to do with humans. Even though a seventy-pound wolf could track, chase, capture and kill an animal nearly ten times its size—a cow moose on Isle Royale, for example—reports of wolves attacking humans were rare. Once a pack of wolves killed an elk or a moose, they often ate everything but the largest bones and some hair. To avoid starvation, wolves had been known to eat muscles, tendons, hides and marrow that humans wouldn't touch.

As they approached the bloody carcass, Kinnear unzipped the other side pocket in her pack and removed a Bendex-King two-way radio. Then she threw up.

"Jesus fuck, Carl, what happened here?!"

Though she was trained as a biologist and had worked with cadavers in college, Kinnear had never seen anything like this. What remained of the body of a large man was on his back, having made a messy crater in the deep snow that covered the lake, as if he'd fallen from the sky. There were bits of bone, brain and ligaments strewn around the body, mixed in with a lot of blood. His torso was just a red-and-black cavity, most of the meat and tissue having been consumed or ripped apart, and his face was nothing but a bony stump with some gray and black hair in its place. His lower legs were chewed up but still intact, blue Nike running shoes dangling from sockless ankle bones.

"Are you gonna be okay?" asked Gruber, placing a gloved hand on Kinnear's back. "I don't get it. Wolves don't attack humans."

"Where did this guy come from?" asked Kinnear. "He's wearing plaid golf shorts, and I can see pieces of a green polo shirt but no winter gear, no gloves, no jacket, nothing. He couldn't survive fifteen minutes out here."

"Let's see if we can find an ID on this poor bastard," said Gruber, removing his right glove and bending over to check the man's pockets.

"Try not to move him," cautioned Kinnear, as Carl pulled a fat brown wallet out of the back pocket of the plaid shorts. "This might be a crime scene."

"A crime scene? Are we going to arrest a pack of wolves?"

"What if he was already dead, lying here in the snow, maybe bleeding, when the pack came upon him? That's what I heard last night. They were partying. A free meal. No chase; no kill. Manna from heaven."

"I suppose that's possible, because nothing about this makes sense."

"Either way, I need to contact base camp and let them know. They'll call the winter headquarters in Houghton and send a helicopter out here. NPS might even get investigative services involved. They'll probably want us to stay with the body until they get here to keep the ravens and other scavengers from picking it apart even more. Looks like snow has partially covered the wolf tracks, but you can still see them heading north across the lake. They could return for a morning snack as well."

Searching the brown cowhide wallet, Gruber found several hundred dollars in cash, a Minnesota driver's license, and an ID card issued by CopperPlus Metals, LLC. "Marcus Howard Dittrich of North Oaks, Minnesota. Says he's the President and Chief Manager of CopperPlus. What are you doing on Isle Royale, Marcus?"

"I suppose we'll find out soon enough," said Kinnear. "Why don't you scout around for some decent firewood while I contact Ranger Pearson. Our hand warmers aren't going to be effective much longer, and it's still colder than a well-diggers ass in Alaska."

"Yes, ma'am."

CHAPTER 4

February 1, 2020
Lake County, Minnesota

NOT MUCH SURPRISED SHERIFF MacDonald, not even a call in the middle of the night from his deputy, Ryan Hokanson, reporting that a small plane had crashed into Split Rock Lighthouse. While trying to steer his Ford Explorer down icy Highway 61 on the way to Split Rock, he received a second call, this time from his detective reporting a deadly snowmobile accident.

"Gonna be a long day," the sheriff mumbled.

A former Air Force officer and Secret Service agent, native son Sam MacDonald had been sheriff of Lake County for about four years. During that tenure, he'd dealt with the county's first murder in over a decade. A woman's fatal plunge into the Gooseberry River triggered at least three other murders, including the unholy demise of an archbishop, the execution of a scheming investment banker, and the revenge killing of a two-timing lawyer.

"Gail, what are you doing up in the middle of the night? I thought you and Brian were taking the boys to the Cities for a basketball tournament."

"Ryan didn't tell you, did he?" said Gail Klewacki, the sheriff's chief and only detective.

"Tell me what? About the plane crash at Split Rock? I'm heading over there now with every volunteer firefighter we could get out of bed. I didn't want to ruin your weekend. The FAA and NTSB have already been notified."

"I appreciate the thoughtfulness, Mac, but I won't be going to the boys' tournament. I'm sitting in the lobby of Overlook Lodge near your neighborhood."

"What are you doing there? Checking out the competition?"

"Ryan and Deputy Mattson responded to a call about a snowmobile accident on the Red Dot Trail near where it intersects with the North Shore Trail. There was a fatality with some unusual circumstances, so they called me. We knew you and Hallie had just returned from Mexico, so we didn't want to bother you. Then the plane crashed at Split Rock. I hope you had a wonderful honeymoon, boss."

"A fatality? Who's out on a snowmobile in this weather?"

"A bunch of diehards, apparently. Brian said we're booked this weekend, and it's not skiers and snowboarders, it's the snowmobilers." Klewacki's husband's family owned Cascade Mountain Lodge north of Tofte, the largest winter recreation operation in the state. "Anyway, a sixty-five-year-old lawyer from Duluth rammed into an old basswood tree going about sixty miles an hour. Have you heard the name Vandenberg?"

"Sure. The heir to the McFadden fortune. Elizabeth, right? And her dad, Bill, represents every tree-hugger in the state."

"That's right, Mac. He's a lawyer, and he's very dead. The twenty-year-old coed sitting behind him is in serious condition down at St. Mark's."

"Oh, Jesus. So that's the unusual circumstance."

"Not even half of it."

"Listen, I just turned into the parking lot at the visitor center. I'll call you back as soon as I can."

• • • • • • • • • • • • • • •

At Split Rock, fire engines and pumpers from Silver Bay, Two Harbors, and Duluth lit up the parking lot and snow-covered grounds near the lighthouse. The visitor center appeared dark and vulnerable, with the nose of a plane lurking eight to ten feet from its back entrance. Wearing a Lake County Sheriff fleece-lined jacket with brown leather gloves and a wool ski hat, MacDonald observed about a dozen firefighters and EMTs in the vicinity of the downed plane, which looked remarkably intact. Though visibility was poor because of swirling snow, he didn't see flames or even smoke.

Wading through drifting snow past the wounded King Air, he saw lights on in the brick caretaker's house and several people, including a couple of his deputies, standing in the kitchen. MacDonald hadn't met the new caretaker and his wife. He wondered what effect this incident would have on their appetite for life on the North Shore. Before he reached the top step of the porch, a tall younger man wearing a sweatshirt and jeans opened the back door.

"Hello, Sheriff, I'm Corey Dalbec, the new caretaker. We've been expecting you."

MacDonald removed his cap as he shook Dalbec's hand and acknowledged the rest of the crew in the small but recently updated kitchen. He knew everyone else: Hokanson and Mattson from his office, Ed Holmgren, Lake County's Emergency Management Director, and Bob Grytdahl, the fire chief from Duluth. He assumed the voice coming from the dining room was Dalbec's wife talking to someone on her cell phone.

"Now that you're here, Mac, Willie and I will take off," said Hokanson. "Ed and Bob can brief you on what they know so far; there's really nothing more for us to do here. We took some photos of the plane and the lighthouse from the outside, and the body, the cabin and the cockpit on the inside, but we'll leave any evidence gathering to the feds."

"Okay," said MacDonald. "I just talked to Gail, so I'm also aware of the snowmobile accident. We'll get together and review everything tomorrow. You guys be careful on the back roads in this weather."

"It's a strange deal," said Holmgren, handing MacDonald a steaming Styrofoam cup of weak coffee. "We've been in contact with the FAA, the NTSB, the FBI and Sky Harbor Airport in Phoenix. The plane took off from Holman field in St. Paul at about seven last night. It's owned by the company that's trying to mine copper up near Ely. Anyway, the pilot, the guy who's slumped over in the cockpit out there with a bullet in his head, filed a flight plan with Sky Harbor, indicating he had three passengers and would arrive in Phoenix about midnight. Instead, the plane shears a wing on the lighthouse and bounces to a stop at about the right arrival time but eighteen hundred miles off course."

"And without the three passengers," added Dalbec.

"Do we know their identities?" asked MacDonald.

"Not yet," Holmgren replied, "but based on some files and correspondence scattered about the plane, we think one of them was the CEO of CopperPlus. It looks like they were headed to Phoenix to attend the Waste Management Open, a professional golf tournament. Duluth FBI says a couple of special agents from the Minneapolis field office are on their way up here. They're thinking multiple crimes may have occurred over US airspace, and that the pilot ejected the passengers at some point. They could be anywhere in a five or six state area, or maybe even in Canada. The flight data recorder should give us some answers, but if you ask me, the pilot murdered the three passengers and then killed himself."

MacDonald looked out at the plane through a frost-covered window over the sink. "Well, Ed, let's not jump to conclusions," he said. "I assume the NTSB will also be here sometime today. Though they're probably coming from Denver, and Colorado is getting pummeled with heavy snow."

Bob Grytdahl had been with the Duluth Fire Department for over twenty-five years and suffered from early-stage emphysema from a lifetime of inhaling fumes. He was struggling to keep his eyes open, and MacDonald noticed.

"Hey, Bob, let's sit down at the kitchen table. Then you can tell me why we have half the fire-fighting equipment in northern Minnesota up here but no fire."

Grydahl sat, graciously accepting a mug of hot cocoa from Rachel, and rubbed his eyes with the heels of his hands. "We'll know more when the experts arrive, but the main reason there's virtually no fire is there's no fuel. The plane's tanks are bone dry. I'm guessing either the pilot dumped some gas or misjudged the amount he needed. It's likely this plane glided into the lighthouse. With a gale-force tailwind from the northeast, who knows how long it floated on fumes."

"And we're leaving the pilot where he is until the FBI arrives?" MacDonald knew the answer already.

"We've got a transport van on-site to take the body to the morgue at St. Mark's for an autopsy," said Holmgren. "The coroner has already been here and left, and the FBI should be here by five thirty."

"I'd like to take a closer look at the plane myself," said MacDonald. "I had some experience in crash-site investigations with the Air Force. I'll wait for the FBI. Some daylight and sunshine should help."

Not wanting to get in the way, Dalbec stood in the back of the kitchen and stared out at the lighthouse from the back storm door. MacDonald could sense the young man was shell-shocked. He walked over and placed a hand on his shoulder.

"Corey, how are you liking your first month on the job?" he asked. "I knew your predecessor, Bill Doty, very well. He and Marlys were a great team at this place since the early eighties."

"So, I've heard," Corey said. "Mr. Doty told me there'd been a few assaults and vandalism on the grounds over the years, but nothing prepares you for this. But we're good, Sheriff. Rachel and I love it here; I don't think this incident will change that."

• • • • • • • • • • • • • • • •

By 4:30, Holmgren and Grytdahl had gone home to get some sleep, and Corey and Rachel were resting in their bedroom before the onslaught of federal officials and media invaded their domain. Only a handful of emergency personnel remained on-site, setting up a makeshift accident-information desk in the lobby of the visitor center.

Suffering from caffeine overload, Sheriff MacDonald fetched a pair of winter boots and a high-powered LED flashlight from the Explorer and walked the perimeter of the crash site. He shined his GearLight S2000 on the lake side of the lighthouse. There were cracked and broken bricks on the upper third of the blond brick base, but the damage appeared minor, not structural. A small section of the starboard wing that had been sheared off by the lighthouse was caught on barbed wire at the top of an eight-foot chain-link fence that ran about a hundred feet along the rear of the property. Its primary purpose was to keep visitors from getting too close to the precipice that overlooked a rocky outcropping and ultimately Lake Superior 150 feet below. As he walked along the fence and looked out over the lake, he couldn't help but consider the irony of what had just occurred. A structure built over a hundred years ago to prevent ore carriers from crashing into the rocky shore in bad weather was itself the victim of a crash.

With the advent of sophisticated radar and GPS, the once life-saving beacon emanating from Split Rock Lighthouse had become largely ceremonial until it was taken out of service in the late 1960s, when the majestic lighthouse and environs had been transformed into a popular historic site and park managed by the Minnesota Historical Society. MacDonald wondered if in the future the lighthouse would have historical significance for something sinister. He also wondered if Dalbec had considered how long he'd have to close the site to visitors in the aftermath of the crash. He'd bring that up in a private conversation.

CHAPTER 5

February 1, 2020
Rock Harbor Lodge
Isle Royale National Park

PARK RANGER KELLY KINNEAR'S speculation about the corpse on Sargent Lake had been well founded. She, along with four other NPS rangers, an FBI special agent, and the Houghton and Keweenaw County sheriffs, were seated at a walnut-veneer conference table in the dining room of the Rock Harbor Lodge. They were listening to park superintendent Nick Sharockman describe events that would necessitate a major recovery mission.

"This morning at approximately zero six hundred hours the FAA and FBI issued a joint bulletin to all Homeland Security contacts that a small, private aircraft, specifically a King Air 250i, had crashed at the Split Rock Lighthouse historic site northeast of Duluth near Beaver Bay, Minnesota. The exact cause of the crash is under investigation by the NTSB, but we know that the aircraft was owned by CopperPlus Metals, LLC, the Minnesota subsidiary of a South American mining concern. Here's where the story gets interesting or weird, depending on your perspective.

"The plane took off from Holman field in St. Paul shortly after nineteen hundred hours yesterday and was scheduled to arrive in Phoenix, Arizona, shortly after midnight with a pilot and three passengers. Instead, the plane lost part of its wing when it hit the base of Split Rock Lighthouse and crashed at the site between midnight and zero one hundred hours this morning with its landing gear up and a dead pilot with a bullet wound in his head. There were no passengers on the plane, but there was evidence that they'd been there—dishes, beer bottles, wrappers, food, magazines, newspapers, duffel bags, jackets, luggage, golf clubs and blood, blood everywhere.

"At about zero seven hundred this morning Ranger Kinnear called in the discovery of a severely mauled and mutilated human body on Sargent Lake. The deceased male has been preliminarily identified as Marcus Dittrich, the CEO of CopperPlus, a resident of North Oaks, Minnesota, and one of the listed passengers on the King Air flight to Phoenix. Our office compared the information we received about Mr. Dittrich with the report of the plane crash and notified the FAA, FBI and the Midwest office of our own investigative services branch. Because at this point it appears that any crimes that occurred were perpetrated on the plane and not in this park or in a particular state, the FBI Criminal Division is exercising primary jurisdiction over the investigation and will be coordinating the recovery of the other two passengers with our office and the Keweenaw and Houghton County Sheriff's Offices in Michigan.

"The Minneapolis field office of the FBI arranged for a medical transport helicopter from St. Mark's Regional Trauma Center in Duluth to pick up Mr. Dittrich's body on Sargent Lake earlier today and transport it to the medical examiner's office in Duluth. We have worked with the FBI, Two Harbors Aviation and Marquette Airways to arrange for three ski planes to search the island for the other two passengers. Each plane will have two spotters and a pilot. The helicopter will return this afternoon if we locate other bodies. The Coast Guard may also be supplying drones and drone operators to assist in the search. You've all been introduced to Special Agent Lance Whitney from the FBI's Minneapolis field office. Agent Whitney will be directing this effort from the ground.

"The two men we are searching for are David Paul Hesse, the president and CEO of Northern Black Gold, a shale oil exploration company headquartered in Minneapolis, and Lawrence R. Severinson, the chairman and CEO of Universal Health Care Corporation, also out of the Twin Cities. Their immediate families are aware they are missing under unusual and likely dire circumstances. Mr. Severinson is sixty-four years old. He has graying blond hair and is five nine and one-seventy pounds. Mr. Hesse is forty-four, bald, stands six two, and weighs one-ninety. I have recent photographs of both men. Obviously, the weather is more favorable this afternoon than it's been over the past few days. But even though it's clear and sunny, it's still ten below zero with a nasty northwest wind, so everyone needs to take appropriate precautions."

Dale DeHut, the wizened old Houghton County sheriff, raised his hand before speaking. "All three of these guys are pretty damn important fellows, especially Severinson; even I've heard of him. I assume you only want one source of information for the media."

"That's right, Sheriff," said Whitney, pointing to himself from his seat near the head of the conference table. "That would be me."

Whitney was a thirty-five-year-old, self-described bodybuilder whose ego was more inflated than his biceps. He was working the potential kidnapping and homicide investigation with Special Agent Michelle Hinton, a twenty-year veteran of the FBI's criminal investigations division. They had driven from Minneapolis to Split Rock, about 190 miles, in three hours in blizzard conditions. Hinton had been at the wheel; she was in charge of the investigation.

"What an asshole," DeHut whispered to Buzz Hackbarth, his best friend and the longtime sheriff of Keweenaw County in the Upper Peninsula, where there were more people than moose, but just barely.

CHAPTER 6

February 1, 2020
Lake County Courthouse
Two Harbors, Minnesota

"YOU SHOULDN'T HAVE COME here," said Thomassoni, looking up at the tall, dark-haired man who'd opened the door to his office without knocking and strode in like he owned the place.

"Why not?" Ricky Holden replied, pulling out one of two tired-looking upholstered chairs that faced the county attorney's bulky oak desk and sitting his privileged fat ass down with a thud. Looking right through Thomassoni, he said, "Our companies do plenty of business with the county, and I deal with lawyers from your office two or three times a month. I've got nothing to hide, Greg. Do you?"

Greg Thomassoni was starting his fourth decade as the Lake County attorney. He was a capable prosecutor, a mediocre administrator, and a well-connected political operative. In fact, no one had run against him in the past three elections. He was also a notorious skirt-chaser; the younger the woman filling the skirt, the better.

"It's just a little soon after the incident last night, that's all. I wasn't out there, way too cold for me, and never made it to the lodge at all. I assume you were there at some point."

"Really, Greg? Have you ever been on a snowmobile in your life? I closed down the bar at three. Most of the members and guests left after hearing about the accident, but some diehards who'd reserved rooms at the lodge, especially people from the Cities, hung out at the bar. Plus, Klewacki, that nosy bitch from the sheriff's office, asked me a ton of questions about the club. But I didn't tell her shit. That's why I didn't call or text you last night. And that's why I'm here this afternoon. Tell me, Greg, what was that rich old hippie doing out there last night? I didn't even know he was in the club."

"He's not," said Thomassoni. "Bill Vandenberg and I were in the same law school class at Mitchell. He grew up in Ely, so we had a lot in common. We actually shared an apartment in Ramsey Hill during our last two years in school. He's a brilliant guy, absentminded at times, but brilliant. He lost his wife about twenty years ago and never remarried. Though I rarely ran into him professionally, we met for lunch or happy hour a few times a year. We had dinner at Larsmont about a week ago. He seemed really depressed. Said his daughter was wrapped up in her foundation and trying to save the world. The only time he sees her is when he's handling legal work for one of her causes."

"Yeah," Ricky interrupted. "She's a fuckin' nutcase. Her green deal, or whatever she calls it, creates a lot of unnecessary roadblocks for real estate development up here. Her ancestors who made millions off the land probably want to snatch their money back from the grave."

Thomassoni cleared his throat audibly and shifted his ample haunches on the worn, high-backed leather chair he'd had forever. "Anyway, Bill told me he'd been diagnosed with multiple myeloma. Said he was lonely and wanted to do something more exciting than snowshoeing before starting another round of blood transfusions and chemo. I suggested one of our club activities and asked Johnny Steele at Beaver Bay Power Sports to outfit him with a nice Polaris Indy rider. I didn't think he'd come up on the coldest weekend of the year."

"Had he driven a sled before?" asked Ricky.

"He had, but not for twenty years. When I heard he'd made a reservation at Overlook for Friday night, I called Megan Holappa and told her I'd pay her five hundred bucks to make sure old Bill enjoyed himself. Now he's dead and she's in serious condition with a broken pelvis, a dislocated shoulder, and an inquisitive friend of the family who's also a PI lawyer."

"I don't think Megan's going to make trouble for us. We've helped finance her college education, and besides, Greg, if you were a private shyster, would you come after a nonprofit snowmobile club or a millionaire lawyer's estate?"

"I'm not worried about a personal injury lawsuit; I'm concerned about somebody snooping around and publicizing certain aspects of an organization that's had a positive impact on this community, not to mention on the profitability of your resort."

"Not to mention tripling the size of your pathetic bank account, Counselor," chided Ricky.

"I'm going to pretend you didn't say that. Anyway, let me know right away if Klewacki or anyone else from MacDonald's office asks any more questions about the club. The plane crash at Split Rock should keep them busy until this whole thing blows over."

Ricky stood and pulled a pair of deerskin gloves from the left pocket of his blaze-orange ski jacket. "I'm getting hungry, Counselor. I don't know why you'd ever worry about MacDonald, especially now that he's married to my ex-wife, who's also your employee, let's not forget."

"All the more reason to worry, Ricky. All the more reason to worry."

• • • • • • • • • • • • • • • •

MacDonald's office in the Lake County Sheriff's Department was located across the street from Thomassoni's on the first floor of the Law Enforcement Center. The sheriff left Split Rock at 8:30, after spending quality time with two FBI agents who assisted with processing one of the strangest crime scenes he'd ever seen. He picked up a fresh cup of French roast, a breakfast burrito, and a bag of scones at the Cedar Coffee Company on his way to the office. As usual, there was only a skeleton crew in the building on a Saturday morning. Before he could enjoy the first bite of the unwrapped burrito, MacDonald fell into a deep sleep slumped at his desk, his head down on his thick forearms.

Klewacki, Hokanen and Mattson found their boss in this position when they gathered at the entrance to his office at 10:15. Klewacki had tried his cell at 9:30 to schedule a meeting to discuss the snowmobile accident. She hadn't slept a wink and was missing out on a weekend trip to the Twin Cities to watch her teenage sons play basketball against the best 14U team in the state. In other words, she didn't hesitate to wake up a man who'd spent most of the last week in the Riviera Maya.

She relocated MacDonald's coffee cup before unleashing her outside voice.

"Hey, Mac, did you get my message about meeting this morning?"

MacDonald had been watching his six-year-old daughter practice a dance routine at the Little Gym in Falls Church, Virginia. His first wife and their daughter had been decapitated when her car slid under a braking semi-trailer during a snowstorm in McLean in January of 2013. The sheriff dreamed about them at least once a week, even seven years later. The sound of Klewacki's voice quickly brought him back to a different reality.

"Sorry, guys," he said, wiping his eyes with his fingers and surveying the threesome. "I must have dozed off. Willie, why don't you grab a chair from the side table and we can talk right here. I guess I'll wait and heat up this burrito for lunch, but I do have some fresh cinnamon scones if anyone's hungry."

He handed the bag to Hokanen and glanced at his iPhone for any missed calls or messages.

"Oh, and before I forget, Gail, there's going to be a briefing of law enforcement and the NTSB and FAA at the Split Rock visitors center at three this afternoon, followed by a news conference. I'll bring you up to speed after our meeting here, but I'd like you to be there with Holmgren and me."

"Sure, Mac, my weekend has recently opened up."

As usual, MacDonald ignored the sarcasm. "So, tell me about the snowmobile crash. What do we know so far?"

"I brought Ryan and Willie along," Klewacki explained, "because they were the first to arrive on the scene, even before the EMTs."

Hokanen and Mattson made a good patrol team. Both in their early thirties with degrees in criminal justice from St. Cloud State and a half dozen years of experience; both from northern Minnesota, and both earnest and polite but a lot smarter than their shyness might indicate at first. Hokanen was short and wiry with a blond buzz-cut and a face like Eddie Haskell's from *Leave it to Beaver*. He activated his iPad to show MacDonald some photos from the accident.

"We got the call from our 911 dispatch at about ten thirty last night. Given the weather, twenty below and blizzard conditions, I did a double-take, but I guess with today's equipment and technology, you can trail ride with these machines in any weather. It was difficult to get our squad anywhere close to the scene. We parked near a trail entrance to Red Dot west of Lax Lake, and I got a ride to the site from one of the other club members while Willie waited for the paramedics, who brought their own sled with a stretcher. Mr. Vandenberg was clearly dead at the scene. His neck was broken and he was unresponsive and had no pulse. Ms. Holappa's injuries were serious but not life-threatening. She was unconscious, so it was easy for the EMTs to get her stabilized for transport. The Polaris machine they were riding was mangled beyond recognition, signifying a high-speed crash. We took a couple of statements on-site, but with the weather conditions everyone wanted to get back to Overlook where the group ride had originated."

"Any observations or opinions on what caused the accident?" asked MacDonald.

"The guy driving the machine directly behind Vandenberg said his sled left the trail and accelerated right into the tree. He speculated that the driver had a medical event, a stroke or heart attack that caused him to lose control of the rig. I think he might be right about that. The autopsy should confirm whether that's the case. As of an hour ago, Ms. Holappa's condition has been upgraded from serious to fair, but no one from our office has interviewed her."

Klewacki washed down a bite of scone with some water. She'd eaten nothing since Friday at noon and knew this sugar fix wouldn't last long.

"The girl's family is from Duluth. A lawyer that does some work for Brian told me the family already hired one of the more infamous PI lawyers from the Cities to investigate the accident. I'll get in to interview Megan as soon as her doctors say it's okay, but I wanted to talk to you about a different issue."

"What you were referring to last night, right?" MacDonald knew this wouldn't be good.

"Six of the eight middle-aged male drivers out on the trail last night had female passengers with them. Every one of these women was a student at UMD, and each one was a member of the same sorority. I tried to interview two of these young ladies last night at Overlook. I thought it was highly unusual for so many of them to be up the North Shore on a stormy winter weekend, especially riding shotgun with men old enough to be their fathers, or even grandfathers in some cases. And why would they be spending the night at an expensive resort when the Bulldog hockey team had a big game in Duluth and winter activities on campus are in full swing?"

"I don't know," said MacDonald, "but I have a feeling you're going to tell me."

"At first, no one would talk to me. They referred me to Megan Holappa, claiming she'd arranged everything; that it was just a girls' weekend, a time to get away from the pressures of school and horny college boys. I knew that was total bullshit, so I stuck around for a few hours. I focused on a girl who sat by herself near the fireplace in the lobby, drinking Diet Coke and looking anxious. Her name was Katy. I asked if she was alright; if I could do anything to help her. She said she just wanted to go home. She said all the girls wanted to go back to Duluth after Megan got hurt, but they had to wait for the van. Mr. Holden had arranged for a minibus to pick up a dozen girls from campus on Friday afternoon and drive them to Overlook.

"She said most of the other girls had done this before, but it was her first weekend. The resort would give them free food and drinks, and Mr. Holden paid each of them two hundred in cash. In return, they would hang out with members of the Sawtooth Mountain Snowmobile Club—at parties in one of the banquet rooms at Overlook, on the back of their sleds, and then, if something more developed, they were on their own. The only stipulation was they had to meet in the lobby at noon on Sunday to be transported back to school."

"I get it," said MacDonald. "While it sounds like an amateur escort service, without more evidence, we really don't have much. What is wrong with Ricky Holden?"

"I was about to ask you the same question," said Klewacki, knowing she was broaching a sensitive area, "but I'll do some more digging. A few of the other girls saw me questioning Katy and came to her rescue before I could ask her about any actual sex for pay. I found Ricky in the bar with a few of the hardcore members. I tried to question him about paying college students to entertain resort guests, but, after telling me there was nothing wrong with 'priming the pump' to create a party atmosphere, he would only answer my questions with 'no comment' until he got irritated and told me to fuck off."

"I assume you'll be talking to this Megan when her condition improves. She might be more inclined to talk after her lawyer tells her family how deep the Vandenberg and Holden pockets are. By the way, have we notified Bill Vandenberg's family?"

"I drove down to Duluth early this morning to tell his daughter," said Hokanen. "She's his only immediate family. She lives in a very cool house on Park Point. It's got huge solar panels and a wall of windows facing Lake Superior. No one was home, though, and she wasn't answering the cell phone number I got from her office at the Vandenberg Foundation."

"Nice try, Ryan. I'm concerned that someone who was there last night will leak his identity to the media," said MacDonald. "I'll call the foundation office today, and if Elizabeth isn't there, I'll tell her top officer or assistant to relay the terrible news and have her call me. If that doesn't work, I'll have to leave a message on her cell."

"I have no idea where she is today," said Klewacki, "but I'm in a book club that meets in Duluth once a month, and Patty Grady, one of Elizabeth's best friends, is in it. She's a big shot in the Minnesota Green Party and a member of Hermantown's city council. She's also kind of a name dropper. According to Patty, Elizabeth is living with the guy who runs that alternative energy company near the Duluth airport. I think it's called *Generosity*. She claims he's going to announce a run for Congress any day now, and Vandenberg's going to bankroll it."

"Wow," said MacDonald. "If that's true, this news is going to hit her extra hard. For her sake, I hope her boyfriend is the real deal. Bill Vandenberg was an authentic, progressive hero. A man who stood up for those without a big bankroll and for preserving what's great about northern Minnesota. Elizabeth won't be the only person who'll miss him.

"Gail, you may need some help to follow up on this snowmobile club fiasco, especially the money trail. Let me know if you want someone from the BCA or St. Louis County to assist. The Duluth police may start sniffing around as well."

"Will do," Klewacki said, as Hokanen and Mattson got up in unison to leave.

"You two get some rest. I have a feeling the next few weeks will be very busy for all of us."

CHAPTER 7

LAWRENCE ROGER SEVERINSON WAS one of the most powerful men in the world. He was CEO and chairman of Universal Healthcare Group, the holding company for not only the largest health insurer in the world in terms of revenue and lives covered, but also for a highly sophisticated medical technology company and one of the most extensive networks of specialty clinics and physician practices in the States, the fastest-growing segment of the conglomerate's empire.

Severinson and his brain trust at UHG were worried about the proliferating attacks against health insurers by politicians, especially those promoting Medicare for All. The status quo, Obamacare lite with lax enforcement of the law's anti-insurer provisions by the Drummond administration, was good for business. While millions struggled to gain access to affordable health care, a few were getting filthy rich in its administration and distribution. Wanting to preserve this environment, Severinson had become a behind-the-scenes supporter and friend of President Drummond, even though privately he thought Drummond was a dangerous, delusional fool.

But, as Severinson well knew, if Democrats took control of the US

Senate and White House and passed legislation mandating Medicare for All or offering a Medicare option for anyone who wanted it, UHG could be royally screwed, unless of course they could become the sole administrator of all Medicare plans on behalf of the federal government, which was why UHG was buying up medical practices all over the country. Ultimately, the health care community would become dependent on UHG's medical technology. That's why he and UHG's political action committee hedged their bets by contributing huge sums to candidates in both parties.

Severinson's luck ran out on February 1, 2020. Late in the day, a park ranger in a low-flying Cessna spotted the body of a man wearing dark-colored shorts and a pink polo shirt, facedown, suspended thirty feet above the ground between two seventy-foot spruce trees whose snow-covered branches were under duress, supporting the weight of a human load. The body was discovered on a densely forested hillside northwest of Siskiwit Lake near the center of Isle Royale. When they finally retrieved Larry Severinson's frozen carcass on Groundhog Day, they found a bullet hole in the back of his head.

CHAPTER 8

February 1, 2020

Visitor Center, Split Rock Lighthouse State Park

THE CRIMINAL INVESTIGATIVE DIVISION, or CID to insiders, was the largest division within the FBI. Among its many responsibilities was investigating violent crimes. Although the CID was headed by an assistant director, the AD was rarely personally involved in an investigation, unless the case involved friends of POTUS.

"I just got off the phone with Assistant Director Epstein," said Special Agent Michelle Hinton, addressing twenty-some law enforcement and government agency personnel seated around a long, makeshift conference table in the lobby of the one-story, brick-and-stone visitor center at Split Rock Lighthouse State Park. "He intended to be with us this afternoon, but a snowstorm on the East Coast has closed both Reagan and Dulles, so he may be participating by phone or Skype later in the meeting."

Hinton knew that was a lie. Epstein was relieved he didn't have to travel to frigid, Bumfuck, Minnesota, and he wouldn't be calling. He knew that his best agent was presiding over a high-profile and highly unusual case, and he believed that any close friend of President Drummond probably deserved whatever befell him. He also believed that Special Agent Lance Whitney was an obsequious, self-promoting blowhard who could be more trouble than he was worth, but that was Hinton's problem.

In her twenty-third year with CID, Hinton was tough, smart, intuitive, and sometimes even funny. She liked her job too much to get married and or even serious about a relationship. Besides, the men who pursued her were either too weak or too self-absorbed.

She'd been one of the first African American women to graduate the Naval Academy and then serve on a Carrier Airborne Early Warning Squadron. She joined the FBI after putting in the obligatory five-year stint in the Navy.

Sitting between Hinton and Klewacki at the conference table, Sheriff MacDonald was impressed with lighthouse keepers, Rachel and Corey Dalbec. With virtually no sleep they'd worked with the FAA, NTSB, FBI and local law enforcement to arrange suitable accommodations and transportation for the army of federal personnel converging on the North Shore. They'd also kept the media at bay by promising that any information that could be divulged about the crash would be available at a 6:00 p.m. press conference at the visitor center. Special Agent Hinton would preside.

"FBI Special Agent Whitney has just informed me that National Park Service and local law enforcement personnel have spotted a second body on Isle Royale from a search plane. A recovery team is headed to the site. As you know, two members of the wolf study group discovered the mutilated body of a man who's been preliminarily identified as Marcus Dittrich, one of the three passengers on the King Air flight. The pilot, Trevor Drake, was the only person on the plane when it crashed early this morning. After we processed the plane's interior, Mr. Drake's body was transported to the morgue at St. Mark's Hospital in Duluth where a thorough autopsy, including a full toxicology screen, will be performed.

"I don't want to taint the investigation that our colleagues at the National Transportation Safety Board will conduct or the final report they will issue, but we at the FBI have a different responsibility. It's possible that multiple crimes were committed on that airplane, and even though all the participants, perpetrators and victims, may be deceased, we will still make every effort to determine who did what to whom and, if possible, why.

"The Duluth Airport was closed at eight thirty last night due to high winds, blowing snow and low visibility. A controller on duty spotted the King Air on Duluth's radar shortly before midnight and assumed the plane was in trouble as it was flying at a dangerously low altitude over Lake Superior about twenty miles northeast of Two Harbors. Try as she did, she could not elicit a response from Mr. Drake. We assume he was already dead, but that's conjecture at this point.

"Now I'll introduce Dan Esbensen, the investigator-in-charge of the NTSB's initial go-team of five for the board's investigation of this crash. Although Dan is from the board's headquarters in DC, he was on assignment in Texas when he got the call early this morning to head to Minnesota. Dan?"

"Thank you, Michelle. Good afternoon, folks. I hope I'm not the only one who thinks this whole thing is bizarre; but, fortunately or unfortunately, understanding what happened here, trying to reconstruct how and why the King Air 250 crashed, falls within the NTSB's mandate."

Esbensen was rail thin and scholarly looking, a balding fifty-something wearing an unbuttoned navy cardigan over an oxford cloth white shirt and tan cords.

"We've located both the cockpit voice recorder and the flight data recorder from the aircraft. They're already on their way to our main office for processing. Over the next week my team will methodically examine, dismantle and transport the aircraft to a research site to be determined. As Special Agent Hinton mentioned, the FBI—*not the*

NTSB—will be leading any criminal investigation. While our final report might not be issued for months, based on the available facts and evidence, the media will assume the pilot is responsible for the death of the three passengers and the ditching of the airplane. But that's just one possible scenario at this point. We haven't even located all the passengers. Data from the recorders, autopsies of the pilot and passengers, a ballistics report on the firearm found in the plane will all be pieces of the puzzle to determine the most likely cause."

Members of Esbensen's team then discussed their roles in the investigation. MacDonald had some difficulty staying awake and hoped no one else noticed that Corey Dalbec's chin was buried in his sweater and his eyes were glued shut. The sheriff respected all the assembled experts but was curious about a few things he'd observed on his own during the early-morning hours. Whatever else was true about this mystery plane that glided into his county on the wings of a nor'easter, that young pilot didn't kill himself.

CHAPTER 9

ALEX JERONIMUS COULD RELATE to the sudden and unexpected loss of his girlfriend's father. Even though Paul Jeronimus was rarely home during Alex's childhood, divorcing his mom when he was three and pursuing the life of a globe-trotting aeronautical engineer and mercenary, he was still his son's hero, teaching him to skate at four, play hockey at six, and even to fly a small plane at sixteen. Paul's murder by Sunni extremists changed the course of Alex's life.

Alex drove Liz's Tesla Model S over the Duluth ship canal via the Aerial Lift Bridge. The couple was heading to her home on Minnesota Point, the longest freshwater sandbar in the world, when she got a call on her Bluetooth. It was Jenny delivering the shocking news about Bill. Liz wanted more details, but all Jenny knew was he'd been in a snowmobile accident Friday night on a trail up the North Shore and he died at the scene. The Lake County sheriff said his body had been taken to St. Mark's. Liz was devastated and dumbfounded.

"My God, Alex," she gasped after the call. "He wasn't a

snowmobiler. Not as far as I knew. What was he doing up there? The weather was horrible Friday night. I thought you were the only one I knew who did stupid shit like that." Then she started sobbing as Alex drove the Tesla into the garage of the ultra-modern home and flipped off the nearly silent electric engine.

"We should cancel the announcement tomorrow," he said, placing a hand on her knee. "We can reschedule after the funeral, after you've had some time to process this."

Liz paused, then opened the door and turned. "No, Alex, everything's set for the announcement. The timing is too good, and Dad was excited about it. Plus, it will be a distraction for me. A good distraction."

CHAPTER 10

MEGAN HOLAPPA HAD JUST finished a Cobb salad and vanilla shake. She was having an animated conversation with her parents, each sitting on a side of her hospital bed, when Detective Klewacki knocked twice on the tan metal door to Room E226 and then entered. Megan's father stood up and greeted a five-and-a-half-foot athletic woman in her early forties. She wore medium-length black hair in a ponytail and smiled pleasantly. He noticed a prominent red scar, the size and shape of a dime, in the middle of her forehead, a scar left by a bullet eighteen months earlier. Klewacki wore a mid-length parka and knee-high black winter boots. The words *Lake County Sheriff* were stitched in white over the county logo on her coat.

"Hi, I'm Vern Holappa, Megan's dad. And this is my wife, Suzie."

"Very nice to meet both of you," said Klewacki, shaking Vern's hand and nodding to Suzie. "I'm Deputy Gail Klewacki. Megan's treating doctor told me her condition has been upgraded to fair. She said I could ask her some routine questions about the accident.

I understand she needs to rest, so I won't stay for more than fifteen or twenty minutes."

"Is that okay with you, sweetie?" Suzie asked Megan. Suzie seemed like a misnomer for this chubby, fifty-something woman, visibly sweating under a full-length faux-mink coat. She farted loudly as she pushed herself off the bed and ambled over to Vern.

"It's fine, Mom. You guys go home. You've been here since yesterday."

Vern and Suzie owned Holappa's True Value Hardware in Duluth Heights. Their business was struggling to compete with Home Depot, Lowe's and Menards, not to mention Walmart, Target and Amazon. They were lifelong Duluthians who'd been married for twenty-five years and lived in a three-bedroom rambler in the Hunters' Park neighborhood. Megan was the oldest of their three children.

"Okay," said Vern. "But we'll be back tonight. Call if you want us to bring you anything." With that, Vern and Suzie left holding hands.

Though Megan's condition had improved, she was still in significant pain, moderated by an intravenous morphine drip. Her chief concern was her face, which was covered with gauze and bandages layered over several sutured lacerations and black-and-purple contusions. She'd asked the doctor about scarring, and to her dismay was told "it's too early to know." Megan's pretty face was her calling card, her most valuable asset.

"What the fuck do you want?" she huffed, catching Klewacki off guard.

"Not a nice way for an elementary education major to talk," Klewacki replied. As usual, she'd done some homework on her subject.

"I don't understand why the police need to talk to me. I didn't kill that old guy. I mean, he was super nice. I feel terrible about this whole thing."

Klewacki could see tears forming in the girl's red, weary eyes. "Megan, I know you weren't responsible for the accident or Mr.

Vandenberg's death. I'm interested in knowing why you and several of your sorority sisters were up at Overlook Lodge in the middle of a blizzard. Who asked you to go up there?"

"It's not a big deal. Usually, Ricky calls me mid-week if there's going to be a big party up there. If we get eight or more girls who want to go, they pick us up from campus on a bus and take us to the lodge. We stay three or four to a suite, and they comp our room and give us free food and drinks, plus some cash. The bus brings us back to campus on Sunday around noon."

Klewacki was thankful for the morphine; there was no way the brash girl would be talking so freely without it.

"Megan, who's Ricky?"

"He's the owner of Overlook Lodge—Ricky Holden. Everybody knows the Holdens. My dad says they own half of Duluth."

"Is Mr. Holden the person who's paying you and the other girls?"

"Sometimes Ricky pays us. Sometimes one of his employees. What difference does it make?"

Klewacki wanted Megan to keep talking, so she had to choose her words carefully. "You mentioned that *they* pick us up and *they* comp our room. Are Ricky and his staff at the resort the only ones involved in setting up these weekends?"

"Pretty much. One other guy gave me money once. He's also the guy who asked me to show Bill—you know, Mr. Vandenberg—a good time this weekend. He's a lot older, but he was there when I first met Ricky at an alumni event I worked last year."

"What work did you do at an alumni event?"

"I'm in a work-study program at UMD. I try to work twenty hours a week to earn some extra money, mostly as a server at faculty and alumni events. Ricky and his friend were both flirting with me a little that first night. Greg, that's his name. And I think he's a lawyer or a judge up in Two Harbors." She paused. "Hey, I'm feeling weak and kind of sick to my stomach. Can we be done for now?"

"You've been incredibly helpful, Megan. I only have two more questions and then I'll let you rest. How much did this Greg pay you to show Mr. Vandenberg a good time?"

"Five hundred. And then Bill bought me dinner and gave me another five hundred."

"And what did they expect you to do for a thousand dollars?"

Megan didn't hesitate. "Just hang out with Bill. There's nothing wrong with that, is there?"

"And that's all any of your friends who were paid to go to Overlook did for the money—hang out with older men?"

"I think you're out of questions, Officer." Megan pulled a sheet over her head and turned away from Klewacki. Then she added from under the sheet, "Hey, I can only speak for myself, but we're all adults and Ricky throws a great party."

• • • • • • • • • • • • • • • •

Distracted by revelations from her interview with Megan, Klewacki slipped on an icy walkway in front of St. Mark's and landed squarely on her ass. One of the hospital's security guards helped her up and brushed a coating of snow off her parka. More embarrassed than hurt, the detective insisted she was fine and thanked him for his assistance. As she shuffled more cautiously to her squad car, a black Explorer parked a block away, Klewacki wondered what her boss would do with the information she'd pried from the partially sedated coed.

"On your way home?" Sheriff MacDonald answered his cell after the first buzz.

"Finally. I'm meeting Brian and the boys at the Pickwick for lunch. They didn't win one game against the big-city boys at the Eden Prairie tournament."

"That's too bad, but it's nothing to be ashamed of. The caliber of play on these AAU teams is incredibly good these days. How did the interview go?"

"Better than expected in terms of information," Klewacki said. "I didn't think she'd tell me anything. But worse in terms of who's been implicated in a stupid, frat-boy scheme that probably crossed a few lines."

"You're surprised that Ricky Holden is involved with college girls?"

"Not at all. But I think his partner in this enterprise might be our own Lake County attorney, Mr. Thomassoni."

"Oh, Jesus! Greg?" said MacDonald. "How bad is it?"

"I'm not sure. Apparently, Ricky has been paying students to spend their weekends partying with members of his exclusive snowmobile club at Overlook Lodge. The girls are juniors and seniors, mostly from one sorority. He's paying each of them two hundred dollars plus free food, lodging and transportation. Many of these girls are under twenty-one, so he's also guilty of serving alcohol to underage women. But that's the least of our concerns. I wouldn't be surprised if some of the girls are making extra money from lecherous old members. Megan said Greg paid her five hundred to show Bill Vandenberg a good time, and Vandenberg paid her another five hundred."

MacDonald was in the kitchen of his modest log home nestled high in the primal forest west of Highway 61 with a view of Lake Superior. He checked on the beef brisket he'd placed in a crock-pot a few hours earlier after adorning it with caramelized onions and his mom's garlic rub recipe. He and Hallie had invited five couples to squeeze into their family room to watch two teams that weren't the Vikings in Super Bowl LIV.

"I wonder what Ricky charges club members for a weekend of partying at his fancy lodge?" he asked. "Greg may have an unhealthy attraction to younger women, but he's no fool. If he's involved in this stupid scheme, there must be more to it. And if there is, we might need to hand off the investigation to St. Louis County. They have more resources and no obvious conflicts of interest. But before we do that, why don't you get a copy of the snowmobile club's legal documentation, if there is any, and let's get a subpoena for all their banking and corporate records under the guise of investigating Bill

Vandenberg's accident. Then we'll have something substantive to give Duluth."

"So, you think there's more to this than just priming the pump, so to speak?"

"I'm glad you said that and not me. I don't know, but we need to put an end to it. While you're tracking down records, I'll have discreet conversations with Ricky and Greg. It would be good to end this without attracting media attention that would expose the students and probably end Greg's career, though that might be a good thing. By the way, are you and Brian still coming down to watch the big game with us?"

"If you're still making brisket. We'll bring beer and Brian's North Shore berry pie."

"Go Chiefs!"

CHAPTER 11

February 3, 2020
Rustic Inn Café
Castle Danger, Minnesota

SPECIAL AGENT HINTON SIPPED a foamy chai tea latte as she read the Monday edition of the *Duluth News Tribune*. A last-second field goal to win the Super Bowl was big news, but the front-page headline wasn't about football:

BODY OF UHG CEO RECOVERED ON ISLE ROYALE
Third missing passenger on mystery plane still not found

Sometime in the mid-1980s the proprietors of the Rustic Inn Café converted a dilapidated log home on Highway 61 into a quaint, simple restaurant that developed a reputation over the next thirty years for making delicious homemade pies and other local favorites mostly from scratch. Seated at one of about a dozen knotty pine tables with red wooden chairs and red-and-white checkered tablecloths, Hinton ordered one of those favorites, walleye cake eggs benedict, while she waited for Agent Whitney. He'd hitched an early-morning ride from Isle Royale to Two Harbors from one of the ski plane pilots assisting with the search. Sheriff MacDonald had volunteered one of his deputies to give Whitney a ride from the municipal airport to the Rustic.

Hinton enjoyed her two-night stay at the Beaver Bay Inn. She had made new friends over pizza and beer at the local muni-bar, the Green Door, while watching the first half of the big game.

There was nothing more for the FBI to do at the crash site, so she and Whitney would drive back to the Cities after breakfast. Looking up from the paper to savor a sip of her latte, Hinton saw her oversized colleague slip his parka over a backrest and sit directly across from her.

"It's about time you got here," she said, raising her left forearm and staring at her Apple watch for effect.

"Very funny," a haggard-looking Whitney replied, not caring whether she was serious. "I've been up since four, and we were bucking a mother of a northwest wind flying across the lake. If I didn't have a fear of flying in small planes before, I do now, especially planes built decades before I was born."

"Did you get to see the game last night?" Hinton was sure he hadn't. She enjoyed being a prick to Whitney.

"No. I picked up a hard copy of the *Mueller Report*. I'm about halfway through it. I'm fascinated by the information on Russian interference with our elections. Richard promised to record the game so we could watch it together next weekend."

"Okay, I won't talk about it then, but I'll be expecting a written summary of the *Mueller Report* on my desk tomorrow morning."

Whitney's only reply was his middle finger.

Their white-haired, seventy-something server had worked at the Rustic since the doors opened in the eighties. She knew all the regulars by name and also knew that visitors from the Twin Cities often left more than the 15 percent tips to which she was accustomed.

She delivered Hinton's plate of food and took Whitney's order—a ham, bacon and swiss cheese omelet with a side of potato pancakes, whole wheat toast with peanut butter on the side, and a caramel roll.

"I hope you're hungry" was her only comment.

"You know you'll have to go back to Isle Royale if they find the other body," said Hinton as she took a bite of the walleye and let it melt in her mouth along with a forkful of egg yolk and cheddar cheese.

"Sure, though I don't know what good it will do."

"Probably no good, other than to show the public that we're on the case and we care. I spent a couple of hours yesterday with a crack team from the NTSB, an FAA investigator, and an air traffic control supervisor from the Duluth airport. They shared some early findings that won't be public until the final report is issued months from now.

"They think the pilot or one of the passengers shot everyone else on the plane somewhere over western Nebraska, which is where they think the plane made a U-turn and changed course. The data and voice recorder from the black box should confirm or alter their hypothesis within the next week. We now know two of the passengers were jettisoned over Isle Royale. They think the plane either ran out of fuel or some of the fuel was dumped. Either way, the plane likely glided from the western edge of Isle Royale until it crashed at Split Rock with nothing in the tanks. That's why there was no explosion, barely any fire. Whoever planned this probably figured the plane would crash through the ice on the lake, sink five hundred feet into the dark abyss and never be found."

"Whoever planned this?" asked Whitney. "But what was his exit strategy?"

"Apparently, President Drummond was tight with a couple of the big shots on the plane. I don't give a rat's stinking ass about that. We're going to conduct the same investigation and get the same answers to this shitstorm of a mystery regardless of who's looking over our shoulder. The pilot's name is, or was, Trevor Drake. He's in his early thirties and has worked as a part-time pilot for CopperPlus for three years.

"I've already talked to the company's HR director—she was good enough or dumb enough to return my voicemail message on a Sunday. She said Trevor had a high opinion of himself as a pilot and a ladies' man. He was single but paying child support for a five-year-old who lives with his mother in Brainerd. He learned to fly airplanes at UND up in Grand Forks and had worked as a co-pilot for UPS for a few years before getting the part-time gig with CopperPlus.

"She thinks he was moonlighting as a personal trainer at a workout studio and spa for rich ladies in Wayzata. He'd recently broke up with his girlfriend, a real estate agent in the northern suburbs. When we get back today, I'll follow up on Marcus and the pilot. You talk to Severinson's wife and his colleagues at Universal Health. We'll tackle the guy with three names together. He's the most complex character, and, since he hasn't been found, it's the most sensitive investigation."

Whitney was listening carefully and taking a few notes on his iPad between bites. Watching him devour a small truckload of rich food made Hinton sick to her stomach. She looked out the window at light morning traffic on Highway 61 and a bright morning sun glistening on the frozen lake.

"Here's an interesting side note," she said, as the waitress quietly refilled their cups and subtly slid the bill to the person she assumed was in charge. "According to Severinson's wife, and this was confirmed by the CopperPlus HR director, these three amigos had only met each other a few weeks ago, yet they planned to attend the Waste Management Open in Phoenix on Saturday and Sunday morning and then fly to Miami to attend the Super Bowl. They had a tee time at Doral National on Monday, and then they'd fly back to St. Paul. Given that itinerary, you can understand why they were wearing shorts and polo shirts. But no matter what they were wearing, that's a lot of face-time to spend with guys you barely know."

"This whole thing is fucked up if you ask me," Whitney sighed, flipping his paper napkin over the crumbly remains of a caramel roll. "Maybe these rich assholes were up there playing Russian roulette with the Ruger semi-automatic and the last man standing lost his nerve. Did I tell you the Coast Guard is bringing a half dozen drones to Isle Royale this week to look for Hesse? The planes can't cover as much terrain as those quadcopters."

"*Did I tell you* the Ruger they found in the cockpit is being examined by our ballistics lab in Minneapolis as we speak?" Hinton couldn't help being a smart aleck. "FYI, the gun was registered to Marcus Dittrich, who had a conceal-and-carry permit. That doesn't necessarily mean he shot anyone. Let's get on the road before I figure this out."

They bundled up for the fifty-foot walk to Hinton's red Lincoln SUV. The temperature had risen ten degrees since sunrise, all the way to ten below. She left a twenty on the table.

CHAPTER 12

February 3, 2020
Beaver Bay, Minnesota

AFTER HIS FIRST DECENT slumber since returning from his honeymoon in the Riviera Maya, Sheriff MacDonald was up at 5:30. He and Hallie rarely ate much when they hosted a party, and last night's Super Bowl gathering was no exception. The good news was their guests consumed everything in sight and helped with the cleanup after the game, so when the last couple left at 10:30, Sam and Hallie had some time to enjoy each other before beginning another week in the deep freeze.

MacDonald brewed a pot of Sumatra and toasted a couple of sourdough bagels that he slathered with veggie cream cheese, while Hallie spooned Greek yogurt into a bowl of blueberries, raspberries and bananas. They sat together at the antique oak table in their tight, cedar-lined kitchen to share a modest but tasty breakfast. Hallie held up the front page of the *News Tribune* to show him the front-page headline, but before he could react, his cell started vibrating on the old Formica countertop.

"George Redman, what are you doing up so early?"

Redman had been a St. Paul homicide detective and then a senior special agent with the Bureau of Criminal Apprehension. A short, wiry man in his early sixties, he'd resigned from the BCA shortly after participating in the investigation of a series of brutal crimes precipitated by the shocking murder of a beautiful young lawyer up at Gooseberry Falls.

"I got a new dog last week, a Husky and Australian shepherd mix from the humane society. His name is Fred. He's an energetic guy who likes early-morning walks along River Road."

"That's great, Red. I'm really glad you got yourself a friend."

"Yeah, well, I admit I've been pretty lonely since Rita left, but I didn't call to cry on your shoulder, Mac. You know I opened a private detective agency last fall, and, truth be told, I have more business than I want, but most of it's not very lucrative."

"With two big pensions, you can do whatever you want, right?"

"I'm not complaining, but I got a call last night from the head lawyer for the Chilean mining outfit that owns CopperPlus. They want to pay me a retainer of fifty grand, plus five hundred bucks an hour to investigate the death of Marcus Dittrich, the guy who was half eaten by wolves on Isle Royale over the weekend. They want to know whether somebody sabotaged their plane."

"You probably know as much as I do about poor Mr. Dittrich. His plane landed here, but he never did. The FBI is leading the investigation into all crimes related to the potential hijacking and crash of that six-million-dollar airplane."

"Hijacking?" Redman hadn't heard about that.

"That's my word," said MacDonald. "When a plane is supposed to fly from St. Paul to Phoenix and it crashes into Split Rock Lighthouse, there must have been a hijacking at some point."

"I get it. These Chileans are deadly serious, Mac. They want a report covering everyone on that plane, why they were there, their relationship with Dittrich, any interests in or opposition to mining operations. I was up most of the night researching them. It's not easy to find information. They're as private and mysterious as Cargill and no doubt more ruthless. What I do know is they're tight with the Drummond administration and their lobbying efforts have paid off. Their proposed copper mine near your county had been blocked before Drummond took office; now their leases have been renewed."

"I've heard about them," said MacDonald. "We monitor and surveil some of the protests by environmental groups to ensure they remain peaceful. The proposed mines are right in the middle of the Boundary Waters, some in St. Louis County and some in Lake. They've been peaceful so far, but if these companies get the green light to mine, things might change. The Polymet/Glencore relationship is similar, but they're not in Lake County, and they're even closer to moving ahead with mining. I'm all for creating good jobs up here, Red, but mining has no place in the BWCA."

"I won't get involved in the politics of it," said Redman. "I've never been camping, canoeing, hunting or fishing. If an activity doesn't involve a ball, a puck or my dick, I don't give a shit about it. I also don't mind taking a few bucks from these South American billionaires. Apparently, the family that controls the company owns a huge mansion in Washington that they rent out to some members of Drummond's family. Now that's what I call influence peddling.

"Anyway, they'll get their fucking in-depth report. I might be driving up to the North Shore for some research in the next week or so. How would you and your new bride like to meet Fred?"

"We'd love to see both of you," MacDonald said, as Hallie smiled broadly and rolled her big brown eyes. "By the way, do you know FBI Special Agent Michelle Hinton from Minneapolis? She's leading the feds in this thing."

"She's a very impressive person. I've met her and actually worked with her on a bank robbery, kidnapping and multiple murder case in St. Paul fifteen years ago. I already have a call in to her."

"I should have known."

• • • • • • • • • • • • • • •

"I can't believe Rita left him for that lecherous sheriff," said Hallie, filling her coffee mug and taking a big gulp.

The past few years had been a rollercoaster ride for Hallie Bell. Her dad died in March after suffering a massive stroke the year before at his condo in Florida. Her mom, only seventy, had early-stage dementia. Hallie had to move her into an assisted-living facility in Sarasota in May. Divorced from Ricky Holden and the Holden real estate empire for five years, she gave up a partnership in his uncle's law firm and moved to Two Harbors. She felt fortunate to land a job as an assistant county attorney in Lake County, where she was the only woman lawyer and the only African American. That's also where she met Sam MacDonald, the man she wished she'd met years earlier. She'd been spending three or four nights a week at his log cabin for a couple of years.

When she returned to Minnesota after moving her mom, MacDonald suggested they make it a permanent arrangement. He also suggested a destination wedding in Mexico at the Vidanta Riviera Maya Resort. There were no guests. It was just the two of them exchanging vows by moonlight at the Havana Moon Beach with an American expat officiant and two Mexican witnesses they'd met at a bar an hour before the ceremony.

"I love George; he's great," said MacDonald. "But he's nearly twenty years older than Rita and set in his ways. It's what happens sometimes. How much older am I?"

"Not quite twenty years, asshole."

"By the way, speaking of lecherous, I need to confide in you about some stupid and potentially criminal activities your boss and ex-husband might be into that could have contributed to Bill Vandenberg's death."

"Oh, shit, Mac! Nothing Ricky does would ever surprise me . . . but Greg? What is it?"

MacDonald told Hallie about Ricky's arrangement with the

UMD coeds and the $500 payment Thomassoni allegedly made to Megan Holappa. He wanted to prepare her for the possibility that Thomassoni or the county board would ask her to step in as acting county attorney pending the outcome of an investigation. Hallie had a predictably strong reaction.

"If all that is true, if those two cretins were soliciting and paying these girls to fraternize with a bunch of rich old bastards, then you need to stop it cold before it gets into the press. Let Klewacki find out what's really going on and then shut it down. Otherwise, these young women and their families will be terribly embarrassed. It could ruin their lives, Mac."

"You're right about that," said MacDonald. "I'll let Klewacki snoop around a little more, but at some point I might have an obligation to involve St. Louis County."

CHAPTER 13

February 3, 2020
Marshall Performing Arts Center
University of Minnesota—Duluth

DESPITE THE DEEP FREEZE outdoors, the electricity inside was making everyone sweat. Marshall Performing Arts Center seated about 800. The fire marshal must have been nervous because people were standing everywhere, in the aisles and in the back. An ambitious campaign volunteer counted over 1,300 in the room. Campus rules required that the three double doors in the back of the auditorium remain open, revealing another 500 or so in the halls. Outside, campus police and private security were turning hundreds of others away as the one o'clock start time approached.

At three minutes after the hour, Alex Jeronimus walked up to the podium without notes or the aid of a teleprompter. Wearing a black cashmere sport coat over a powder-blue oxford cloth dress shirt, open at the neck, and tan khaki pants, the trim but muscular six-foot-two former Army officer looked as much like an authentic Viking as any candidate in recent memory. His thick, close-cropped blond hair was a few shades from white, and his pale-blue eyes were highlighted by yellow specks of pigment. A strong, square jaw and his father's prominent long nose framed a sober and sometimes brooding affect—until he started to speak. And then he could be spellbinding and mesmerizing, not like any local candidate ever.

Sipping a glass of cold Lake Superior tap water, he scanned the overflowing crowd and smiled, revealing perfect white teeth.

"Thank you so much for coming today. Before I begin to talk about our future, I want to thank my friend and strongest supporter, Elizabeth Vandenberg, for helping to get the word out about our gathering. As many of you know, the Vandenberg family and friends are heartbroken today, mourning the loss of a wonderful man and one of the great environmental lawyers and conservationists of our time, Elizabeth's father, William Vandenberg. Bill lost his life in a tragic accident close to the North Shore of Lake Superior, an area he loved passionately and fought courageously to preserve for future generations. Let us pause for a minute of silence for Bill Vandenberg.

"Thank you.

"It won't take long for me to tell you why, why today, I'm announcing my candidacy for the Democratic-Farmer-Labor nomination for your Eighth District seat in the United States House of Representatives." The crowd erupted into applause.

"Civilization is on the precipice of an historic crisis. It's not about immigration, though we need to revamp our immigration laws and policies to ensure we are treating everyone with dignity and compassion. We need a permanent fix to protect the DACA kids from deportation and to keep them where they belong, right here."

More applause.

"We need to create a fair pathway to citizenship for all undocumented individuals, especially those who are hardworking taxpayers. And we need to use available technology, not walls or guns, to secure our borders. No child should ever be separated from his or her parents in the name of border security. We are a country of immigrants and a country that welcomes refugees from every race and every region of the world, and if we don't recognize that soon, we are a country of bigots and a country of fools."

Rows of onlookers stood and cheered.

"We are living in a time of incredible impending crisis. It's not about health care, though we need to reengineer our health care system so all private health insurers and hospitals are not-for-profit organizations, subject to closer public scrutiny and oversight. In addition, we need to make a public insurance option available, so anyone who doesn't qualify for Medicare, Medicaid or private coverage can purchase high-quality, affordable care. Medicare for All is a trap for those who want an easy answer but not the right answer. Government should regulate, not operate our health care system.

Again, the crowd cheered.

"We are on the verge of a devastating crisis. It's not about the War on Terror, though we need to divert and reinvest the hundreds of billions we are spending fighting useless, futile wars and occupying regions where most of the citizens want us out. We can avoid tragedies like 9/11 by utilizing this country's superior technology and covert intelligence capabilities to keep closer watch on the operations of our enemies and to act decisively when appropriate, but always, always trying diplomacy first. There are ways to topple tyrants like Assad without occupying foreign nations and overseeing regime change.

"The United States should never again have to engage in conventional warfare, exposing ground troops to the ploys of soulless, evil terrorists. I have witnessed the very worst that can happen, and I refuse to accept that we can't do better. We should strive for a smaller, more efficient, more technologically-driven military. And— and this is critically important—the medical and mental health care we administer to our soldiers and veterans must be extraordinary. Today it's ordinary and fraught with delay. That's unacceptable."

Jeronimus waved his hands signaling for the now roaring crowd to sit and allow him to continue. After nearly a minute of unmitigated applause he took another sip of water as the audience calmed.

"We are on the cusp of a crisis. It's not about income inequality or wealth redistribution, though we need to create more opportunities for families living from paycheck to paycheck, families stuck in a cycle of poverty, and especially for people of color. Free community college for everyone? Forgiveness of student loans? These are popular campaign slogans, empty promises made in exchange for votes. The problem is no one will be able to deliver the goods. We should be ensuring opportunity and affordability, not giveaways. Should a billionaire's child be entitled to free community college or student loan forgiveness? I don't think so.

"If I had my way, we would outlaw the granting of stock options to corporate executives or place a fifty percent federal tax on any gain from the sale of the stock. But I won't get my way on that issue because too much wealth and too many special interests are controlled by the stock- option generation. No CEO in America is worth more than a million dollars a year, period. The fact that the boards of directors of every Fortune 500 corporation in America would disagree with that statement is what's wrong with corporate America."

Jeronimus paused again, allowing admirers to vent their enthusiasm as he built toward a crescendo.

"Before I tell you about the looming crises, I need to make a few disclosures. I am the president and chief executive officer of Generosity Energy, one of the largest renewable energy project managers and producers in the United States, headquartered right here in Duluth. We are a public benefit corporation. All profits are reinvested in our mission, which is to replace fossil fuels with renewable energy alternatives. We don't grant stock options to employees. We have no stock. I have persuaded my board of directors to limit executive compensation. We pay everyone well, but no one, including the CEO, makes more than three times the median salary of our employees.

"I have always been an environmentalist and an avid outdoorsman. Since leaving the Army in 2010, I have dedicated my life to preserving a habitable, beautiful, bountiful planet for future generations. Starting today, I am taking a leave of absence from my position at Generosity. If elected, my leave of absence will become a resignation.

"Climate change presents both the greatest challenge and the greatest threat mankind has ever known. According to a recent report prepared by the foremost conservation scientists in the world, human activity—think auto emissions and coal-fired power plants—has put a million species on the verge of extinction. This threat is in a category by itself in the annals of human history. And if we don't take dramatic action now, right now, this activity will put us all on the verge of extinction.

"I don't have time to delve into all the horrific details of what our world will become if we don't reduce our toxic emissions by twenty-five to thirty percent in the next ten years. But think about this. Even if the planet only warms by another two degrees Celsius in the next forty years—and we're on pace to warm more than that—hundreds of millions of people will suffer from water scarcity, and many populated areas along the equator will become unlivable. And that's just the beginning. If you want to learn more, I recommend David Wallace-Wells's readable book, *The Uninhabitable Earth, Life After Warming*. This is scary stuff. Last July was the hottest month ever recorded in human history. I guarantee you, this record will be broken soon, and that's not good. If our planet is destroyed, then what is the value of a good education and a good job? What kind of world will your children and grandchildren inherit?

"In my view, the Green Deal is a clever term and a good start, but its agenda doesn't go far enough. Our goal should be the eradication of all fossil fuels in America and their replacement by renewables by 2030. That's right, by 2030. Not only will the US go from being a laggard to a leader in the war against global warming, but we will create a new world of opportunities for jobs and economic prosperity, the world of renewable energy. Its costs are competitive with fossil fuels today, but the biggest benefit—we will be protecting our planet and future generations from desolation and destruction.

"Let's face it, the protection of our air, water and wilderness areas has been severely compromised and, in fact, has regressed as a result of the policies and actions of the Drummond administration. They exited the 2015 Paris Agreement in 2017 and have exposed many wilderness areas to mining and oil-drilling interests. In our own region, they have reversed the fed's prior ruling to prohibit copper and other non-ferrous mining in the Boundary Waters Canoe Area and have renewed the mineral leases of CopperPlus, which exposes the wilderness to degradation for generations to come and is a travesty.

"Whether or not you elect me as your representative in Congress, I will do everything in my power to stop non-ferrous mining in or near our wilderness areas and to replace fossil fuels with renewables. I will also do everything in my power to ensure that Ronald A. Drummond, a pathological liar, the worst president in the history of our republic, and the most immoral, narcissistic leader the modern world has ever known, is not reelected. I'll wait until I'm fortunate enough to capture the DFL endorsement before I say much about the incumbent. Suffice it to say, he's an ardent supporter of the president.

"We're a month away from the Super Tuesday primaries, and my party still has a handful of candidates vying for the nomination. Incredibly, polling shows that Drummond would likely defeat any one of them. That's not right. That's not the America that I love and fought for, so please, if you agree with my agenda, support my candidacy, volunteer on my campaign, and let your voice be heard. Even if you don't support me, if you love America and want to restore justice, fairness and opportunity for everyone, you must do everything in your power to remove President Drummond from office, once and for all."

.

Jeronimus smiled broadly, seemingly elevated by the roars of approval.

"We are fortunate to live in a state and region where unemployment is low, education is good, and diversity is increasing. Besides jobs in renewable energy, our Arrowhead region has been increasing employment in the hospitality and tourism industries, and we can still boast that Duluth is the busiest inland seaport in the world. The new low-silica iron pellets created up Highway 61 at Northshore Mining are an environmentally friendly and more efficient component of modern steel manufacturing.

"Life is good in northern Minnesota, but unless we act now, it won't stay that way. Join jeronimus2020.org and let's work together for a better tomorrow."

• • • • • • • • • • • • • • • •

Bellisio's Italian Restaurant had operated in the shadows of the Aerial Lift Bridge in Canal Park for twenty years. Liz Vandenberg believed their wine list was the best in the state and often scheduled important meetings with colleagues and potential donors in the intimate, dimly lit bar. After an exhausting Monday that included an emotional session with a pathologist from the medical examiner's office, Alex's big announcement, and a fundraising meeting with some of the DFL's heaviest hitters at her dad's law office, now the Jeronimus for Congress headquarters, she'd invited Jenny to enjoy a quiet happy hour and catch up.

Their server brought a bottle of Marchesi Fumanelli Valpolicella along with an artisan cheese plate and buffalo shrimp with fried green tomatoes. The intensity of Jenny's amorous feelings for her boss hadn't subsided, even though she was reminded almost daily of Liz's romantic involvement with Jeronimus. She liked Alex and supported his candidacy, but she was confident his relationship with Liz wouldn't last. And when it fell apart, she'd be there.

"This tastes so good," said Liz, finishing a small crust of Italian bread combined with a hunk of Gouda. "What did you think of Alex's speech today? Most big donors and party people loved it, except for some labor union leaders and mining supporters. I think he'll appeal to thousands of young people who've probably never voted."

"He's good, Liz. He's self-assured and authentic, at least he seems authentic. Even though I'm super busy at the foundation, I'd like to help with the campaign, maybe do some research, write some speeches and call on leaders of the LGBTQ community."

Liz reached across the table and gently touched Jenny's wrist with her open hand. "You're vitally important to the success of the foundation, Jen, especially now that I'll be spending most of my time on the campaign. But working on a political campaign can be as satisfying as running a mission-driven foundation, so I'd love for you to dedicate ten to twenty hours a week to the campaign. After all, I think the foundation will be even more effective if he wins."

Jenny felt warm inside from a combination of the wine and touch. She couldn't help but notice tears welling in the corners of Liz's eyes. "Are you crying?" Jenny assumed she was feeling a surge of emotion over Bill's unexpected death.

"I'm okay," she said, wiping a wet cheek with the side of her hand. "It's just that everything with Alex and my dad is overwhelming. I met with Dr. Higgins, the head pathologist in the medical examiner's office. He'll perform the autopsy. He said there's no question in his mind Dad had a massive heart attack seconds before he lost control of the sled and slammed into the trees. He said it should be a comfort to me that he was doing something he loved, especially since the cancer would have killed him within a year. I told him my dad was a cross-country skier and distance runner and played an occasional round of golf, but I didn't think he'd ever been on a snowmobile before last Friday. I didn't tell him Dad never told me about the cancer."

Jenny didn't know what to say. Bill Vandenberg was one of her heroes. Even now, she had a hard time believing he died in a snowmobile accident with a twenty-year-old tethered to him.

"I'm so sorry," she commiserated. "What do you think brought him up there in the first place?"

"I'm not sure, but I have my suspicions. One of Dad's best friends from law school is Lake County attorney Greg Thomassoni. They both grew up in northern Minnesota and even lived together for a few years. I know they met for lunch last week; it's on Dad's calendar. Greg's been divorced multiple times. He's also tight with a real estate developer named Rick Holden, who goes by Ricky even though he's over forty. Holden's family owns more property in Minnesota and Wisconsin than the state and federal governments combined. They're multimillionaire Drummond supporters with no regard for the environment. You won't see any Holdens on our donor or prospect list.

"Ricky is a typical third-generation, pampered prick. A guy who was born on third base but thinks he hit a triple. He's cocky, keeps himself in shape, and used to be married to a black lawyer named Hallie Bell. She left him about five years ago when she discovered that a twenty-year-old drink-cart server at Ridgeview Country Club was having his baby."

"How do you know so much about him?" asked Jenny. "I know you grew up in Duluth, but still."

"My mom and dad knew his parents. They all belonged to the Kitchi Gammi Club and Northland Country Club. Rick is five or six years older than me, so I didn't know him well, but shortly after his divorce he hit on me at a fundraiser for St. Mark's Foundation. Let's just say we weren't a good match.

"His family owns the new mega-resort on the North Shore, Overlook Lodge. It's been Ricky's pet project, and he spends a lot of time up there with other trust-fund babies, rednecks, and landed aristocrats from the Twin Cities. Apparently, either Greg or Ricky introduced Megan Holappa to my dad and arranged for his stay at the lodge and his use of a fancy snowmobile. Now, Jenny, you can't tell anyone about this."

"You know I won't." Jenny felt happy that Elizabeth would trust her with such juicy information.

"A detective with the Lake County Sheriff's Office called me this afternoon, right after Alex's announcement. She's a friend of a friend through a book club and is a tough, successful woman in a profession dominated by men. Ironically, her husband's family owns Cascade Mountain Lodge, one of Overlook's main competitors. She called to give me a heads-up on a matter related to the investigation of Dad's accident. She said if it became public, it might be embarrassing to my family. The gist of it is that Holden and Thomassoni have been arranging for female students from UMD to spend weekends at Overlook Lodge to party and who knows what else with a bunch of horny old men who are members of a snowmobile club. They're paying the girls a couple hundred dollars and comping their food and lodging. She said Megan admitted Thomassoni paid her a thousand bucks to befriend my dad."

Jenny thought "befriend" might not be the correct verb, but kept that to herself. "It sounds like a prostitution ring," she said, disgusted by the thought of crusty old men touching college girls.

"She's most concerned about protecting the reputation of the students," Liz explained, "but she wanted me to know in case someone leaked the story to the media. If it's true, it would end Thomassoni's career. She's not sure a crime's been committed, but it's a scandal regardless and could have a negative impact on the campaign if it implicates my father.

"That would be so unfair," said Jenny, shaking her head and downing half a glass of wine. "We can't let that happen. Those men are pigs."

"Promise me you won't breathe a word of what I just told you to anyone."

"Of course."

"And on top of everything else, I'm worried about Alex. He's a special man, Jen, but I can see why at thirty-eight he hadn't had a serious relationship. He's kind and thoughtful but eerily quiet most of the time. He has nightmares and flashbacks about the war almost every night. When I finally convinced him to talk about it, we both broke down and cried when he described the worst of it. His best friend from officer candidate school was a lieutenant on his intelligence team during a mission in northeastern Afghanistan. They were in a Humvee on a dirt road near Bagram Air Force base. Alex was in the front seat with the driver; his best friend was in the back. They drove over an IED that destroyed the back of their vehicle, killed two enlisted soldiers, and blew the head right off his friend. That was in July of 2009. He left the Army ten months later."

"That's horrible," said Jenny, confirming her belief that their relationship wouldn't last. "It sounds like he's unstable."

"Maybe schizophrenic," Liz said, but then wished she hadn't. "I don't mean clinically schizophrenic. He has this need for total isolation. He spends ungodly hours working on position papers for the campaign and trying to keep up with what's going on at Generosity, but then is obsessed with going off by himself for days winter camping, hiking and snowshoeing."

"Winter camping?"

"Yeah. My dad liked to do it when he was younger. No bugs, few if any humans. Just you, the wildlife and the weather. This past weekend, as cold and windy as it was, Alex took a huge backpack and had his security guy drop him off near Grand Marais, so he could climb Eagle Mountain and camp on the highest peak in Minnesota. I drove up there to pick him up and have dinner yesterday."

"Did he get hurt up there? I noticed he was limping today."

"He claims he lost his balance on some ice near the top of the mountain but nothing serious. The massive purple bruise down the side of his leg might say otherwise, but he'd never complain about it. Jenny, once we get him into Congress, we'll remain close, but I don't see us staying together as a couple. Again, that is strictly between us."

"Of course."

CHAPTER 14

February 3, 2020
Duluth, Minnesota

YEARS AGO, WHILE REHABBING an old apartment building off
Mesaba Avenue, Ricky Holden drove by a *For Sale by Owner* sign in
a yard that had the most spectacular view of his beloved city and lake
he'd ever seen. The 1950s Rambler taking up space in the yard was
owned by an elderly couple who'd already moved to an assisted-living
complex. Ricky offered them $20,000 over the asking price and tore
the place down a week after the closing. He hired an eccentric local
architect to design his dream house, a contemporary bachelor pad
perched inconspicuously in the heart of Duluth's central hillside. He
acted as the general and took advantage of subcontractors beholden
to the family business.

Two million dollars later, in late 2015, he moved into a structure
that, with the help of a taconite retaining wall, appeared to float over
a rocky outcropping the locals call Observation Hill. On a street
map or GPS, it was known simply as West Fourth Street. Glass walls
dominated the floor plan, held together with a minimum of steel

and concrete. There were breathtaking views of Lake Superior from the great room and master bedroom, not to mention the incredible vistas from the composite deck off the kitchen and the six-person hot tub built into a bluestone terrace off the finished lower level. Heated floors throughout and a two-sided, wood-burning stone fireplace inserted between the great room and master made Duluth winters more than bearable.

Ricky was too cocky to be nervous, but he was pissed. His banker, a second vice president and charter member of the Sawtooth Mountain Snowmobile Club, had called earlier in the day with unwelcome news that a detective from Lake County had served North Shore National Bank & Trust with a subpoena. The bank held millions in Holden loans and deposits, and Ricky's dad served on its board of directors. The subpoena demanded copies of all bank statements, signature cards and applications associated with the Sawtooth Mountain Snowmobile Club. He would have to comply within a few days but wanted to give Ricky an opportunity to have his counsel intervene.

The club was more fun and more successful than Ricky had ever imagined. It had attracted wealthy businessmen and outdoor enthusiasts from throughout the Midwest.

The idea of inviting dozens of coeds to the weekend festivities came to Ricky during the coldest weekend of 2018. Five women in their early twenties had reserved a suite for Friday and Saturday night for a wedding shower. By ten o'clock Friday evening, they were singing Jimmy Buffett songs and leading a line dance in the bar. Ricky walked through on his way to the club room and invited them to join the bigger party, where food was free, and they would never pay for a drink. That party didn't die down until 3:00 a.m., and bar revenue was 50 percent higher than the previous record.

Only casually concerned about the legalities of paying young women to have fun, Ricky consulted the big brother he never had. Thomassoni, a politician and prosecutor but not a legal scholar, opined that so long as there was no *quid pro quo,* no requirement or expectation that the women perform any sexual acts or favors in exchange for the cash and other freebies, it did not constitute prostitution. Having been married and divorced four times, Thomassoni thought himself an expert on women. He was also in serious financial trouble because of them.

His government salary barely covered his three alimony payments, the monthly payment on his used Range Rover, and his credit card debt. After the dissolution of his most recent marriage, he was forced to sell his townhome in Two Harbors to pay off his thirty-year-old spouse of three years and retain his pension. He would be sixty-five in less than a year and was desperate to build a nest egg for retirement.

Based on a hunch, Ricky increased club dues from $1,000 to $5,000 a year. Once Megan and her friends started showing up, membership increased by 25 percent, notwithstanding the hike in dues. After covering the club's expenses for snowmobile rentals, food, booze, insurance and cash payments to their special guests, the club netted nearly sixty grand a year. Half stayed in the club's capital account for future investment and half was paid to GHT Consultants, LLC, whose sole owner, manager and employee was one Greg Horace Thomassoni. Ricky didn't need the money; Thomassoni would ensure the *legality* of club activities.

Ricky got home late from a Duluth city planning meeting he'd attended with his dad. The city was proposing to sell a portion of Lester Park Golf Course, prime real estate for development with mature trees, rolling hills and views of Lake Superior. The Holdens were salivating over it. Washing down a slice of cold Sammy's pizza with a Castle Danger Cream Ale, Ricky sat at the kitchen table and worked some numbers on his laptop. He wanted to build million-dollar homes on that golf course property, but he had to convince Rick Jr., better known as Richard, that there would be a substantial return on the family's investment.

At 11:15, he closed the laptop, filled the dishwasher, and tapped off the kitchen and great room lights with a universal remote. He'd lived in the fishbowl, as his mom called it, for five years, and he could count on one hand the number of times someone had rung the digital doorbell. Hearing a synthesized version of "Black Magic Woman" on his chime speakers, Ricky didn't bother checking his iPhone app, assuming it was either his dad or Thomassoni.

He was pleasantly aroused when he opened one of the birch double doors. Standing before him was a tall woman with long, flowing blonde hair, the color of Elly May Clampett's. She was wearing black high heel pumps, black leather driving gloves, and a black, full-length fleece-lined puffer coat. The scent of her seductive perfume drew him closer. She kept her head down, looking at her feet. Then she opened her coat to reveal a shapely, athletic body with nothing covering it but a black-lace bikini bottom.

"May I come in, Mr. Holden?" the woman asked softly.

Ricky backed up without saying a word; she stepped forward, following his lead. He swung the door shut as they embraced and kissed.

CHAPTER 15

February 3, 2020
Plymouth, Minnesota

HINTON AND WHITNEY ARRIVED at the FBI's field office in Brooklyn Center a few minutes before noon. Hinton told her boss, the special agent in charge, that Whitney had been working fifteen-hour days on Isle Royale and needed some time off. He didn't argue. She, on the other hand, was eager to start collecting evidence that she could piece together into the portrait of a killer. A woman had left an intriguing message on the FBI's tip line over the weekend. It was the only message out of 200 that Hinton would pursue, though she'd probably ask Whitney to follow up on a few others. The woman claimed to be the ex-girlfriend of Trevor Drake. She said she had information about Trevor that might be related to the plane crash. She left her first name, Kari, and her phone number. Based on her conversation with the CopperPlus HR director, Hinton knew Drake had broken up with his girlfriend, but now she had a name. It was something.

Only thirty-three, Kari Swanson was already a successful real estate agent for Minnetonka Realty, selling thirty homes in the previous seven months. She had a 6:30 closing in Golden Valley so agreed to meet Hinton in the spacious, usually empty lobby of her luxury Parker's Lake apartment complex at 9:00. She started the conversation by disclosing that Trevor had been her personal trainer at Iron Buns Fitness before he was her lover. Turns out, he'd also been the personal trainer for Lona Dittrich, Marcus's wife.

"I was attracted to Trevor. He was cute, really built, and had a warped sense of humor that I liked. He didn't take himself too seriously, and he thought most of the executives he flew around the country were total assholes."

"Did you ever see him use or carry a firearm?" asked Hinton, sitting on a leather sectional and nursing a can of Fresca.

"Never. I don't think he'd even know how to load a gun. He was a lover, not a fighter. Unfortunately, the horny little bastard was smitten by Lona 'Pillow Tits' Dittrich. She lived up in North Oaks but drove all the way across town to Wayzata to work out. Trevor met her at a company holiday party last year, and it was lust at first sight. Let's face it. Marcus was over sixty with a bad heart and probably a shriveled dick. Lona looks like a fucking goddess. She already had a personal trainer who came to the house, but Marcus insisted that it be a woman. Trevor invited her to work with him at Iron Buns on condition that Marcus never know about it. Within a month of that holiday party, Trevor had dumped me for Lona. We stayed friends, though, and he was still my trainer.

"I don't know what kind of pilot he is, but there's nobody better at teaching strength and endurance workouts. When I heard about the crash, my first thought was that Marcus found out about Trevor and Lona. According to Trevor, he was insanely jealous of anyone who showed the slightest interest in his trophy wife. Trevor said Marcus always carried a loaded pistol, but probably didn't know how to use it. Trevor was more afraid of the Chilean mafia who owned the company and controlled Marcus like a puppet."

Hinton was impressed with this young woman and was beginning to think that Trevor wasn't a serious suspect. "What else can you tell me about these Chilean owners?"

"I don't know any of them by name, except for one guy that Trevor referred to as Ramon. He's the son of one of the owners. Trevor always called them *Fagos*. That must be an abbreviation. Anyway, I remember one time Trevor flew Marcus and some other execs down to a big meeting in Santiago. The heads of all the Fagos companies were there. Some Brazilian guy got into an argument with Ramon during dinner at a fancy resort, called him a third-generation, know-nothing idiot. Trevor said Ramon just ignored him. Then, as dessert was being served, Ramon walked over to the guy and shot him right in the balls. The guy started screaming and calling Ramon a filthy Latin pig-fucker. That's Trevor's translation. Ramon lifted a machete from the front of his pants and with one powerful whack sliced the guy's head right off. A couple of guards carted him away, and everyone got back to dessert, cigars and cognac as if nothing had happened. Trevor said he ran to the nearest bathroom and threw up."

"When's the last time you had contact with Trevor?" Hinton asked.

"I saw him and Lona leaving Iron Buns together last Thursday night around seven thirty. I was just getting there for my workout. Trevor said the usual, 'How's it goin' Kari, baby?' Lona completely ignored me."

"As far as you know, did Trevor have any close family or friends in the Twin Cities or elsewhere? People he kept in touch with regularly?"

"He had an older sister who drowned at a Girl Scout camp when she was eleven or twelve. His mom and dad divorced when he was a teenager. His dad moved out to California and remarried. Trevor didn't have much to do with him, but he was close to his mother. She's got a good job with an insurance company in Bloomington and lives in a townhouse or condo in Eden Prairie. I never met her, but I think her name is Cathy. He also has a five-year-old daughter from a one-night stand in Brainerd. He visits her a few times a year and sends her mom five hundred a month for support. As for friends, Trevor was a loner. He had a couple of pilot friends who went to aviation school with him at UND, but they don't live around here."

"You knew Trevor pretty well for someone who dated him for only a few months," said Hinton.

"I do my homework," said Swanson. "These days you never know what you're dealing with in a man unless you check out his family and history on Google and social media. I really liked Trevor. It's too bad he had to fall for such a complete bitch."

"I don't know about that," said Hinton, "but you've been very helpful, Ms. Swanson. I'm going to give you my card. If you think of anything else that might be important regarding Trevor or the Dittrichs, you can call, text or email me. By the way, have you shared this information about Trevor with anyone else?"

"Only one other person. I got a visit at work from a gruff little man who said he was investigating the crash for the owners of the plane, so I'm not sure if he's working for Fagos or somebody else. He wouldn't say. His name was Redman."

CHAPTER 16

February 3-4, 2020
Two Harbors, Minnesota

DESPITE BEING THE COUNTY seat, Two Harbors was a small town. The population has hovered around four thousand for over a century, although it peaked at nearly five in the halcyon lumber and iron mining days when Teddy Roosevelt was president and five local men started a company called Minnesota Mining and Manufacturing that would later be known as 3M.

Greg Thomassoni was born in Two Harbors in the 1950s. His dad was a salesman for Two Harbors Bottling and his mom a librarian. Despite four divorces, Thomassoni still attended Holy Spirit Catholic Church, where he'd been baptized and married once. He loved the little Lake County railroad town on the shores of Lake Superior.

Well over six feet tall, young Thomassoni had been a standout basketball player for the Two Harbors Agates in the early 1970s, but after years of overindulging, he tipped the scales at close to three bills. His weight and severe lower-back problems prevented most forms of exercise except walking, an occasional round of golf, and an even less frequent romp in the sack if he could find a willing partner. He'd also been struggling with negative cash flow until his friend Ricky devised a way to infuse his bank account with club benefits. Oddly enough, the attorney's name never appeared on a club financial statement or membership list or even in the club's newsletter because Thomassoni had never been on a snowmobile in his life.

Like his finances, Thomassoni's world had shrunk in recent years. He rarely drove the Ford Edge Lake County provided for its elected attorney. He didn't need to drive. His two-bedroom suite at the Agate Bay Apartments on Sixth Street was only blocks from his office in the county courthouse, and his office was only feet from the Backwoods Grill, his favorite eating and drinking establishment. Knowing he might have a drink or five, he was careful never to drive to a bar in Two Harbors. The walk home, especially in the cold, would serve him better than a career-ending DWI.

Thomassoni stayed at the office late, trying to figure a way he and Ricky could head off an investigation into the club's finances. It was 9:30 when he sat in the bar at Backwoods and ordered a Kettel One martini with three blue cheese–stuffed olives and an order of calamari. A basketball game between UCLA and Stanford caught his attention. He watched it until the end, eating a bacon cheeseburger with fries and downing a couple Bud Lights and a snifter of cognac. After slipping old Jed the bartender a ten-spot and taking a leak, Thomassoni left the bar at 12:30 a.m. The walk to his apartment was a straight shot down Sixth. The sidewalk was glare ice, so he walked down the middle of the street, not expecting to encounter either pedestrians or cars.

He never heard a thing and never saw the car that ran him over in the middle of the street in the middle of the night.

CHAPTER 17

February 4, 2020
Duluth, Minnesota

A NIGHT-SHIFT SUPERVISOR FROM the water quality lab in Knife River had been driving down Sixth Street in Two Harbors at three in the morning when she saw a large object in the middle of the road. She pumped the brakes of her Subaru Outback and slid to a stop twenty feet from what appeared to be a large man facedown in the middle of the rutted, icy road. Leaving the engine and headlights on and activating the emergency flashers, she grabbed a flashlight out of the glove box and exited the Outback. As she approached, she saw blood oozing from a deep cut near the older man's temple. Shining the flashlight on his face, she was stunned to see the Two Harbors icon who lived just two doors down from her apartment.

"Greg! For fuck's sake, Greg!" she cried out. Kneeling on the cold road and removing a glove with her teeth, she felt a weak pulse on his neck. Pulling her smartphone from the pocket of a down jacket, she tapped 911 with her thumb and told the dispatcher that the county attorney had either slipped and fallen hard on the ice or been hit by a car.

Deputy Hokanen was the second emergency responder at the scene. Two paramedics told him that a car must have hit Thomassoni from behind, that his spine might be severed at L-4 from the impact. His right side hit the pavement first, breaking his right hip and right arm in multiple places and mangling his jaw. His skull had also been cracked open at the temple. And that was the preliminary assessment of two inexperienced EMTs. Hokanen relayed this information to his boss.

Sheriff MacDonald decided to wait until 8 a.m. before calling Thomassoni's only immediate family member, a son who lived in Portland, Oregon. He sipped on vending machine coffee from a paper cup and was one of three weary souls sitting in the waiting room of the intensive care unit at St. Mark's Hospital and Trauma Center in Duluth. Doctors had stabilized Thomassoni, but the lawyer was in a coma. The sheriff was about to leave the hospital in search of breakfast and a decent cup of coffee when the hospitalist in charge of Thomassoni's care burst through swinging double doors separating intensive-care patients from a small lobby for their families and friends.

"Good morning, Sheriff MacDonald. I'm Toni Bagley, the doctor coordinating Mr. Thomassoni's care. I understand he has no family in the area." Dressed in light-blue hospital scrubs and carrying a clipboard, Dr. Bagley was a handsome woman in her mid-forties, with a boyish salt-and-pepper haircut and a cheerful demeanor, despite sleeping about four hours a day.

"Not unless you call four ex-wives family," said MacDonald, regretting the cheap shot before he finished delivering it. "I really appreciate everything you're doing, Doctor. How is the tough old barrister?"

"He'll likely survive, but he's facing a long, painful recovery and potential paralysis in his legs. He'll need good friends like you. We expect him to be awake by the end of the day. Given the way he was bleeding, he wouldn't have made it if he'd been discovered an hour later. There's not much you can do here now, Sheriff. You should go home and get some rest."

"I'll probably do that, Doc, but can you tell me anything about the probable cause of Greg's injuries? Could he have simply slipped and fallen on the ice?"

"That's not my area of expertise, but to use a clinical phrase, *hell no*. Because you showed up to be here for your friend, I'll give you my best guess. He was run over by a vehicle. Probably not a heavy truck; that would have killed him for sure. But he was definitely hit by a blunt force that knocked him to the ground and then ran over his body. In other words, Sheriff, I believe someone was trying to kill him."

CHAPTER 18

February 4, 2020
North Oaks, Minnesota

GEORGE REDMAN HAD LIVED in the Twin Cities for fifty-plus years. As a St. Paul cop and BCA agent, he'd been virtually everywhere in the seven-county metro area, but he'd never been to North Oaks, a swanky suburb in the northernmost reaches of Ramsey County. The Dittrichs lived on a cul-de-sac at the end of a tree-lined, winding road called Catbird Circle. *Fagos must have liked Marcus,* thought Redman. They had to be paying him a shitload to be able to afford the limestone-and-granite castle he beheld while giving Fred a dog biscuit and exiting his aging Jeep Wrangler.

It was nine in the morning, and the air temperature was already a balmy three below. A Minnesota heat wave. The bright morning sun and endless blue sky made Redman smile as he jogged up the paver driveway, climbed the porch steps two at a time and rang the bell. He was surprised when Lona, and not some servant, opened the ten-foot maple doors that guarded the manse.

"Mr. Redman, right?" she asked politely.

"Yes, ma'am," he replied, respectfully.

"I'm Lona Dittrich. I'll take your coat," she said, not giving Redman an option to keep it. He knew she'd be expecting him. Julian Bande, the lawyer at Fagos, had set it up. He'd told Redman that Lona would be very cooperative.

Marcus had been born and raised in Cologne, Germany, and attended Aachen University in North-Rhine Westphalia near the Belgian border, where he met his first wife, Hilda, and earned a master's degree in metallurgical engineering. He'd worked for Fagos thirty-eight years, living on four different continents and raising two daughters with Hilda, a tremendous cook and wonderful mother who was a type-1 diabetic. She died of kidney failure at fifty-three when they were living in Ecuador. Five years later Marcus was having dinner at Providence in Los Angeles. Lona Mendez, a twenty-year-old marketing student at UCLA, was his server. He left her a $500 tip and a note, and three weeks later they were married. Redman knew that Lona had signed an iron-clad prenup that would take care of her for the rest of her life if she did exactly what Fagos told her.

Lona led the private detective through a massive great room with marble floors and a twenty-foot vaulted ceiling to a study or library with mahogany-beamed ceilings and coffee hand-scraped bamboo floors. Floor-to-ceiling bookshelves dominated the room. Most were filled with impressive volumes, many of which the studious curmudgeon had read. Redman was sure Lona had cracked open a few of the notable classics like William Prescott's *Conquest of Mexico* and Churchill's *A History of English-Speaking Peoples*. He had a hard time thinking ill of this gorgeous woman, not because of her looks, though the tight red cashmere sweater she wore over even tighter black suede pants didn't hurt, but because he hadn't eaten breakfast and she'd laid out a spread of croissants, scones, bagels, fruits and yogurt together with aromatic black coffee, which was Redman's version of crack. The morning feast occupied a long, glass-topped table framed by two gold leather couches.

"Would you like coffee, Mr. Redman?"

"Yes, please," he said. "Just black for me."

Lona put cream and sugar in hers and told him to fill a plate with food. Redman wasn't bashful when it came to filling his belly. He spread cream cheese and raspberry jam on a wheat bagel and grabbed a ripe banana and a string of grapes before sitting across from Mrs. Dittrich.

"It's weird," she said. "I'll never see Marcus again. I'm glad I talked to the medical examiner before I read the gruesome description of what happened to him in the *Star Tribune.* They said I could see his body if I really wanted to, but then that would be my last memory of him."

"I don't blame you," said Redman. "I wish I could erase a few memories of scenes from the past. I'll try not to take up too much of your time, Mrs. Dittrich. What did your husband tell you about his trip to Arizona?"

"The same thing he told me about most of his business trips, almost nothing. Look, Mr. Redman, despite what you may think or think you know, Marcus and I had a good marriage. He was basically a good, generous guy who worked eighty hours a week. He was also thirty years older and couldn't get it up half the time. So, yes, I had some fun with Trevor, and no, Marcus never knew about it. He got a hand job once a week and a little more on his birthday and holidays, and he was happy with that. Even though he carried a gun, he didn't know how to use it, and he never would. He'd been paranoid that I'd leave him for someone younger since before we were married. If he'd found out about Trevor, some thug from Fagos would have cut his balls off and stuffed them down his throat, but my husband was incapable of violence. What else do you want to know, Mr. Redman?"

"Wow," said Redman. "That sounded like a prepared speech, but I appreciate the information and the honesty, I think. Did Trevor say anything to you about this trip?"

"Just that he was excited to see the Super Bowl. He didn't play golf and didn't care about it. To him, it was just work. Trevor was a fun, likeable guy, but we had no future together."

"Okay," said Redman, beginning to understand why Marcus might have been paranoid. "What did you know about the other men on the plane—Larry Severinson and David Hesse?"

"I've never met Hesse and know nothing about him. Mr. Severinson and his wife sat at our table at a Children's Hospital fundraiser a few years ago, but they probably don't remember us. They were very pleasant, about Marcus's age. I recall she bid over ten grand for a couple of the live-auction items. I remember thinking at the time that they must be loaded."

"I think you're right about that," Redman agreed. "Did your husband have enemies? Anyone who threatened him or your family?" Redman knew that a lot of conservationists and environmentalists opposed CopperPlus's proposed mines, but was curious about Lona's perception of the situation.

"I can show you tons of hate mail, horrible emails, negative voicemails, all by people who don't know me or my husband. I totally get that they don't want copper mining in their backyard or in their campground or in the forests. But I'm biased. These are the same people who want the products that are made using these minerals. Having said that, I don't think Marcus felt any of these people would physically harm us or sabotage his plane, if that's what you're getting at. I just don't understand this, Mr. Redman. Trevor and Marcus wouldn't hurt anyone. I can't see Larry Severinson capable of violence, and why would he be? He's a gazillionaire. I didn't know the other guy at all, but he must be the guy, right? Right?"

Mrs. Dittrich covered her face with her hands and started blubbering. Redman wasn't sure the tears were real, or if they were for Marcus, Trevor, or both, but he also didn't think she knew much that could help him. If she did, why did Fagos need him?

"That's what I'm trying to figure out, Mrs. Dittrich. I won't take up any more of your time." Redman stood and waited for Lona to do the same. This time he led her through the great room, collecting his coat from the front closet. He opened one of the double doors and turned to face her, extending his right hand.

"Thank you for meeting with me and for your candor. I know this is a difficult time for you."

Lona ignored his hand, wrapped her arms around his neck, and gave him a meaningful hug.

"I apologize for losing it, Mr. Redman. Please let me know if you find out anything, okay?"

"Of course, I will," said Redman, handing her his business card before descending the porch steps, feeling a little ashamed for sprouting a woody during the brief embrace.

• • • • • • • • • • • • • • • •

Back at his place in St. Paul, Redman recognized the number on his cell. He was nervous but didn't know why.

"Hello, Special Agent Hinton. Thanks for returning my call."

"What's this Special Agent Hinton bullshit, George? Have you become more formal now that you're a high-paid private dick?"

"It's been a long time, Michelle," said Redman, sitting at the small desk in his apartment. "I wasn't sure you'd remember me."

"Only good memories. I'm not trying to blow smoke up your ass when I tell you that you were one of the best, George Redman. I'm not sure why you'd want to sully a great career by working for the Chilean mafia."

"For now, let's just say curiosity and a nice payday. Chilean mafia? I heard you're the FBI's lead in the CopperPlus plane crash investigation. I thought we might want to work together or at least share information."

"Oh, sure. I share information with you until you get something big and then go on radio silence. I generally don't team up with private investigators; it's against FBI protocol, but in your case I might make an exception. What did you have in mind, exactly?"

"I've got tickets to the Wolves game tonight. Meet me in the lobby at six thirty and we can compare notes over a beer after the game."

"My husband might not be crazy about that idea, George."

"I didn't know you were married."

"I'm not. I just wanted to know whether this was all business, or you were asking me on a date." Hinton loved fucking with shy guys like Redman, especially if she liked them.

"All business." That was a lie. But for his relationship with Rita at the time, Redman would have asked Hinton out when they'd worked together years earlier.

"Perfect," said Hinton. "I'm about to leave my office to interview Trevor Drake's mother. I'll meet you at the skyway entrance to Target Center above Second Street. You'd better have something I don't already know or you're buying me dinner."

CHAPTER 19

February 4, 2020
Duluth, Minnesota

AFTER LEAVING THE HOSPITAL, MacDonald called his eighty-year-old mother and offered to pick up pastries and coffee. Maggie MacDonald had been a registered nurse at Lakeview Hospital in Two Harbors. After her husband died, she retired and moved to a one-bedroom condo in Duluth's Kenwood neighborhood near St. Scholastica College. She accepted the offer of pastries but insisted on making a pot of Folger's rather than having her son spend four dollars for a fifty-cent cup of coffee.

MacDonald told her about Thomassoni's accident, the reason for his early-morning trip to Duluth. They sat at Maggie's kitchen table, enjoying her scrambled eggs with diced ham and cream cheese along with a Danish almond kringle, her son's contribution.

"What do the doctors say about Greg?" Maggie asked. She'd known Thomassoni since he was in middle school.

"They think he'll survive," said MacDonald, "but he's got a difficult road ahead. It's likely he'll be paralyzed from the waist down. That might only be in the short run or it might be permanent."

"Any leads on who was driving the car that hit him?" she asked, filling both mugs with Folger's made extra strong for her son.

"Not so far. Klewacki will work with an investigator from the Two Harbor's PD on the case, but unless a witness comes forward or we catch a break, I'm not confident we'll ever know. We'll talk to Greg when he's able; maybe he saw something."

"What about his job? Do you think he'll ever return to work?"

"I think he's done as county attorney, Mom. The commissioners meet tomorrow night, and they'll choose an interim for now. It'll either be Pete Begich or Hallie. Hallie's the only lawyer besides Greg who deals with the board, but she doesn't have any criminal law experience, and that's all Peter does. Hallie probably has the inside track, but I'm biased."

"That would be wonderful, Sam. She deserves a good break."

"You mean being married to me isn't everything a woman would ever want?"

"I think you know the answer to that. Why are you putting on your jacket? You just got here."

MacDonald was concerned about Thomassoni's partner in crime. Though it wasn't quite nine, the sheriff had called Ricky Holden three times and texted him twice with no response. That wasn't like the smarmy bastard, so MacDonald thought he'd make good use of his time in Duluth and visit Holden at his glass house on the hill.

"Sorry, Mom, but I need to check on somebody before he leaves the house. Remember, Hallie and I are taking you to brunch on Sunday at the Lake Avenue Grill." He kissed her forehead and gave her the kind of hug that a 230-pound man gives to the one and only mother he'll ever have.

"Thanks for breakfast. You still make the best scrambled eggs in town."

• • • • • • • • • • • • • • • •

Parking the Explorer in Holden's driveway, MacDonald had to admit he was envious of the magnificent view and one of the most spectacular homes he'd ever seen, occupied by one of the biggest fuckups he'd ever known. Ascending the steps to the granite front porch, he sensed something was amiss. It was a gloriously sunny Tuesday morning, and four floodlights, one above the porch and three on the garage, were shining uselessly. That wouldn't be unusual; Ricky might be in bed recovering from a wild Monday night, but MacDonald could see that one of the front double doors was ajar and the chandelier in the entryway was also on. He didn't bother ringing the bell or knocking. One step inside was all it took. Ricky Holden lay facedown, sprawled on the marble entryway floor.

MacDonald called out Ricky's name reflexively, not expecting a response. He knelt and checked for a pulse on Holden's wrist and on the carotid artery in his neck. Not only was there no pulse, but Holden's body was cold and rigid, and his face was a bloodless hue of grayish white. A rivulet of blood had trickled from Ricky's mouth and dried on the floor. It was too late for CPR, too late for an ambulance. Richard Holden III was dead.

Punching 911 on his cell, MacDonald wondered how Hallie would react to news of her ex-husband's death. "This is Sheriff MacDonald from Lake County," he told the dispatcher. "I'm at the Holden residence up on East Fourth Street, the glass house on Observation Hill. I'm afraid Mr. Holden has expired, so you should send the closest squad and a couple of homicide detectives. There's not much blood and no sign of forced entry, but I think we might have a crime scene. The crime being murder."

CHAPTER 20

February 4, 2020
St. Paul, Minnesota

THE TIMBERWOLVES WERE BEATING Sacramento in a rout, so Redman and Hinton left at the end of the third quarter. Hinton had taken a Lyft to the game, knowing Redman would drive and offer to take her home. The first thing he did was cross the Mississippi River to St. Paul where he was more comfortable, where he'd spent most of a lifetime.

When Hinton said she'd be up for beer and a burger, Redman suggested the Blue Door on Selby. The host seated them at a quiet table for two in a dark corner of the bar. Redman had to squint to read the menu by candlelight. They both ordered the house salad and a cheeseburger. Hinton ordered a Diet Coke and Limón; Redman, a Grey Goose martini up with a twist. They'd managed to be together for three hours without saying a word about the case. They talked about failed relationships, bad bosses, the case they solved together, and their shared disgust for the commander in chief.

"Red, I think it's great that you've got this private gig, but aren't you concerned about the true motives of the South Americans?"

"True motives, Michelle? They want to know who murdered one of their star employees and destroyed their fancy plane. Isn't that what you and the FBI want to know as well?"

"Of course. But the difference is what they do after they have the information. They've been known to take justice into their own hands, and with our current leadership we might not be in a position to stop them."

Redman sucked down his martini and ordered another. "If I didn't do their bidding, someone else would. I don't see anything wrong with their interest in pursuing this. Quite the contrary. Does this mean you don't want to work together?"

"*Quite the contrary*? Are you a cop or a British spy? Of course I want to work with you. If I didn't trust you and your judgment, I wouldn't be here. You're not that cute, George. I'm ready to compare notes." What she didn't tell him was the AD wanted to keep tabs on Fagos.

"You might just be playing me, Michelle, but that's okay. I've been doing my homework. I've interviewed the pilot's ex-girlfriend and his lover, who also plays the part of Marcus Dittrich's wife. I'm heavily discounting the possibility that Trevor Drake committed a violent crime. I've done background work on the three businessmen and their companies and have a meeting scheduled with Wanda Hesse and the lawyer for Northern Black Gold. The UHG people have been very cooperative, but I don't have anything scheduled with Mrs. Severinson. Understandably, she's grieving and isn't terribly interested in meeting with the private investigator for a mining company."

"Special Agent Whitney is meeting with Mrs. Severinson tomorrow. She'll be insulated by an army of executives. They're meeting at UHG headquarters, not the family's estate on Lake Minnetonka. I don't expect to get much from that, but you never know."

"That's for sure," Redman agreed. "Right after I talked to you this morning, I got a call from the risk manager for Infinity Life

Insurance. David Hesse took out a five million term life policy two weeks ago and used company funds to pay the first year's premium. And get this, the company has a key-man policy on Hesse's life with even higher limits. This guy wanted to hire me to investigate the circumstances of Hesse's death. I declined, of course. They offered about a third of what Fagos is paying."

"Five million dollars?" Hinton almost choked on a breadstick. "Hesse works for a company that's lost money in three of the last four years. He hasn't been paid a bonus in five years, and his options are underwater. His three teenage kids go to the Blake School at forty grand per kid, and he lives in a ten-thousand-square-foot mansion on Interlachen Golf Course. All that on three hundred and fifty grand per year?"

"I'm impressed, Michelle," said Redman, who loved nothing more than sticking it to self-absorbed, egotistical rich guys. "You think Mr. Hesse may be overextended? I think we should make a joint visit to the Hesse compound. I'd like to get access to all their financial records. I already have copies of the three mortgages on their home, the deed and mortgage on their lake cottage in Wisconsin and townhouse in Bonita Springs. I'm pretty sure the FBI can come up with a credit report under these circumstances without Wanda's consent."

"I'll see what I can do," said Hinton, tongue in cheek. "So, Hesse is leveraged to the hilt. Why not just take your own life? Why involve three innocent men?" Hinton had her own theories but knew she'd be amused by her cynical colleague's perspective.

"First of all, if he commits suicide within two years of taking out that Infinity Life policy, his family gets nothing. But if no one can prove who pulled the trigger on whom on that plane, they'll be forced to pay it out. Kind of brilliant if you ask me, especially if he's got an enemy in the bunch. Of course, what would really be fucking brilliant, crazy but brilliant—"

Redman stopped midsentence when their gaunt but pleasant bearded server set a plate down in front of him with a still-sizzling, mountainous cheeseburger dominating a tiny green salad. For the next five minutes, Redman and Hinton enjoyed each other's company while attacking their food in rapturous silence.

Hinton was the first to come up for air. "This is great," she said, washing down a particularly large bite with the dregs from her second drink. "Good choice, Red. By the way, don't you live close to here?"

Redman had been hoping she'd give him an opening to invite her to his place for a nightcap. "A couple miles east but relatively close. I picked up a fresh apple pie from Woulet's if you'd like to see it for yourself."

"I shouldn't on a weeknight, but if you make me an Irish coffee and introduce me to Fred, I might make an exception."

For the first time since he started dating Rita nearly twenty years earlier, Redman felt like a teenager. After pie and Redman's version of Irish coffee, heavy on the Irish, Hinton spent what was left of the night in St. Paul.

• • • • • • • • • • • • • • •

David Paul Hesse was born in 1975 on the eve of the US bicentennial. It was fitting, then, that he was born in London to Thomas Paul Hesse, a commander in the US Navy who was a defense attaché in the US Embassy, and his spouse of less than a year, Lydia Swift, a British citizen who'd recently taken a break from a job as an interior designer to start a family. Lydia developed preeclampsia and suffered a fatal stroke while giving birth to David. Because Thomas was a career Naval officer, he sent his son to live with his parents, both high school teachers in Albany, New York, rather than have him raised by a nanny. Tom visited his son at least once a month until he remarried five years later and secured a permanent position with the defense department in Washington, DC. Hesse spent the rest of his childhood in Bethesda, Maryland, where he gained two half siblings and a stepmother who treated him as her own blood.

Hesse excelled in math and science and lettered in soccer in high school and at William & Mary College, where he majored in chemistry. He went on to get a master's in chemical engineering at Georgia Tech in Atlanta, where he would meet his future wife, Wanda Stanton, a marketing major and Georgia Tech cheerleader whose father was an unsuccessful Atlanta stockbroker and whose mother was a professional social climber.

Hesse could never make enough money to cover Wanda's needs and desires, so debt became a natural part of their lifestyle. Wanda stopped working outside the home after the twins were born, and Hesse's progressively better jobs at Chevron, Mobil Oil and Atlantic Richfield kept them out of bankruptcy, barely.

When Hesse was offered the CEO position at a growing shale exploration company in 2015, he jumped at the chance to be the master of his destiny and to own a meaningful share of a growing organization. Though Wanda wasn't thrilled about moving from Houston to the Twin Cities, when she found out NBG's main operations were in western North Dakota and eastern Montana, she was relieved to be in Minnesota. The problem was they assumed the job would be worth millions in bonuses and options, but that all depended on the price of crude and the costs to extract it. When the price became depressed for three years and the extraction costs increased, they were in serious trouble. With a quarter million in credit card debt, two million in mortgages, and private school tuition for their three kids, they were forced to borrow the max from David's 401k and over fifty grand from Wanda's parents, who charged the same interest they were paying on their credit cards.

Hesse was desperate. In late 2019, oil prices rose to levels where Northern could capitalize on increasing production levels, but the board of directors, which included the principal investors, was cautious, especially since rising crude prices were primarily due to a series of Iranian-led attacks on Saudi oil fields and Drummond's reactionary foreign policy.

Hesse wanted to be more aggressive; he needed to be more aggressive. To protect his family, he convinced the board at NBG to pay the first year's premium on a big life insurance policy payable to his wife. He readily accepted Dittrich's invitation because he wanted access to his Chilean bosses. If he could convince them to buy out the Minnesota investors and take over NBG, he could double or triple the company's profitability and the value of his incentives and shares. He also wanted to talk to his father, but Tom Hesse didn't recognize his son. He was suffering from severe dementia and living in a long-term care facility in Bethesda. That would never happen to David. If he couldn't find a deep-pocket investor soon, he'd have to take more drastic measures.

CHAPTER 21

February 5, 2020
Duluth, Minnesota

DR. THEODORE HIGGINS WAS president and CEO of Midwest Medical Examiners, the largest professional pathology and forensic medical practice in Minnesota. Higgins, or Dr. Ted as he was known by local law enforcement, was a big man with a big resume. He'd studied medicine at the University of Wisconsin and Mayo Clinic and enlisted in the Marines as a medic during Desert Storm. Early in his career, he recognized that his gruff, dismissive bedside manner was more effective interacting with corpses than with living, breathing humans. His examinations were exhaustive, and his autopsy reports detailed and unassailable. Once he reached a conclusion, he was open to new approaches and ideas but not to intimidation by a cross-examining lawyer or an angry family member.

As meticulous and formal as he was professionally, he was crude, loud and sloppy personally. In his mid-fifties, Higgins had long, unruly gray hair and a bushy gray beard. Stuffing 250 pounds into his six-foot frame, he often wore light-blue scrubs with a large tear, or maybe it was a flap, over his butt cheeks, and expensive high-top Jordan basketball sneakers. He played tennis with Sheriff MacDonald once a week and lived in a renovated five-bedroom brick Tudor on the lake side of London Road with his wife, four daughters and two uppity shih tzus.

Higgins and his loyal staff had worked around the clock to keep pace with the winter carnage. He invited Klewacki, MacDonald, Special Agent Whitney and Detective Sargent Ahmed Ali of the Duluth PD to his office in the bowels of St. Mark's for a sneak preview of his findings before releasing anything to the media.

MacDonald brought pastries and coffee from Amazing Grace Bakery in Canal Park. After brief introductions, everyone sat in folding metal chairs around a long metal table that formerly was used for postmortem examinations. Just one example of Higgins's sick sense of humor. He distributed a four-page memo that covered the salient points of the dissertation he was about to give.

"Okay, everybody, it's already after nine, so let's get started. We'll discuss these cases in chronological order, starting with William Vandenberg. Mr. Vandenberg had clear indications of atherosclerosis, a plaque buildup in his major arteries. That doesn't mean he couldn't or wouldn't have lived several more months when blood cancer most certainly would have killed him. However, the excitement of driving a snowmobile sixty miles per hour in a blinding blizzard with a twenty-year-old woman's warm hand wrapped around his withered penis was just too much for old Bill. He had an arrythmia-triggered infarction of the heart muscle when, or immediately after, he ejaculated into his boxers. He probably lost consciousness and control a few moments before crashing into a large tree. Was he already dead when he broke his neck or did the crash kill him? Does it matter? You tell me. Our report will include all the clinical details, of course."

Klewacki gave MacDonald a look that said *holy shit.* Higgins continued.

"The three gentlemen from the ill-fated King Air presented fairly simple, straightforward cases for us even though one of them was half eaten by animals. The two older men had been shot in the back of the head at close range, and the third, the young pilot, was shot a few centimeters below the temple. I can't say for certain that they were killed instantly, but the two who were recovered on Isle Royale would not have survived the fall if by some quirk they had survived a small explosion inside the cranium."

Special Agent Whitney spoke up. "I'm curious. Given the condition of Dittrich's body, with most of his head missing, how could you tell he'd been shot? We know the only gun we've recovered was his Ruger, so an obvious connection to make is that he was the most likely shooter."

"Good question," said Higgins, though in truth he thought it was amateurish. "Fortunately for our purposes, Dittrich must have landed on his back. In any case, the animals left the back of his head and neck intact. Though we never recovered a slug, there was a visible entry point that matched the entry wound of Larry Severinson. I assure you, Dittrich was not the shooter, or, more to the point, he didn't shoot himself."

"So, if we find David Hesse, we should have our killer, is that what you're saying?" asked Whitney.

"That's for you folks to figure out," said Higgins, as he paused to enjoy part of an apple fritter. "Let's move to the most interesting and most difficult case— Richard Holden III. It may take weeks before we have a final report on him, but you should know that his entitled, arrogant, rich-fuck father has already been hounding me for answers. I've told him that it's highly unlikely his son died from natural causes like a stroke or heart attack, but without a detailed toxicology screen, I can't issue a definitive cause of death.

"Having made that disclaimer, here's what I think. Rick Holden was murdered. Someone stabbed him in the neck with a syringe containing both a powerful anesthetic like propofol, and a deadly poison like strychnine or curare. I'm leaning towards curare, a short-acting neuromuscular blocking and paralyzing agent, because Mr. Holden died of organ failure and general paralysis leading to heart failure. The big question is this: how did someone get this deadly mixture? I'm guessing it's someone who works in a hospital or large pharmacy, or someone who knows someone who does. I won't speculate on how the murderer got into Mr. Holden's house."

Detective Ali spoke up. "We've reviewed the video and photos from the CCTV cameras on the front porch and garage. Whoever murdered Holden knew what he or she was doing. She was quite tall if a woman, with platinum-blonde hair that may have been a wig and a long down coat. Ricky didn't hesitate to let her into the house. She didn't park a vehicle in Holden's driveway even though there's no on-street parking for at least two blocks on either side of his house, and it was fifteen below zero at midnight that evening. She was also wearing black gloves and was careful never to look directly at either of the cameras. Other than the photos and video, there's no evidence of her ever being in the house, no fingerprints and nothing left inside. According to the video, she entered at seven minutes after eleven and left twelve minutes later."

"She also must be quite strong," added Higgins. "Ricky was over six feet tall, yet she had enough leverage and strength to penetrate the tendons in his lower neck with a syringe and to keep the needle embedded while she delivered the deadly mixture into his bloodstream. I'm sure he passed out and collapsed immediately, but he probably didn't die for an hour or so."

"I don't think it's a coincidence that Ricky Holden and Greg Thomassoni were attacked on the same night," Klewacki said, standing and lifting her heavy parka from the back of her chair. "Excuse me, everybody, but I'm late for a meeting with Holden's banker. I've got a window of opportunity to get the records for Sawtooth Mountain Snowmobile Club's accounts before the elder Holden figures out that Ricky was mixing business with pleasure at Overlook Lodge. This is related to last Friday's snowmobile crash, but if I discover any connection to Ricky's murder, I'll call you, Ahmed. Thanks for the info, Doc."

When Klewacki left, the meeting was over. After a brief discussion about the release of the autopsy reports, Ali and Whitney left, but MacDonald stayed to finish his coffee and have a chat with his friend. A nurse from intensive care texted him that Thomassoni was alert enough to have a visitor.

"You've been busy, Ted. I can't believe what your team has accomplished in the last five days. Greg Thomassoni's fortunate he's not in one of your drawers."

"We've got a good group here, Mac, but to be honest, except for Holden, these cases are straightforward. Speaking of Holden, I haven't come across curare poisoning since my days as a medic."

"Isn't that a plant-based poison that some Southwestern tribes rubbed on their arrows to kill large animals?"

"Including human animals," said Higgins. "I forget sometimes that you're a student of history. If it turns out to be curare, I'm curious about how the killer knew about it and mixed it together with an anesthetic. You need to have special expertise to get it right or have access to a Native American medicine man."

"Maybe whoever wanted Ricky Holden dead had the resources to commit the perfect murder. Anyway, I think I'll head up to intensive care and check on our county attorney."

"Tennis or squash Friday afternoon?"

"I'll call you."

• • • • • • • • • • • • • • •

The head nurse in the ICU told MacDonald he could visit with Thomassoni for fifteen minutes, tops. *Ten minutes will be enough,* thought MacDonald, as he surveyed the sterile, white room with a window overlooking a parking lot and several monitors and med tech devices taking up more space than the hospital bed and visitor chairs. *The View* was airing on a small color TV suspended from the ceiling, but it was either on mute or the volume was set below a whisper.

Pale, with three days' growth of his salt-and-pepper beard, Thomassoni wore a blood pressure cuff on his left arm and had multiple intravenous lines infusing his bloodstream with pain medications, antibiotics and whatever else his team of doctors prescribed. His nurse had used the bed's remote-control device to prop him into a sitting position, at his request. He was awake, staring at his hands, fingers intertwined and resting on his diaphragm.

"What the fuck, Mac? Who did this to me?"

Thomassoni's voice was weak and breathy, not reflecting the ferocity of his anger. MacDonald sat on the chair closest to the bed and set his jacket on his knees.

"What have you been told?"

"The only people I've talked to since I've been awake are my doctors and nurses, my son and Doug Priley. None of them has told me anything except that some cocksucker in a car mowed me down at one in the morning."

"Unfortunately, that's about all we know. Gail is working on it, but we haven't located any witnesses, and there are too many overlapping tire tracks to identify even a type of vehicle. Do you remember anything from your walk home that night, Greg?"

"It was a beautiful night, clear and cold. There were millions of stars visible over the lake. I've walked those four blocks a thousand times, maybe more. That time of night, especially on a Monday, I didn't expect to see or hear anyone, except maybe one of Two Harbors' finest on patrol. Here's what I don't understand. The wind was at my back, yet I never heard a thing, no engine, no muffler, nothing, and then boom! After that, the lights went out."

"How much did you have to drink that night?"

"A few beers with my dinner at Backwoods. Is it a crime to walk home over .08?"

"Hey, that's pretty funny, but what I'm trying to get at is whether you were too drunk to hear an engine. If not, then perhaps you were hit by an electric car, a Prius or Tesla or Leaf?"

"I'd say that's possible, maybe even likely. There was nothing wrong with my hearing that night."

"Okay, Greg, I'll pass this information along to Gail. How are you feeling other than justifiably pissed?"

"That's the problem. Right now, I can't feel anything below my waist. I've got some broken bones on my right side, so my arm and jaw are sore. But, hell, Mac, I know I'm lucky to be alive."

"What did Doug Priley have to say?" Priley was the chair of the Lake County Board of Commissioners.

"I called him right before you came in. I told him I'd be laid up recovering for a month or two, so my duties should be split between Hallie and Pete."

"You should call him back, Greg. Tell him you're going on disability leave or retiring, whichever is more advantageous to you financially." MacDonald didn't want to upset Thomassoni, but his time as county attorney was over.

"Why should I do that?" Thomassoni protested. "I've still got twenty months left on my term, and who knows, I might run again in 2021."

"Gail is reviewing the banking records of Rick Holden's snowmobile club as we speak. If there's nothing in those records that might embarrass you, then maybe you should run again. Of course, there's also the matter of some UMD students being paid to entertain club members."

"Oh, for shit!" said Thomassoni, covering his eyes with his hands. "And what do Ricky and his lawyers have to say about all this?"

"Ricky's dead, Greg." Before MacDonald could expand on that bombshell, the lead ICU nurse was standing between him and Thomassoni's bed.

"I gave you an extra five minutes, Sheriff MacDonald. Mr. Thomassoni needs his rest."

MacDonald walked over to the door, keeping his eyes on Thomassoni. "Think about what I said, Greg. You can call me later if you feel up to it."

CHAPTER 22

IT HAD BEEN TWO days since the big announcement, and Jenny Pierce was already inundated with campaign work. She'd literally begged Liz to put her in charge of recruiting, training, and managing volunteers. They needed volunteers to send emails and make phone calls to solicit contributions; volunteers to go door-to-door distributing campaign literature and lawn signs; volunteers to write letters and blogs; volunteers to research the opponent; and volunteers to manage the website and Twitter feed. The Vandenberg Foundation would be taking a back seat to the campaign, but Liz and Jenny agreed the campaign was worth it.

Jenny lived in a newer three-bedroom condominium just east of Woodland Avenue and north of Clover Street near the UMD campus. There were only a handful of units in her building, occupied mostly by graduate students, professors, and young professionals. Jenny shared the condo with two roommates—Justin, a transgender third-year medical school student who worked part time at a funeral home; and Christina, a recent elementary education grad who taught second grade at Holy Rosary Catholic School even though she was a lesbian. Pretty and petite, Christina was careful not to wear an embroidered *L* on the blouses and sweaters she wore to work. Occasionally, Christina would end up in Jenny's bed after a night of overindulging with alcohol or pot, but both women wanted nothing more than a friendship with benefits.

Christina and Justin were psyched about working on the Jeronimus campaign; both took a day off in the middle of the week to help their friend organize the 400-plus volunteers who'd signed up since Monday afternoon. The three roommates and five veteran DFL activists sat around a conference table like an NFL team's front office and scouts on draft day, comparing the strengths and weaknesses of various volunteers, reviewing resumes, emails, texts and letters, and creating teams of campaign soldiers. Jenny orchestrated the effort, though her thoughts drifted elsewhere. Her bosses, Alex and Liz, were campaigning together in Hibbing. Jeronimus was giving speeches at a couple of junior colleges and Hibbing High School while Liz met with donors and the media. They were a good team.

CHAPTER 23

February 5, 2020
St. Paul, Minnesota

REDMAN FELT SOMETHING WARM and wet on the back of his neck. Struggling to wake up, he opened one eye and saw *5:35* in red, two-inch numerals that even he could read on his digital alarm clock. Then he remembered why he was so tired and why he'd only been sleeping for three hours. *Michelle.* He turned to his left expecting to see her, to feel her warm body touching his. But it was Fred. Fred licked his face and whined.

"Where'd the lady go, Fred?" he asked rhetorically, as he lifted the sheet and comforter and swung his legs out of bed. He noticed a fresh text on his iPhone, fully recharged on his nightstand. It was from Hinton.

Thx for the fun evening, Red. Got Lyft home—busy day.
See u @ Hesse house @ 10. I love Fred.
MH

Redman made a pot of mud-butt coffee. He scrambled three eggs with onions, tomatoes and swiss cheese, then scooped the concoction onto two pieces of sourdough toast. Fred got his usual dry dog food garnished with a spoonful of the eggs. Redman didn't like reading newspapers online. After all, the *Pioneer Press* took only twenty minutes to read from stem to stern. He retrieved his daily paper from the first-floor lobby of the fourplex and sat at the kitchen table to eat his sandwich and keep tabs on the evil in the world, while Fred laid his head on Redman's knee, a signal that he'd like a morning walk.

The lead story in the paper continued to be the Split Rock crash and its aftermath. A memorial service for Marcus Dittrich was scheduled for Friday morning at North Oaks Country Club. Larry Severinson's funeral at Mount Olivet Lutheran Church would be standing-room only on Saturday afternoon. There were a lot of questions but few answers about what transpired aboard the King Air 250 after it left Holman Field. Three men shot in the head and one missing and presumed dead. Three murders and a suicide? That was the prevailing opinion. Might make for a good movie, but Redman didn't buy it. *David Hesse is capable of murder,* he thought. *Who isn't? But kill himself so Wanda and the kids might collect on the big insurance policy?* He'd know more after interviewing Wanda.

Weather.com on his smartphone said it was partly cloudy and five below with an expected high of twenty. The sun wouldn't be up for an hour. He dressed for conditions, making sure he wore lined boots, insulated gloves and a wool ski cap, and reached for Fred's retractable leash on a hook in his front closet. The dog's tail banged against the closet door in anticipation.

Redman had a handful of routes for walks with Fred. Today, it was the Summit Avenue promenade, a three-mile walk covering a mile on the historic parkway down to St. Paul Cathedral and John Ireland Boulevard and then back to his apartment near Ramsey Hill. Redman was contemplative as he observed the emergence of the morning sun. Rays of yellow light shot through cracks in low-hanging cumulus clouds in the eastern sky over the Mississippi.

His life as a cop had been tumultuous, a string of cleared cases that didn't come close to making up for a dead partner, gunned down in the line of duty when Redman was on the only two-week vacation he'd ever taken. He still blamed himself for not being there.

He'd never been married, except to his work, and then, twenty years ago, he was sitting at the bar in the St. Paul Hotel having a club sandwich and a beer on a Saturday night. He'd spent most of a sweltering day as a negotiator in a domestic hostage situation that ended badly. Watching the Twins lose to the Angels in a late game, Redman became distracted by a chatty bartender. She was beautiful. Wearing Converse All-Stars, she was tall, taller than Redman, with dark-red hair, pinned up in the back, wonderful freckles everywhere, and a wide, toothy smile. She was husky, or, more artfully stated, big-boned; she definitely outweighed Redman, and he loved every single inch of her. To him, the most unusual thing about the twenty-something woman was her attraction to a squirrely, sweaty, foul-mouthed forty-five-year-old cop. Throughout their twenty years together, he never fully accepted the fact that she loved him, but that didn't help much when she left.

Within two months of his resignation from the bureau, G. B. Redman Investigations had a website, an office on Grand Avenue, a professional private-eye license, and a part-time receptionist. Redman needed something to do. He'd been close to his dead partner's family, especially his two boys, who called him Uncle George and would be starting college in the fall. When Fagos called him, his initial reaction was to say no, *no fucking way*. But he'd opened a college savings account for the two boys, and $50,000 would pay for a year of private college or two years of a good state school. It might be the best thing he'd ever done.

Fred took a juicy dump in the driveway of a wealthy suit who'd told Redman before to "keep that fuckin' ugly dog away from my property." Redman hadn't bothered to get into it with the arrogant prick, but he also didn't bother to pick up after Fred.

Back at his apartment, he filled Fred's water bowl, shaved, showered and finished some background prep for his interview with Wanda Hesse. He wanted to be at his best to impress Michelle. Wanda had to be desperate for some answers and maybe for some cash.

• • • • • • • • • • • • • • •

Redman parked the Jeep near the back of a circular concrete driveway. Two stone lion sentinels that must have been six feet long and five feet tall guarded the entrance to the Hesse compound on Bywood West, one of several mansions in the upscale Rolling Green neighborhood of Edina, a solid eight iron away from historic Interlachen Country Club. The all-brick Georgian-style home sat in the middle of a wooded, two-acre lot. It had five bedrooms, seven bathrooms and nearly 10,000 square feet of living space, including a theater room and sauna.

As usual, Redman was early, but he wasn't the only old bird after a worm. There were three other vehicles in the driveway. He assumed the BMW 550 belonged to the Hesse family lawyer, the Cadillac XT5 belonged to NBG's chief operating officer, and, by process of elimination, the older Lincoln SUV had to be Hinton's. He peeked in a window of Hesse's four-car garage and saw a Mercedes SUV, a '65 Mustang convertible, and a newer Audi A8. He wondered whether it was worse to be stinking rich or to want to be rich so badly that you stunk. He wouldn't fret about the answer; stinking rich was better.

Although the driveway was bone dry, the stone sidewalk leading to the front door was icy and slick. Redman surmised that family members entered the house through the garage. Given the prominence of the two large signs on the front porch, one banning solicitation and the other advertising a wireless security system, he also surmised that the Hesse family had few visitors. Or maybe they were preparing for an invasion of creditors.

Between the time he located a well-hidden doorbell and raised a finger to press it, Wanda Hesse opened the front door and greeted him with a distinctive Georgia drawl. "Why hello, Mr. Redman. We've been waitin' on you." She was a tiny woman, about a head shorter than Redman and barely a hundred pounds. She waited for him to remove his boots, then took his jacket and led him through the two-story foyer and spacious family room to a dining area with a long, oval mahogany table where Hinton and two gentlemen in suits were seated, both cradling coffee mugs and staring at laptop computer screens. While Wanda disposed of his jacket, Redman introduced himself and sat next to Hinton, across from the suits. He opened a small, leather portfolio that contained a notebook and a Cross ballpoint pen that had been a parting gift from the BCA. Hinton subtly pinched his knee under the table while continuing to stare at her laptop.

Wanda sat at the head of the table and offered Redman coffee, tea or water, which he politely declined. She was the quintessential junior leaguer, and she intended to be in full control of the proceedings.

Hinton was about to take the lead; after all, she was the one who'd asked for the meeting. But the older suit, Alan Wineblatt, a heavyset fellow with a manicured white beard, black and navy–striped tie and black-rimmed glasses, lifted a meaty right hand and cut Hinton off at the pass.

"I just want to make it clear at the outset that I represent both the Hesse family and Northern Black Gold in this particular matter, and I will continue to do so unless and until there is a conflict in their respective interests. My clients intend to cooperate with all legitimate investigations into this unfathomable tragedy, which we believe is a case of a pilot who, for whatever reason, went batshit crazy, murdered and disposed of his passengers, including David, and then committed suicide. We have been hoping and praying for the speedy recovery of David's body. We're also considering all of our legal rights and remedies, including a wrongful death action against

CopperPlus for the negligent hiring and supervision of Trevor Drake. Mr. Redman, I know you're investigating this incident on behalf of the company, so I want you to be aware of our position."

"Duly noted," said Redman, wanting to say more but deferring to Hinton. He noticed that Wanda seemed irritated with her counsel and that the younger suit was sweating profusely while taking notes on his laptop.

Hinton patiently waited for her turn. "Mrs. Hesse, I have some questions for you, but I'd like to start with a few questions for Mr. Lundegard, if I may."

Terrence Lundegard was what is known in business parlance as a "number cruncher." A finance major in college, Lundegard was a certified public accountant who married his high school sweetheart from Pine City at twenty-two and accepted a job as an auditor with a big-four accounting firm. From there he rose to audit manager, then audit partner. He was the opining partner for NBG's independent audit in 2017, when the company's chief financial officer was caught texting photos of his private parts to the president of the United States. He did it as a joke, with the caption *From one big dick to the biggest dick of them all.* No one on NBG's board thought it was funny, and Hesse replaced him with Lundegard, a no-nonsense financial wizard who worked seventy hours a week and read the tax code in the company's bathroom to increase his personal productivity.

The directors loved Lundegard, so they readily acquiesced with Hesse's plan to promote him to chief operating officer, in line to succeed him as CEO in five to seven years. Neither the board nor Hesse had a clue that Lundegard was not only a financial genius but also a complete fraud. He'd been siphoning small amounts from each of the company's drilling and exploration operating accounts every day, which, if undetected, would net him three million-plus in the next five years.

"Mr. Lundegard, I want to confirm with you that Mr. Hesse had a company-issued cell phone, an iPhone X, is that right?" Hinton and

Redman knew that, so far, no cellphones had been recovered from the King Air or from Isle Royale. Even the pilot's phone was missing.

"That's right," Lundegard acknowledged. "He may have had a personal cell phone as well, though I never saw him use it."

"He had no other phone," Wanda chimed in. "He didn't like textin' and didn't have any use for a smartphone. He was always on his laptop or iPad."

"Thank you, Mrs. Hesse. Could you tell me then when was the last time you talked to your husband? Was it during the flight?"

"During the flight? Are you fuckin' kiddin' me, sweetheart? David hugged me and the kids on Friday morning before he left and told us he'd call before the Super Bowl on Sunday. That's it, honey; that's it. He wasn't much for phone calls." And then the tears came.

"I am so sorry, Mrs. Hesse. Would you like to reschedule?"

Redman gently kicked her under the table. He had a feeling the tears were manufactured.

"No, no. I'll be fine. I just want y'all to know that David went on this trip to save his company. He wanted to invest in more drillin' cuz he knew crude prices were on the rise, but others, like the Fargo numbnuts who control the voting shares and Lunderfuck over there, wanted to hold back and refinance the debt first."

"That's a lie!" Lundegard blurted. "David didn't like taking orders from the Hatton brothers; he thought they were second-generation morons who would lose the fortune their father amassed from cattle ranching in Montana. He wanted to sell his soul to Chilean mining devils. That's why he befriended Marcus Dittrich. The Chileans pretty much let Dittrich run the show at CopperPlus; David wanted a similar situation and access to unlimited capital."

Wanda stood and leaned across the table, nearly biting Lundegard's long nose with her flapping gums. "You were taking it up the ass from both Hatton boys!"

Redman got into the act. "Hey, folks, let's take a deep breath and think about why we're here. Special Agent Hinton and I are trying to figure out what happened on that plane. I doubt the internal politics at NBG had much to do with it, but you're welcome to continue this conversation when we leave. You say David Hesse knew Marcus Dittrich. How about Larry Severinson? Were the two of them acquainted before this trip?"

"I have no idea," said Lundegard. "He talked a lot about CopperPlus and what an advantage it was to have the Drummond administration on your side in dealing with the EPA and Interior Department."

"He knew who Severinson was," said Wanda. "Everyone in town with a brain knows he's the head of UHG, but David didn't know him socially. I know he was excited for the chance to talk to him about health care on the plane."

Wineblatt had pieces of a chocolate donut in his beard and was either sleeping or reading the label of the zipper that was heading south on his fly. Hinton pulled a file out of her briefcase and removed copies of some key correspondence. She paused for a moment to consider how best to phrase her next question.

"So, at some point in the future, Mrs. Hesse, it is highly likely that you and Northern Black Gold will each be making a demand on Infinity Insurance for several million dollars, primarily because of two term life policies that were issued less than a month ago. Can you tell me why the company and family wanted this level of protection?"

"I can explain the company portion," said Lundegard. "Out of the blue, David announced that he'd signed up with Thomson Treks to climb Mount Kilimanjaro in Tanzania in May. It's a ten-day climb at a time of year when the weather is unpredictable. Although David has been frustrated with the board and the brothers, they still believed he was the right guy to lead NBG, so they directed me to increase the key-man policy on David's life from three million to eight million to cover the cost of replacing him. When David was asked to undergo a physical to qualify for the additional five million key-man policy, he asked the company to pay the first year's premium on an additional five million for his family, and, against my recommendation, the Hattons agreed."

"Sure, they agreed," Wanda butted in. "Those pricks promised my husband the world to get him to move up to this frozen wasteland, and now we're up to our eyeballs in debt, and my poor David is probably a human popsicle for some polar bear. If I have any problems collecting the insurance he got to protect us, I will rip a new asshole into each of them Hatton brothers and burn down their mansions on Lake Minnetonka."

"Have you talked to anyone from the insurance company?" Hinton asked Wanda, trying to alleviate some of the tension between her and Lundegard.

"Why would I?" Wanda sneered. "He's not been found dead yet."

Hinton removed more papers from her briefcase, put them in proper order and placed them in front of Wanda. "These are authorizations permitting the FBI to gain access to your and David's credit, banking, investment and insurance accounts to assist our investigation. We can subpoena the records if we need to, but I'd prefer to have your permission and cooperation."

Wineblatt cleared his throat. "You don't need to sign those, but eventually they will get access to your account information."

"I've had enough of this shit for one day," Wanda cursed as she stood and pointed in the direction of the front door. "Everybody out," she yelled. "Everyone get the fuck out of my house now!"

Lundegard stood without saying a word, collapsed his laptop, snatched his overcoat and stalked through the house and out the front door. Hinton and Redman were more deliberate. They'd seen this kind of reaction before. Redman winked at Hinton while zipping up his leather portfolio. She packed her briefcase and followed Redman, who was following Wanda towards a large closet in the foyer where she'd hung their coats. The lawyer sat in his chair without moving a muscle, except for smirking. He, too, had witnessed this behavior, but he was the only one who'd witnessed a Wanda meltdown.

"I'm truly sorry if we've upset you, Mrs. Hesse, but I have a job to do, and that job is to gather all relevant information on the lives of the men on that airplane and then to develop a supportable theory about what crimes were committed and by whom and, if we're very fortunate, why. I appreciate that you and your family are going through a difficult time, so I will honor your request to leave, but if we determine the FBI needs to question you again, one of my colleagues or I will be back, do you understand?"

"Fuck off," Wanda said as she slammed the front door in Hinton's face. Redman was already halfway down the driveway, but he heard it all and then waited for Hinton to catch up.

"What did you make of that?" asked Hinton, playfully punching Redman in the shoulder.

"I'm not sure, but I think I know why David Hesse killed himself."

"That's awful, Red, even if it might be true. I think it's a combination of grief and frustration; the latter she's been dealing with for quite a while. We need to recover her husband, then we'll know a lot more.

"We've got three memorial services in the next five days. I know you'll attend Dittrich's on Friday and the pilot's on Monday. Lance and I will go to Severinson's Saturday afternoon. I think I told you Lance has a meeting at UHG headquarters early next week with their senior executive team and Severinson's wife. They've been cooperative so far. After that meeting, the three of us should get together and compare notes."

"That's fine," said Redman, "but maybe the two of us should get together at my place on Saturday night to watch the Gophers and enjoy the best spaghetti with sausage in the Twin Cities, my Irish mother's recipe."

A reliable voice in her head told her to say no; she didn't need to get in deep with another cop. "I can be there around seven thirty. I'll bring a bottle of red to go with your pasta and maybe a special dessert."

"Perfect." He leaned over and kissed her cheek, something he'd never have done in broad daylight with Rita. Maybe he wasn't too old to learn.

CHAPTER 24

February 5, 2020
Two Harbors, Minnesota

THE LAKE COUNTY BOARD met every Wednesday evening at six. The meeting on February 5, in the Split Rock River Room, was short on agenda and long on gossip. A plane had crashed into Split Rock Lighthouse, and a legendary county attorney had nearly been killed by a hit-and-run motorist. Sheriff MacDonald presented reports on both topics, indicating the NTSB and FBI would be leading the investigations into the cause of the crash and any crimes that were committed on the plane. On the other hand, Detective Gail Klewacki was handling the investigation into the attempted murder of Greg Thomassoni, who was now in fair condition at St. Mark's Hospital. She had not yet identified suspects.

Board Chair Priley reported that he'd had a phone conversation with the county attorney an hour before the meeting. He was shaken by the call mainly because Thomassoni was emotional and upset and asked him to inform the board that he was resigning as Lake County attorney effective immediately. He regretted that his recovery would take months if not years and that he would not be in a position to serve his constituents in the foreseeable future, if ever.

Given his years of service, he qualified for a pension equal to 75 percent of his average salary over the past five years, which Commissioner Priley noted he richly deserved. He didn't mention that Thomassoni might be paralyzed below the waist.

The final order of business was the appointment of an interim county attorney, who would hold the position until a special election could be held in November. Priley reported that Thomassoni didn't think either of the two assistants in the criminal division had enough experience to lead the office and represent the people of Lake County. He recommended the appointment of Hallie Bell MacDonald as interim county attorney. After Priley placed her name in nomination, there was a brief discussion about the propriety of appointing a county attorney who was married to the sheriff. Since the county's current authority on legal matters had recommended her, and voters would get to decide in November, the board appointed her by acclamation.

CHAPTER 25

February 6, 2020
Duluth, Minnesota

RICKY HOLDEN HAD MORE flaws than a counterfeit painting, but to his dad, he was the perfect son, the apple of his eye, a source of pride, a like-minded soul. Richard Holden was grieving and halfway through a bottle of bourbon before eight in the evening. He sat alone in his penthouse office atop the sixteen-story Holden Towers, the tallest building in Duluth. In the wake of his son's death, Richard had become obsessed with two things: revenge and revenue. He needed to find Ricky's killer and dump the white elephant the boy had built on Shovel Point. Looking through floor-to-ceiling windows at the lights on the ship canal and the steel-colored lake beyond, Holden made a call for help at the highest level.

"Hello, Rudy?"

"Yes."

"Rudy, this is Richard Holden up in Minnesota. We met at a fundraiser at that fancy Florida resort last fall."

"Sure, I remember. Your family owns most of the Midwest. The

Boss keeps talking about extending the Organization's franchise into the heartland. What can I do for you, Dick?"

"It's Rick, Rudy."

"Right. What's on your mind, Rick?'

"I need some help, and I think your boss may be interested in a deal."

"I'm listening."

"My son, Ricky, was murdered in his home last Monday night. According to the coroner, he was poisoned. The local cops have nothing on a suspect so far. They don't even know if it's a man or a woman. I want the feds to get involved; I want whoever killed my son to be brought to justice, whether that means life in prison or, even better, gunned down and gutted like a deer."

"My oh my, Rick. I am so sorry for your loss, and I'd love to help, but I'm not as connected to the president as I used to be. He doesn't even return my calls half the time."

"You're the only one I know who has the background and access to help with this."

"I'll talk to some folks I know over at Justice and get back to you, but I can't promise anything."

"That's all I ask, Rudy. The president may be more interested in the second reason for my call. My son invested over forty million of our money developing a luxury resort on Lake Superior. It's called Overlook Lodge and Conference Center at Shovel Point. If you've been to Twin Farms up in Vermont or the Cliff House in Maine, you've got a good idea about its style, incredible setting and amenities. I know the president is planning a visit to northern Minnesota before Super Tuesday. I'd like to invite him to stay overnight at Overlook, maybe bring some members of the Drummond Organization to spend a few days and experience our North Shore. Maybe even hold a fundraiser in our Palisade Room. Overlook was Ricky's dream. Now that he's gone, I've decided to sell the place, and I want to give your boss an opportunity to buy it."

"Rick, I think I told you I'm not really on the inside anymore, and I've got my own problems to deal with, but I'll do my best to give the Boss and his family your message."

"Thanks, Rudy. That's all I can ask."

CHAPTER 26

February 7, 2020
Finland, Minnesota

HALLIE BELL MACDONALD HAD lived in northern Minnesota for nearly fifteen years. She'd been up Highway 61 beyond Grand Portage and across the Pigeon River into Canada. She'd been to most of the celebrated lodges, restaurants and historic sites in Lake and Cook Counties, including Sven & Ole's Pizza in Grand Marais and the Lemon Wolf Café in Beaver Bay, but she'd never been to the Trestle Inn Saloon in the middle of nowhere.

Located twenty miles north of the township of Finland on Lake County 7, the Trestle Inn was a stone's throw from Crooked Lake in the heart of the Superior National Forest. The family that built Crooked Lake Resort in the 1940s added a saloon in the eighties to make use of massive Douglas fir timbers they'd extracted from a railroad trestle that had been abandoned more than fifty years earlier in a forgotten section of the woods. The result was a unique, two-story structure that drew snowmobilers, three-wheelers, hunters, fishermen, hikers, campers and plain old tourists for a variety of libations and delicacies like the Trainwreck, a marriage of beef and bratwurst patties with bacon and cheese. Every weekend hundreds of snowmobilers skied down the Tomahawk trail from Ely to the front door of the Trestle. The North Shore State Trail brought hungry riders from the south and east.

MacDonald had been walleye fishing in Crooked Lake as a teen and had been to the inn a few times in his capacity as the chief law enforcement officer of Lake County, but he'd never enjoyed a meal at the Trestle.

After a crazy week of crashes, murders, and Super Bowl parties, MacDonald surprised Hallie by popping into her office in the county courthouse an hour before closing, announcing he was taking her out to a new place for dinner, a place they'd never been before, to celebrate her appointment as Lake County attorney. They'd leave her Renegade in Two Harbors and take the Explorer to dinner.

She was sure it would be a restaurant in Duluth, maybe Va Bene, a new Italian place overlooking the lake, or the new steakhouse on Miller Hill, but then MacDonald turned right at Highway 61 and drove north, away from Duluth and towards the wilderness. Of course, there were a few good options for fine dining north of Two Harbors, but she thought she'd been to all of them—the Cascade Tavern, Blue Fin Bay and Cove Point. He'd never take her to one of the restaurants at Overlook, especially now that Ricky was gone.

When her husband turned left onto Highway 1 and headed northwest, she started thinking about restaurants in Ely. She'd been to the Ely Steakhouse but not to the new fusion place on Sheridan Street. But those thoughts were quickly dashed when MacDonald turned right at County 7 and entered uncharted territory.

"Okay, Mac. I sat here enjoying the winter scenery, thinking about places to eat in Beaver Bay, Tofte, Lutsen and even Grand Marais, and then you took Highway 1, and I was all in for Ely, but now I swear you're driving into the twilight zone. What's even out this way? . . . I don't even have cell service on this road. The least you can do is tell me how much longer before we get there."

"Fair enough," said MacDonald, clicking on the high beams so she could see a broader swath of the dark, empty road. "We'll be there in fifteen minutes."

"Doesn't seem like anyone else will be," she giggled, causing MacDonald to smile broadly, knowing that she would soon be in for a treat.

They sat in relative silence for the rest of the trip, listening to MacDonald's "80s Rock Playlist" on Spotify. Duran Duran's "Hungry Like the Wolf" was starting to play when the night sky lit up.

"Look to your right," said MacDonald, pointing to suspended strings of holiday lights illuminating a dozen rustic cabins near the shore of Crooked Lake as well as several makeshift fishing shacks out on the snow-covered lake. On the south side of County 7, about a hundred feet behind the cabins, were a convenience store and bait shop, a parking lot filled with pickups and snowmobiles, and the best damn place to eat and drink in a twenty-mile radius, the Trestle Inn and Saloon.

"Holy shit!" Hallie exclaimed. "I had no idea there was a place like this way out here. Have you been here before?"

"Responding to some calls in the last few years. And I may have been here with my girlfriend when I was a teenager."

"Good to know."

MacDonald let Hallie out near the entrance and wedged the Explorer between two RVs at the back of the packed lot. On his way in, he couldn't help but notice a silver Tesla sedan parked between a Dodge Ram pickup and a nine-passenger van. Instinctively, he checked the front bumper and grill. Some ice and snow but otherwise unblemished.

There were no tables available, so the MacDonalds sat in wooden captain's chairs at the bar. They each ordered a Castle Danger Cream Ale and asked for menus.

"I'm curious," said Hallie. "Why'd you pick this place?"

"Three reasons," MacDonald said, squeezing her knee with

his right hand. "First, since you're going to be county attorney for everyone in the county, I thought it would be good for a girl from Chicago to mingle with some fine folks you may not see very often. Second, I thought about taking you to some fancy place in Duluth but figured that might remind you too much of your deceased ex-husband. I mean, RIP Ricky, but tonight's about us. Third, I just thought it would be something different, something fun."

Hallie leaned over and was about to kiss the big man when a shouting match broke out at the other end of the bar. Two heavyset men in snowmobile suits were yelling at a man and woman seated in captain's chairs.

"No copper mining in the BWCA? No fossil fuels in ten years? Are you fucking nuts, pal? Why not just tell all the workers and families on the Iron Range to pack up their shit and move out now? Because if we follow your plan, there will be no jobs up here, and the Chinese will be eating our lunch!"

"I know that guy," said MacDonald, getting out of his chair to make sure the yelling didn't escalate into something worse. "It's Mark Petrich."

Petrich grew up in Eveleth. His dad worked in the mines for forty years. He played high school football against MacDonald in the late 1980s and went on to play backup center for a couple of championship teams at UMD before graduating with a degree in labor relations. He'd been a labor organizer and negotiator with the steelworkers' union for years. MacDonald had run into him at a few demonstrations against CopperPlus near Isabella, but their interactions had always been cordial.

After riding down the Tomahawk in their sleds, Petrich and one of his union buddies had stopped at the Trestle for a few beers and a burger. He recognized both Alex Jeronimus and Liz Vandenberg sitting next to each other at the bar, trying hard to keep their cool. The local union was solidly behind the Republican incumbent, and Petrich was determined to keep him in office. But neither the candidate nor his rich girlfriend were taking the bait. As MacDonald approached, Petrich's face was within spitting distance of the former Army officer.

"I suppose you want to take our guns, too. People like you two are ruining the Democratic Party. Before the last election, I never voted Republican. Now rich tree huggers and pussies like you have hijacked my old party."

Liz turned back to the bar, choosing to ignore the rube. It was clear to MacDonald that Petrich had been drinking heavily on the trail, but he was taken aback by Jeronimus's response.

"Listen, fellas, I'm sorry that you haven't accepted the science of climate change and the value of protecting our wilderness areas, but there's never a good excuse for being rude or using vulgar language. How about I go outside with you two gentlemen and we can continue this conversation without bothering anyone in this fine establishment." Jeronimus stood. He was taller than Petrich and gave him a look that showed no fear, a look that made even MacDonald flinch.

"Hey, Mark. Why don't you just move along and find yourself a place to sit and have something to eat. I'm sure Mr. Jeronimus would rather get back to his meal than go out in the cold with you. I know I'd rather have dinner with my wife than arrest somebody for disturbing the peace."

"Hi, Sheriff," said Petrich. "Didn't expect to see you here. We don't want any trouble. I just got a little carried away. You folks all have a good evening." And with that he and his quiet companion stomped out of the saloon, relieved that the sheriff had intervened to save them from getting their asses kicked.

MacDonald couldn't quite believe what he'd just witnessed. He had no doubt that Jeronimus was capable of killing both men with his bare hands.

"I don't think we've met. I'm Sam MacDonald, sheriff of Lake County." MacDonald shook the hand of a man who was at least as powerful as he.

"Good to meet you, Sheriff. I'm Alex Jeronimus, a candidate for the DFL nomination for Congress up here, and this is my friend, Liz Vandenberg."

"Hello, Sheriff. I've heard a lot of good things about you, and I've met Detective Klewacki from your office. She's an impressive person. I'm hoping we can count on your vote."

"You can be sure I'll vote, and I promise to give your candidacy serious consideration."

"That's all we can ask, Sheriff," said Jeronimus. "Do you come here often? I was sure we'd have to drive all the way to Tofte or Silver Bay to have dinner, but Liz knew about this place. We were campaigning in Virginia, Eveleth and Ely today."

"To tell the truth, I haven't eaten here in years," said MacDonald, "but there's no good reason for that; I've heard the food is great. I'm not a snowmobiler, so I just haven't thought about coming up this way. I'll remedy that in the future. You folks heading back to Duluth tonight?"

"We're spending the night at Cascade Mountain Lodge up near Tofte," said Liz. "We might get in an early-morning ski before driving to Grand Marais for a rally Saturday afternoon."

"Well, you two have a good evening and drive safely on these icy roads."

"Thanks, Sheriff," they said nearly in unison.

"By the way," said MacDonald, turning back towards the couple, "I noticed a newer Tesla Model S in the parking lot. I think it's silver. Does that belong to one of you, perhaps?"

"Why do you ask, Sheriff?"

"Just curious. You don't see a lot of those up here."

"It's mine," said Liz. "I rarely drive it, but it's been great for campaigning."

MacDonald returned to his date. She was busy attacking a Trestle cheeseburger with a side of onion rings. "Hey, Mac. I couldn't wait for you to order. I got you a Minnesota burger. It's what I'm eating topped with two of your favorite things—tater tots and cream of mushroom soup. What was all the commotion down there?"

"Liz Vandenberg and your future congressman, Alex, were having a peaceful dinner at the other end of the bar when one of the union reps I know got in their face. He might have had a beer or two out on the trail. Anyway, he was rather hostile and a little too vocal about their positions on copper mining and climate change."

"Until you came to their rescue?" She smiled broadly and blinked, mocking him just a tad.

"I did suggest that they move along, but I think Mr. Alex could have handled things without my help, and, unfortunately, I think he would have preferred that. He's not your stereotypical liberal politician, Hallie."

"Whatever that means, Sheriff."

• • • • • • • • • • • • • • • •

Jeronimus drove the Tesla while Liz reread the demand letter from Megan Holappa's attorney, a personal injury lawyer from the Twin Cities.

"We need to bury this now," said Liz. "I won't have this asshole impugning my father's character and good name with these tawdry accusations. He's asking for five million; Jim thinks we can settle for three and a half with Holden's estate contributing a million."

"You know this is extortion," said Jeronimus. "This was simply an unfortunate accident that never would have happened but for worthless, scheming Ricky Holden. His daddy should step up and pay the whole thing."

"That's not going to happen, Alex. He's lost his only son, and he's pissed and bitter. Jim convinced his lawyer, who's also his brother, to throw in a million to protect the family name. I hear the Lake County attorney is close to destitute and might be paralyzed, so he's in no shape to contribute."

"I hate to say this, but those two clowns got what they deserved. By the way, what do you make of the sheriff's comment about your car?"

"He doesn't seem like the smart-ass type, so maybe it was just curiosity or maybe Jenny lied about hitting a deer when she borrowed the car on Monday. Then we've got bigger problems, but that would be totally out of character."

Jeronimus fluffed his thick hair with his fingers as he considered the potential consequences. "You can't even imagine what some people are capable of, Liz. Good thing we got the car fixed right away in either case. What time is our meeting at Overlook?"

"Eight. Jim was going to be there at seven thirty to have a discussion with Holden and his brother. Though we don't agree on much with those people, we need to present a united front on this. To me, it's not about the money—though that kind of money could do a lot of good in other ways. It's about these Holappas and their lawyer taking advantage of the situation for a big payday. Jim thinks she's not going to have much in the way of permanent injuries, so under normal circumstances her case would be worth a half million at most."

"As I said, it's extortion."

"I hope they have something decent to eat at this fancy resort," said Liz. "There wasn't one vegetarian item on that menu."

CHAPTER 27

February 7, 2020
Near Illgen City, Minnesota

AS SOON AS THEY entered the sparkling, three-story lobby of Overlook Lodge, Liz Vandenberg and Alex Jeronimus were greeted by a vivacious, twenty-something concierge in a revealing silk blouse. She directed them to the Baptism River meeting room on the second floor of the main building. It was ten after eight, and everyone else was already seated in padded, brown leather chairs at a marble-topped conference table, except for a surprise attendee—Megan Holappa. She sat in a motorized wheelchair, gauze and white bandages covering most of her face and neck, an oversized blue flannel robe covering the rest but open down the front to expose at least a third of her very white, very large breasts.

Vern and Suzy Holappa were dressed in their Sunday best next to their attorney, Clint Boyer of Dyckman & Boyer, a five-lawyer litigation powerhouse from Minneapolis. Matthew Dyckman and Clint Boyer played small college football together in the early 1990s. Dyckman, a handsome, agile African American from Milwaukee, played quarterback, whereas Boyer, an imposing physical specimen with a quick mind but slow feet, played center. They both ended up in law school at the University of Iowa, where they roomed together and made plans to kick ass and make millions. Even the two associates in the firm cleared over a half a million in 2019, so mission accomplished. Unlike his clients, Boyer was relaxed and casual in a plaid flannel shirt and khakis.

Richard Holden and his younger brother, Bruce, were seated across from the Holappas. With nearly identical shaved heads, white goatees, black cotton turtlenecks and gray wool pants, they could have passed for twins, except it was obvious that one had either been crying, not sleeping, or both. Boyer thought they might be part of a secret society or were simply creepy.

Jim Baxter sat at the head of the table. He looked the part of a confident professional, which he was, in a Brooks Brothers tweed sport coat over a navy collared sweater. In his early seventies, Baxter had been Bill Vandenberg's personal attorney for over thirty years. He was the consummate solo practitioner, well versed in multiple areas of the law. He handled introductions as Liz and Jeronimus, still dressed in business casual campaign outfits, sat next to the Holdens, leaving an empty chair between them for several good reasons. Baxter took charge of the meeting with his deep, gravelly voice and calm but authoritarian demeanor.

"I want to thank everyone for getting together on short notice. We've all had an opportunity to read Mr. Boyer's letter and memorandum on behalf of his client, Megan Holappa. He's demanding five million dollars to compensate her for injuries suffered in a snowmobile accident that occurred a week ago. Now, normally this kind of demand wouldn't be made for months after the accident so the parties could make a reasonable assessment of the extent of any permanent injuries and future medical expenses, but we all know that this is not a normal case; it's all about two prominent families and a political campaign trying to keep certain information and allegations out of the press and public domain to the extent that's even possible."

Baxter thought Boyer might object to this characterization, but he was content to lean back in his chair with his arms folded across his chest. Richard Holden was not so content. He leaned in toward the Holappas.

"This is extortion, plain and simple. Your daughter was hurt, but she's obviously recovering; my son is dead. If I ever find out you had anything to do with his murder, I'll—"

Bruce interrupted his brother's outburst by simultaneously pushing him back in his chair with his forearm and talking over him.

"Please excuse my brother. He's had a rough week. We came here to listen and try to resolve this situation, within reason."

"Let's get on with it, then," said Baxter. "Mr. Boyer, I've been authorized to offer your client a million dollars to be paid over a one-year period in four quarterly installments of two hundred fifty thousand and memorialized in a settlement, release, and confidentiality agreement which I will prepare. The payment of each installment is contingent on your client's compliance with the confidentiality agreement."

"We understand the need for the installment payments and the confidentiality agreement, but the amount is unacceptable," said Boyer. "My client has been traumatized as well as physically injured. A million dollars is chump change to you folks."

"A million dollars isn't chump change to anyone, Mr. Boyer," said Liz. "I only have so much patience to sit here, so let's cut to the chase. If poor little Megan spills her guts to the world, it might cause embarrassment to our families and hurt our foundation and Alex's campaign, I grant you that . . . and we want to avoid that. But Megan will also have to admit that she accepted money to *entertain* a bunch of old men. Are her parents really okay with her doing that?" She looked at Vern and Suzy Holappa. "So, what's the bottom line on this, Mr. Boyer? Let's get to the bottom line, and we'll either have a deal or go home without one."

Boyer wrote something on a yellow legal pad and showed it to his clients. Vern looked at him and nodded. Megan wasn't consulted; she was too busy making eye contact with Jeronimus. Boyer looked over at the Holdens, then at Liz Vandenberg, and then faced Baxter.

"Megan would accept four installments of $750 thousand, or $3 million. That's the bottom line. Take it or leave it."

Baxter scribbled something on his own legal pad and then made eye contact with everyone in the room before saying, "I think we have a deal, Mr. Boyer. I'll prepare the documents and send drafts to you and Mr. Holden. If there are no other questions, we are done here."

With that, Boyer thanked everyone for their cooperation, and he and the three Holappas left the room before the rest figured out they'd just been scammed out of three million dollars.

Everyone else got up to leave at a pace commensurate with losing a big game. Baxter put some items in a worn leather briefcase and shook hands with the Holdens and with Alex and Elizabeth.

"I'll be in touch," he said to Liz, lightly patting her shoulder before walking out of the conference room.

"That fucking bitch gets millions for being a little whore," Richard said to his brother as they left. "That'll be the last time we sit on the same side of anything with those two crazy fuckers"—referring to Liz and Jeronimus. His brother didn't say a word.

CHAPTER 28

February 8, 2020
Temperance River State Park

WITH BRIAN AND THE boys on their way to Duluth for a basketball tournament, Gail Klewacki was free to get in an early-morning ski on the groomed trails near Temperance River before resuming her investigation into the attempted murder of Greg Thomassoni. She often sought the solitude and beauty of one of the North Shore's many cross-country ski trails to contemplate the details of an investigation and decide her next move.

She arrived at the park before sunrise and hit the intermediate trail, the one with the best views of Lake Superior. The trail followed a tree-lined ridge above the lake. It would be the warmest day in a month in northern Minnesota, with temperatures climbing into the twenties.

On the positive side of the ledger, Klewacki could prove that Ricky Holden was funneling close to $40,000 a year to Thomassoni out of the club's operating account. He was also making cash withdrawals of $2,000 to $3,000 a week, most likely representing payments to the young ladies attending club parties and events. On the negative side, MacDonald convinced Thomassoni to retire in exchange for his promise not to refer the potential criminal case against Greg and Ricky to the St. Louis County sheriff.

Klewacki didn't disagree with her boss's rationale or decision. She understood it was probably in the best interest of the young women for the case to go away. As for the attempted murder case, she didn't believe it was an accident or a random act; she was convinced that someone who knew Thomassoni wanted him dead. Probably the same person who murdered Ricky Holden or arranged to have him killed. On that front, she'd called Detective Ahmed Ali to check on any leads in the Holden case. Ali was frustrated. No useful video footage, no witnesses, no physical evidence at the scene. All he had were a few still photos of a tall woman—or man dressed as a woman—who never faced the camera.

Klewacki had spent two days calling every auto body shop in a forty-mile radius of Two Harbors asking about vehicles with front-end damage, especially electric cars. In the middle of a cold, snowy winter, there were about 200 accidents a week with front-end damage that was repaired by a body shop. However, only two of the repaired vehicles in the vicinity were electric. One was a Tesla and one was a Nissan Leaf. Klewacki would visit those shops on Monday.

When she thought of potential suspects who might want to kill both Thomassoni and Holden, the list included land developers and contractors in Lake County who'd had run-ins with both, and perhaps a member or ex-member of the snowmobile club who'd figured out their scheme. But the most obvious person was Elizabeth Vandenberg, who was also one of the smartest and most philanthropic women in the state. Unfortunately, all the brains and money in the world wouldn't bring her father back, and but for the antics of Ricky Holden and Greg Thomassoni, Bill Vandenberg would still be alive.

One thing Klewacki knew for sure—if she kept poking around, asking questions, looking for leads and witnesses and connections, eventually she'd find the truth. Perseverance and resilience; they had always been the keys to her success.

As Klewacki packed up her equipment, she saw two familiar faces untethering skis from a rack on top of a Volvo wagon. It was the Dalbecs, the young couple who lived in the keeper's house at Split Rock.

"Corey and Rachel, what brings you to a competing state park?" she teased.

"Hi, Gail," said Corey. "We needed to get away. We're closed for another week while the NTSB finishes their on-site work and disassembles the plane. We haven't been able to clean up the grounds or do much of anything, so we thought we'd get some exercise and experience a different view of the lake."

Rachel snapped on her skis while Corey talked. Then she added, "We had some scary visitors last night, Gail. We thought about calling the sheriff after they left."

"Really?" Klewacki asked. "Tell me about them."

"They showed up at the residence at about eleven last night," said Corey. "Two men in black suits and dark ties. At first, I assumed they were FBI, but they said they represented the owners of the plane, some company from Chile. One of them was a lawyer from a firm in Washington, DC. His name was Anthony. The other man was Ramon."

"He was the scary one," said Rachel. "He was as tall as Corey but twice as broad, with black eyes and a thick accent. They wanted to inspect the plane. Said they had permission from the government. They produced a letter signed by the administrator of the FAA. We thought the NTSB was in charge, but we weren't going to argue with these guys. Corey thought he saw a gun in a holster under Ramon's suit jacket."

"So, did you let them inspect the plane?"

"What's left of it," said Corey. "Some parts had already been hauled away in a semi-trailer. Here's the weird thing: they spent almost no time inspecting the plane. Instead, Ramon walked to the front of the fuselage with an electric screwdriver and removed a four- or five-inch plate from the nose of the plane. Then he took something out of a small compartment and put it in an inside pocket of his suit. It's below zero and neither one of them is wearing a coat or gloves. It was like a spy movie."

Rachel curled an arm around Corey's waist. "Before they left, they said if we were smart, we wouldn't tell anyone about their visit. That's why we didn't call Sheriff MacDonald or Agent Hinton. We don't want any trouble, Gail."

"I understand you guys," said Klewacki. "I totally get it." But she was already thinking about what she would do with the information.

CHAPTER 29

February 8, 2020
Near Grand Marais, Minnesota

SATURDAY WAS A GREAT day for the Jeronimus campaign. A thousand enthusiastic supporters and only a handful of protesters showed up for a rally in the gymnasium of Cook County High School. Jeronimus gave an inspiring speech about the urgent need for millennials who cared about the future of the planet to get involved. Then he invited everybody to join him on a snowshoeing adventure up Devil Track River. More than 300 trekkers accompanied the candidate and his staff on a day when twenty degrees above zero felt like sixty, and the winter sun accentuated the majestic beauty of the red rock cliffs, the shimmering whites of the birches and aspens, and the variant greens of the spruce, balsam and pines.

At six that evening, the campaign hosted 200 contributors and friends at a reception and dinner at Naniboujou Lodge, where Liz Vandenberg made two announcements. First, the only other candidate seeking the DFL endorsement, a St. Louis County commissioner from Virginia, dropped out of the race and would be throwing her support behind Jeronimus. Second, and likely one of the reasons for the first announcement, some incredible results from a *News Tribune*/Northland Public Radio poll of 900 registered voters in the Eighth District. When asked about their preference if the 2020 Congressional election were held today, 61 percent picked Alex Jeronimus, and just 34 percent chose the Republican incumbent. Jeronimus did especially well with young voters and women.

Yes, Alex Jeronimus struck a resounding chord with the voters of northern Minnesota. Was it because the message was delivered by a handsome, athletic war veteran whose oratorical skills rivaled Bill Clinton's? Or was the message of a worldwide climate crisis finally moving from ears to brains to action? Did twelve disciples follow the message or the messenger? Abraham Lincoln, John F. Kennedy, Ronald Reagan, Barack Obama. Message or messenger? In the 2016 presidential election, a multitude voted for the message—not the messenger.

President Drummond and his minions devised a strategy to strike again with a divisive message. They visited swing states hoping to rally their base and weaken Democrat hopefuls, among them Alex Jeronimus. Drummond would try to ignite the crowd at a rally at the Duluth Entertainment and Convention Center on Saturday afternoon and then appear at a fundraising dinner at Overlook, where he'd graciously agreed to spend the night and perhaps negotiate a backroom gentlemen's agreement to add a North Shore property to the Drummond Organization portfolio.

The Drummond White House was feeling good about the Democrats' failure to deliver a knockout punch. Democrats in the House had impeached the brash, lying New Yorker, but Drummond had been acquitted in the US Senate, and his enabling Justice Department managed to thwart or stall a bevy of civil lawsuits and criminal investigations that would have exposed him for the soulless fraud that he was. Depending on the media source, the Drummond presidency was either hanging by a thread or on its way to an improbable, unbelievable second term.

• • • • • • • • • • • • • • •

Though Saturday was a good day for the Jeronimus campaign, it wasn't nearly as good for Jenny Pierce. She'd hoped to travel to the Iron Range and Grand Marais with Liz and the candidate, but Liz asked her to meet with two key environmental groups, Water Legacy and the Center for Environmental Advocacy, to discuss short-term plans for opposing nonferrous mining near Hoyt Lakes, Babbitt, and the BWCA. More particularly, these groups were interested in the foundation's willingness to fund their efforts. That took up Friday. On Saturday, she met with leaders of the Fond du Lac Band of Lake Superior Chippewa, whose lands would be impacted by one of the proposed projects, an ugly open-pit mine that could damage wetlands and wildlife habitats.

Jenny was instrumental in creating cooperative working relationships with tribal leaders throughout the upper Midwest, and she was grateful for the opportunity, but the work was mundane compared to the excitement of campaign life, especially spending long days and nights with Liz. Jeronimus was so focused on the campaign he didn't seem to care about their relationship, at least that was how Jenny saw it. Sitting by herself in the campaign office in Lakeside and eating leftover pasta salad, she regretted not accepting the invitation from her roommates. They were spending the evening at one of Duluth's craft breweries, sampling micro drafts and eating pizza. Jenny's dilemma—whenever she went out with friends, she imagined doing whatever she was doing with Liz, and that made her anxious and depressed. If only she could tell Liz what she'd done for her; that would change everything. Someday.

CHAPTER 30

SHE SAID HER NAME was Eva, Eva Olerud, and something about her voice, maybe its urgency, convinced Sheriff Sam MacDonald that he needed to meet with her, soon. She'd left a number and a long message on his office phone Friday evening. She was in her eighties and lived alone, afraid to drive farther than into Grand Marais. She'd been a reference librarian at the Cook County Library but had been retired for years and lived in a modest home east of Hovland off 61. She'd read about the plane crash and the bodies discovered on Isle Royale. She'd witnessed something very strange on Lake Superior in the early-morning hours of February 1. She thought the Lake County sheriff should know about it.

MacDonald called her Saturday morning and agreed to drive the eighty or so miles to her place that evening. She said she wanted him to see the view from her sitting room at night, in the dark, so he'd have a better idea of what she'd seen. He hadn't been on Highway 61 past Grand Marais since he'd rescued Redman after the Fallon murder.

Eva lived in a two-bedroom cabin that her father, a local carpenter, built in the early 1950s on Chimney Rock Point, about halfway between Grand Marais and Canada. MacDonald parked in the driveway of a one-car, detached garage. A halogen floodlight activated by a motion detector on the garage lit up the driveway and narrow concrete walkway leading to the front porch. The unseasonably warm daytime sun had melted the ice on the shoveled path.

Sitting by the window at her kitchen table, Eva watched the Explorer ease into her driveway. She opened the heavy storm door before MacDonald could reach for the brass knocker. Barely five feet tall, she wore a long-sleeve, red and green–embroidered housecoat with fur-lined red suede slippers.

"You must be Sheriff MacDonald," she said, looking up in the stratosphere and pleased to see the kind face attached to the giant lawman.

"Yes, very pleased to meet you, Ms. Olerud," said MacDonald, reflexively sticking out his right hand. Eva reacted by grabbing his right thumb with her tiny hand, noticeably trembling from early-stage Parkinson's, and directing him into a small foyer where she took his wool parka and draped it over one of two mismatched antique maple chairs that fit under a newer butcher-block table in her kitchen. Then she led him down a narrow hallway, past a sitting room and into a cozy, cedar-paneled study that had picture windows with breathtaking views of Lake Superior on three sides and a secretary desk flanked by floor-to-ceiling bookshelves on the wall. Above the desk were a dozen professional-quality color photographs of the lake taken during both summer and winter storms.

"What a wonderful room," exclaimed MacDonald, trying to take in the photographs, the titles of the eclectic collection of books on the shelves, and the view from about eighty feet above the frozen lake. "Where did you get these amazing photographs?"

Eva blushed. "It's been a hobby of mine for years. My mom died when I was a girl, and my dad and granny raised me in this very house. Dad knew my two favorite things were reading and photography, so he built this room to facilitate my hobbies. Though I've had my share of maladies, I've been fortunate to retain excellent visual health. In fact, I think my eyesight is better today than it was fifty years ago. Which brings me to the reason I contacted you. Let's sit over here in the northeast corner of the study where I spend hours watching this awful, wonderful lake.

MacDonald obliged and discovered a teacup and saucer as well as a dish of homemade chocolate chip cookies and vanilla bean scones. "I'm not an accomplished baker," Eva said, "but I've heard my oatmeal chocolate chip cookies are better than Sweet Martha's in the Cities. You can judge for yourself, but they're better with some green tea; I think it's still hot."

The cookies were better than advertised, and though MacDonald wasn't a tea drinker, the strong green brew was hot and better than he'd expected.

"Some nights I don't sleep at all," said Eva, "so I come in here and either read or turn the lights off and monitor activity on the lake. On the night of the plane crash down at Split Rock, I woke up at two in the morning and was sitting in here with the lights off drinking tea. At about three thirty, I thought I saw a tiny light flickering in the distance, right out there towards Isle Royale." She pointed in a northeasterly direction.

"Sheriff, there are no lights out on the lake at three thirty in the morning. Not this time of year. At first, I thought it might be a seaplane making an emergency landing. We're about eighty feet above Lake Superior on this point. I can see twelve to fourteen miles out there—not all the way to Isle Royale, but within about five miles. When I saw the light, I grabbed these binoculars." She lifted a compact pair of Olympus PRO binoculars off a side table and handed them to MacDonald.

"It's a clear, star-filled sky with nearly a full moon, so there's a lot of natural light close to shore. But look as far as the eye can see out there, and it's dark, even on a night like this. That night, or early morning, I should say, it was snowing hard and the wind was swirling, mostly from the northeast. I focused on the twinkling light with my binoculars and couldn't believe what my eyes were seeing. The light was getting closer. Slowly, incrementally, but it was definitely getting closer. I took several photos with my digital camera and my iPhone over the next five hours. I'll let you see them in a minute. It's too bad that the light didn't keep inching toward Hovland. Instead, it moved west and maybe slightly northwest near the Grand Portage reservation.

"Sheriff, you will see in the last few photos that I took with my zoom at the maximum a shadowy figure. I'm convinced a human being walked across the ice from Isle Royale, or in that vicinity, to Grand Portage in a blizzard. I don't know if anyone else saw what I saw, but I calculated this person was moving at less than two miles an hour, which might seem slow, but not when you consider they would have to be wary of breaks and crevices in the ice and stretches of open water, all in the dark and during a storm with strong winds and temperatures below zero. It's absolutely incredible."

"I read that a couple wolves walked from Canada to Isle Royale last winter," said MacDonald, "but I can't imagine a human even trying to do it, especially at night with low visibility. Could I see those pictures?"

Eva hobbled into the kitchen and returned a few minutes later with a pot of hot water to refresh their tea and an iPad on which she stored her photos. She handed the device to MacDonald and filled his teacup. He slowly swiped through the photos as he recalled Eva's account of her discovery.

"You're right about the light," he said. "Too bad whoever it is moved away from your view right before dawn. This is amazing. If I give you my card with my email address, could you send me these photos?"

"Yes, of course," said Eva. "But what do you think this means, Sheriff? Do you think this could be the third passenger from that plane? The man who's still missing?"

"I don't know," MacDonald admitted, though he was thinking the same thing and, drawing on his military background, trying to figure how it could have been accomplished. "Maybe someone living or working near the shore north of here observed whoever this is in the daylight."

"You know, I love and hate that old lake," said Eva, lost in thought.

"Really? The way you say that, I assume there's a story behind it."

"Not one that many have heard, Sheriff, and not one that I've told in years."

MacDonald sensed that she'd like to tell it now. "I'm all ears if you're up to it."

"You may have guessed that I've never been married. Just a spinster librarian living in the house my father built. Back in the late 1950s, during the first summer after I graduated from St. Benedict's and started working as a teacher in Grand Marais, I met a young man named Harold Louis Weeks III, who was known by everyone as Hal. Hal's grandfather was a commercial fisherman on Lake Superior for many years. He and his wife, Marie, owned a beautiful cottage on the lake between Lutsen and Grand Marais. I say *beautiful* because my dad built it for them right after the war, and Harold and my dad, who served in the Navy together during the war, became close friends.

"Harold and Marie had a son, Harold Jr., who married a woman from Connecticut while attending Yale Law School. He ended up staying out East and joining a law practice in Hartford in the middle of the Great Depression. Hal was born in 1937, a year after me. He and his family visited Harold and Marie at least once a year during the early fifties, and when Hal went to college to study art history at Northwestern, he started spending summers up here. He worked at a small gallery in Grand Marais. That's where I met him.

"I can't speak for him, but I fell for him on the day we met during a two-hour argument over which book is better, *East of Eden* or *Atlas Shrugged*. Even though he wasn't a fan of Ayn Rand, he said her writing was more original than John Steinbeck's. I disagreed, of course, but he was so polite and so passionate about his beliefs, that even when we argued I wanted to wrap my arms around his skinny blond neck and kiss him. I'd dated a few boys from St. John's when I was a Benny, but no one who made me want to spend every waking hour with him. That's how I felt about Hal. During the summer of 1960, we were inseparable. We were both big fans of JFK, even though Hal's dad was one of Nixon's biggest supporters in Connecticut.

"One Friday afternoon in late July—it must have been ninety degrees in the shade—Hal's grandparents were in Silver Bay for a barbeque with friends. I had my dad's '57 Ford Fairlane, since he usually drove an old Chevy pickup, and I drove Hal and me over to his grandparents' place after work. We'd talked about getting married after he graduated from Northwestern, and that day we were simply reveling in each other's company. Walking up the driveway, I spotted two Old Town green canoes leaning against the side of his grandparents' garage.

"'What a great day for paddling a canoe,' I said, wondering why Hal had never suggested that we do something together on the lake during the two summers we'd hung out with each other, especially since his grandfather worked out on the lake every day.

"'If you want to,' he said with no enthusiasm.

"'Okay,' I said, 'why don't we just take a walk along the shore and then come back here and have dinner.' Sensing my disappointment, he quickly changed his tune.

"'I'll get the paddles from the garage, and we'll have ourselves an adventure on old Gitchee Gumee,' he said with mock enthusiasm but good humor.

"As we were shoving the canoe in the water, he conceded that he'd never been in a canoe in his life; that, unlike his grandfather, he and his father loved the water from a distance. 'But that needs to change right now,' he said, 'because I love you more than my grandfather loves this lake, and more than all the water in it.'

"'Even so,' I told him, grabbing his white polo shirt and pulling him close for a kiss, 'I'll steer from the stern and you just do what I tell you up there in the bow. Don't even put your oar in the water unless you're told.'

"He climbed in with his useless paddle and we were on our way. We headed northeast towards Grand Marais. Sensing Hal's unease, I stayed within a couple hundred yards of shore. He turned to face me a couple of times saying, 'This is great, Eva.' And then in an instant, everything changed. The sky in the west was turning black, but I didn't see it. I was paddling east and enjoying the warm sun on my back. I felt the wind pick up and saw we'd drifted about a half mile from shore. Finally, looking back at the western sky, I was horrified. The black storm clouds were overtaking us and the waves and wind were growing by the second. 'Hal,' I cried out, 'we need to get to shore now!'

"He turned his head sideways and nodded. Then, before I could steer us towards shore, an ill-timed gust from the northwest flipped the Old Town over and dumped us into the lake just as it started to rain. The lake was suddenly transformed into a vicious serpent. 'Forget about the canoe, Hal,' I screamed while gulping and choking on water. 'We need to swim to shore!'

"Those were the last words I ever said to him, Sheriff. You see, I assumed he knew how to swim. He was the grandson of a professional fisherman, for God's sake. But he didn't. He'd never learned how to swim out there in Hartford, Connecticut, and yet he went canoeing on Lake Superior without a life jacket. Incredible as it may seem, they never found his body. I blamed myself for his death, but I also blamed that unforgiving lake. Over the years I've learned a lot about fate, about harsh, random fate, and now I just accept it."

MacDonald was familiar with loss but not as comfortable with fate. "Well," he pondered, "it seems that our mystery ice walker might have gotten one over on the lake, assuming he made it to shore alive. I will do some investigating and, if you'd like, let you know what I find."

"I'd like that very much, Sheriff. I think you're going to find a connection between that plane crash and this mysterious light. I'll give you my gmail address so it'll be easier for us to keep in touch."

MacDonald stood with dirty dishes in hand. "That sounds good, Eva. Thanks for sharing this with me. I don't think I would have believed it without your camera work. I enjoyed our conversation and your hospitality. That's the best green tea I've ever had, and your cookies are better than any I've bought from a bakery."

CHAPTER 31

February 8, 2020
St. Paul, Minnesota

GEORGE REDMAN WAS DEFLATED when he read Hinton's text. She couldn't make it over to watch the Gophers and enjoy his Irish-Italian cooking. No reason given and no follow-up call, so Redman could either call her or stew about it. He chose the latter. The only good thing—he could order a large four-meat pizza from Carbone's rather than spend the afternoon in the kitchen. He overindulged on a thick crust with extra cheese and then sipped on Green Spot Irish whiskey while stretched out on his leather recliner with Fred draped over his legs fast asleep. The Gophers were up seven at the half, and Redman was drifting off to dreamland when he felt something vibrating in the pocket of his sweats. Hoping for Hinton, he was surprised to see MacDonald's number on the caller ID.

"Doesn't a newly married man have something better to do on a Saturday night than call me?"

"Hello, Red. I just spent a few hours with a single woman who's not my wife. She's old enough to be your mother and sharp enough to be your boss. Fortunately for you, she's not."

"Sounds like a riddle, Mac," said Redman. "I suppose she's got a hot tip on my cold case."

"That's good," said MacDonald. "I'd say it's more than a tip. She lives in a house overlooking Lake Superior between Grand Marais and Grand Portage. She's also an accomplished photographer. I'll cut to the chase, Red. I think she's got compelling evidence that someone hiked the twenty miles from Isle Royale to Grand Portage in the early-morning hours of Saturday, February 1, the same early morning that a King Air crash-landed at Split Rock, and you know the rest of that story."

"Wait a minute, Mac. You said someone *hiked*. Are you saying someone walked over twenty miles across that lake in the middle of a fucking blizzard? You'd have better odds playing Russian roulette with five bullets and one empty chamber. I've read about the ice formations in Lake Superior. They're not stable. There could be open water anywhere. It'd be a fool's game in good weather."

"Could it be that David Hesse was desperate enough and resourceful enough to try it?" MacDonald had been pondering this since leaving Eva's. "I mean, they haven't found his body."

"Don't think I haven't thought of it, especially after the way his wife acted during our interview the other day. Hesse was—or is— millions in debt. Without a lifeline of some sort, he'd have eventually been forced to file bankruptcy, win the lottery or steal from his company. Faking his death for a life insurance jackpot could bail out his family, but if it is Hesse, where did he go? And did he have to kill three men to accomplish it?"

"I have no idea, George. I don't know the man. I'm giving you a head start on this and expecting you to follow up with your friends at the FBI. I'll forward the photos and video, and you can pass them along to Special Agent Hinton.

"A couple of things to keep in mind, Red. First, the only way Hesse could have exited the plane safely is with a parachute. I'm not sure he had any Ranger or paratrooper training in the service or elsewhere, but I'd check that out. Second, the two big shots they've recovered were dressed in summer attire. Obviously, Hesse couldn't have been if he's the guy in these photos. What did his compatriots think when he arrived at the hangar with all his winter gear?"

Redman got up to get Fred some water and refresh his drink. "Maybe the cockpit recorder will provide some clues on that. If this mystery ice walker is Hesse, did he involve his wife in the scam, or is he protecting her from the truth? Either way, he's an asshole. I still can't believe that someone could pull this off." Redman started making a to-do list in his head; one item not on the list was sharing this information with Hinton, at least not yet.

"Let me know if you'd like any help on my end. Klewacki is busy working the hit-and-run on Greg, but both of us can spare some time on a case like this. By the way, Gail ran into the new lighthouse keeper and his wife on a cross-country ski trail today. The only reason she called me with that news is that a couple of suits representing your client were snooping around Split Rock examining the remains of the wreckage. She said they removed something from a compartment in the nose of the plane. I assume you didn't know about their visit."

"Never got the memo on that," said Redman. "I'll do some more research on Hesse. I might also head out to Holman Field in St. Paul to see what they have for surveillance cameras in the hangars and out on the tarmac. Someone working that Friday night have seen something. For all I know, the feds may have been out there already."

"Good idea, Red. I'm turning into the parking lot at the Green Door. I ordered a pizza for Hallie and me, half sausage and mushroom and half veggie."

"I didn't know Hallie was a sausage girl."

"That's funny, George. Funny and original. Enjoy the rest of your weekend. And by the way, remember the name Eva Olerud. She's the amazing eighty-something whose insomnia and sharp eye are responsible for this new evidence. She might be a little old for you, but you'd love her oatmeal chocolate chip cookies."

CHAPTER 32

February 9, 2020
Isle Royale National Park

THE WOLF POPULATION ON Isle Royale had grown from two to twenty over eighteen months with the latest infusion coming from Canada in late 2019. The big unknown—would the wolves stay and prosper or try to escape and die off? And what about the moose population? It had swelled to more than 2,200 for the first time in decades, eliciting calls for a controlled moose hunt by the Michigan Department of Natural Resources and big-game hunting enthusiasts. The 2020 wolf-moose study would provide statistics and perhaps some predictions about the future of the predator-prey experiment.

Kelly Kinnear and Carl Gruber were traveling across the middle of the island with their team of six, a mix of rangers, research scientists and volunteers. They had spent a week monitoring pack movements, assessing the condition of fir trees in areas with heavy moose traffic, and trying to get anything accomplished while drones buzzed overhead. As of Saturday evening, drones and ski planes had not discovered evidence of the third passenger, David Hesse.

Technically, Sunday wasn't a workday for the team, but they were trekking from Mott Island to Washington Harbor over a five-day period, and today's hike on snowshoes or skis with fifty to seventy liter packs would cover six miles at a leisurely pace. They took turns dragging a sled laden with equipment and provisions. The plan was to travel along Greenstone Ridge to the southeast corner of Lake Desor and then cross the lake diagonally to reach Minong Ridge Trail. They would follow Minong to an open field near Washington Creek where a search drone camera had captured the most recent wolf arrivals feeding on a moose carcass.

As usual, Gruber was in the lead, about twenty yards ahead of the other five, three men and two women who covered the frozen tundra in two pairs gliding on cross-country skis while Kelly straggled behind with bright-red poles and matching snowshoes. It had been an exhilarating day on the island. A cloudless sky and temperatures in the thirties for the first time since early December energized the team, so much so that everyone enthusiastically assented to Gruber's suggestion to traverse the two miles across Lake Desor into a beautiful setting sun rather than making camp in the sunlight and waiting until Monday to cross.

Within a hundred yards of shore, Gruber's head swiveled back toward his colleagues. "The ice is uneven up here!" he called and then cried out something unintelligible as he disappeared into the lake.

"Oh, Carl! Carl!" Kelly yelled. "Carl went through the ice!"

Kelly started running awkwardly, passing the skiers even though she was still wearing snowshoes. Within seconds, all five were hovering over a misshapen opening in the ice about six feet long and four feet wide. There was no sign of Gruber. He'd been swallowed up by the lake.

As the senior ranger in the group and Gruber's bedmate, Kelly didn't hesitate to take charge. Before anyone else did more than gasp and look for movement in the dark water, Kelly removed her backpack and undressed down to her thermal underwear. She removed a high-powered stiletto LED flashlight from her backpack.

"Do any of you have any strong rope or cord to tie around me? Carl's wearing a heavy pack and snowshoes. I'm sure he's disoriented and panicking and can't find this fucking opening."

Dr. Willis, a fifty-something MTU research scientist with the physique of a distance runner and more knowledge of wolves than any living human, pulled two three-foot bungee cords and a hundred feet of tightly wound non-dry rope out of a toolbox tethered to the sled. "I don't think the bungee cords will help much, but I never go hiking or climbing without this rescue rope."

"You're a genius," said Kelly, as she wrapped an end of the rope around her waist and secured it with a bowline knot. "Doc, you and Paul hold on to my lifeline. If I tug it, pull me up. If I don't resurface with Carl in two minutes, pull me up."

Before anyone could argue or object, she dove into the freezing water, knowing she only had about a minute to find Carl and avoid hypothermia and death. With over a foot of snow covering most of the ice, there was almost no natural light under the water. With the high-intensity light, Kelly quickly found a moving target and focused on her large companion. Gruber had jettisoned his backpack and poles and was pushing against the ice in what seemed like slow motion. The big veterinarian had run out of air and stamina and was about to give up.

Kelly scissor-kicked over to Carl and grabbed his wrist. She wasn't sure he was conscious enough to recognize her, but that didn't matter. She tugged on the rope while maintaining a firm grip on his arm, and then wrapped her flashlight arm around his waist. Gruber was limp.

Waving her flashlight at the rocky darkness below, Kelly observed that the water wasn't deep, maybe twelve to fifteen feet. Then she saw it, a body floating or, more accurately, gently bobbing just above the lake bottom. It was facedown and appeared to be wearing shorts, since its bare white legs were easy to distinguish in the artificial light. Before the image fully registered in her brain, she and Carl were being hoisted up through the opening in the ice.

"Are you okay?" Paul Jusczak asked Kelly, as he literally set her down on the snow and untied the rope around her waist. "We found another pair of thermals in your pack," he said, taking the underwear out of his jacket pocket and handing them to Kelly. "I'll examine Carl and start CPR if it's necessary. Doc got out some blankets and is searching for some clothes that might fit him. The other three headed for shore to set up camp and build a fire."

Jusczak was a forty-two-year-old registered nurse from Ironwood, Michigan. He was also a medic in the Army reserves who'd done multiple year-long stints in Iraq and Afghanistan. He'd been a volunteer on a dozen wolf studies and might have been the most valuable nonacademic on the island. He'd come out as trans fifteen years earlier but hadn't experienced much in the way of discriminatory treatment in the reserves, at his day job as an emergency room nurse, or on the wolf-study teams, where he was valued and respected.

Kelly dried off and dressed quickly, wrapping a wool blanket over her shoulders. Jusczak worked on Carl, performing a combination of chest compressions and mouth-to-mouth resuscitation. Within a minute or two, Gruber started spitting up water and coughing. Jusczak helped him sit up and firmly patted his back with an open hand as he spit up more water. Once he started breathing, Kelly and Doc helped him into clothes that were a few sizes too small, sat him on the dry sled and covered him in blankets.

"Holy fucking Christ, I thought I was a dead man," a hoarse, shaking Gruber gasped between coughing fits. "It was pitch black under there and I got disoriented." Overcome with emotion, he leaned over and bear-hugged Kelly. "I can't believe you jumped in after me. Are you nuts?"

"It's getting dark," said Dr. Willis. "Let's secure Carl on the sled and get to camp. You've both probably got hypothermia."

"Wait a minute!" a wide-eyed Kelly cried out, pointing at the hole in the ice. "There's a body down there! I saw a body at the bottom of the lake!"

"That could explain a lot if it's the missing passenger from that plane," said Willis. "A two-hundred-pound body falling from a few thousand feet or more and hitting a weak spot in the ice could smash through several inches of thickness. The warmer weather this week didn't allow sufficient ice reformation to handle Carl's weight."

"That makes sense," said Kelly. "In any event let's mark this spot with a flag, and when we get to shore, I'll call Park HQ in Houghton. They or the feds will bring a recovery crew out here."

• • • • • • • • • • • • • • • •

By the time Kelly and the three men arrived at the campsite, the team's main tent had been erected, a fire was blazing, and a cauldron of black bean and chicken chili was hanging from a tripod and bubbling over the flames. Dr. Willis's assistant, a graduate student, and a newly minted park ranger on his first assignment had completed about ninety minutes of tasks in a half hour.

"Great work, you two," said Kelly. She could see the relief on their faces that Gruber was alive and appeared to be okay. "Let's set Carl up in one of these folding chairs near the fire. After we get some food in him, I'll work on his body temperature in my bag."

The two rookies exchanged a look that spoke volumes. "Whatever you say, chief," said the young ranger, "but we'll expect to hear your account of the rescue around the campfire at some point tonight."

"Sure, if I'm up to it. Why don't you help me put up my tent while I call Houghton on the radio."

"To tell them about Carl?"

"About him, but mostly about the body I saw at the bottom of Lake Desor. It might be the missing passenger from that plane."

"Can we assist in the recovery?"

"Let's not get ahead of ourselves. You pitch the tent; I'll let you know what HQ says about the recovery. Carl may need some medical attention that we can't give him, so our trip to Windigo may have to be aborted for now."

CHAPTER 33

February 9, 2020
Beaver Bay, Minnesota

HALLIE WAS EXHAUSTED. SHE nursed a glass of Jack London cabernet, sitting at the round oak table in the kitchen of a home her spouse called a "work in progress." The partially refurbished log cabin was perched on a densely wooded hill overlooking Lake Superior and Palisade Head, an enormous rock formation rising more than 300 feet above the lake. MacDonald had depleted his Secret Service 401k to purchase the rundown, two-bedroom structure built in the 1920s as a hideaway for a gang of bootleggers from St. Paul. If the property had been on the lake versus a mile above it, MacDonald wouldn't have been able to afford it, nor would he have wanted it. He loved that his closest neighbors were the deer of Tettegouche Park and the black bears of the Superior National Forest. On most days, he could see the roof over Holden's monstrous lodge near Shovel Point from his screened-in side porch. On a clear day, his binoculars could catch a peregrine falcon feeding her young or a bald eagle soaring above the tree-covered Palisade rock.

Hallie spent most of the weekend getting acclimated to her new job as Lake County attorney, which meant a crash course in criminal law and ongoing paranoia about skeletons or worse in Thomassoni's office. He'd called on Saturday morning to congratulate her, offering to get together, after completing rehab, to share valuable inside information. She asked if he remembered anything new about the attack. He said no and reminded her that Klewacki was checking in with him a few times a day to ask the same thing and to ensure the Duluth police were guarding his room 24/7.

MacDonald had his second glass of wine. After spending Saturday night with Eva Olerud, he went for a five-mile run early Sunday and then drove to his office with a thermos of Colombian supremo and a couple of his mother's homemade caramel rolls. He had two early-morning voicemails. The first was from Jayson Harris, the assistant director of the Secret Service's Office of Protective Services. It was highly likely the president would be visiting Lake County on Saturday, February 15, after his rally at the DECC in Duluth. It was protocol for someone in Harris's office to coordinate POTUS's visit with local law enforcement, and because Harris knew MacDonald from his stint at the Agency, he was making the call himself. After all the commotion surrounding the plane crash, the sheriff wasn't excited about dealing with a visit from POTUS, especially the current one.

The other message was from the attorney for Megan Holappa. The family had settled with the Vandenbergs and Holdens. As far as the Holappas were concerned, the matter was closed. MacDonald wondered if the matter would stay closed, or if some curious journalist would convince one of the other coeds to disclose what really happened during weekend parties and hookups with members of the Sawtooth Mountain Snowmobile Club. Could one of these girls, an athlete perhaps, have poisoned Ricky Holden? *No crime is flawlessly executed*, thought MacDonald, *but the Duluth cops are at a dead end. And what about Thomassoni's attacker?*

Klewacki had nothing very promising so far. Greg Thomassoni

may have had four wives, but amazingly they all still liked him. MacDonald pondered various scenarios as he halved some heirloom tomatoes and chopped romaine lettuce on a cutting board. He divided the result into two glass salad bowls, poured just the right amount of a Caesar dressing and shaved fresh Parmesan cheese over the top, all to the delight of his wife, who shared his love of tasty, quasi-healthy recipes but preferred to have him make them.

"Did you by any chance talk to Greg today?" MacDonald asked.

"He called this morning to congratulate me and, I think, to get a read on everyone's reaction to his retirement. He's worried about his legacy."

"Let's hope it doesn't include operating an escort service. I've been wracking my brain trying to think of someone who had a motive to attack him. Someone other than Liz Vandenberg, who had plenty of motive but was seen by fifty people at a campaign event after midnight when Greg was hit, and the Holappas, whom I've eliminated as suspects because they spent the entire night at St. Mark's. Klewacki will be interviewing body shop operators next week trying to track down an electric car with front grill damage. It's a long shot. First, I'm skeptical about Greg's account of his walk home. He claims there was no engine noise before the car hit him, but it was after midnight, and he'd been drinking. Second, if it were an electric car, and we know there aren't many up here, what if the owner has decided to hide the car rather than get it fixed? Unfortunately, it's all we have right now."

"And it's more than the Duluth police have on Ricky's femme fatale."

"I'll bet you breakfast at the Rustic that whoever poisoned your ex either ran over Greg or knows who did."

"Are you sure you can afford to lose that bet? I'll bet you a new Tesla that we'll never know who committed either crime," Hallie said with a twinkle in her eyes and an impish grin.

"I'll take that bet, Ms. County Attorney."

• • • • • • • • • • • • • • •

The Jeronimus for Congress brain trust sat on a taupe corduroy sectional in the three-story great room of Vandenberg's ultramodern home on Minnesota Point. The wall of windows running the length of the room afforded them an incomparable view of a full moon and infinite black sky that spawned an endless array of twinkling stars over Lake Superior. But none of them noticed. It was midnight, and they were drinking—green tea for Jeronimus, white wine for Liz and Jenny—and prepping Jeronimus for a key speech on Monday. He'd be unveiling his version of a Green New Deal at a joint meeting of the Duluth Chamber of Commerce and Rotary Club, two groups that supported the incumbent in the last election but respected Jeronimus for what he'd accomplished at Generosity Energy and paid attention to his stunning performance in the polls. And besides, he'd recently joined both organizations.

"You need to emphasize that renewables can provide both more *and* cheaper power, not at some point in the distant future, but now," Jenny said. "Xcel, Minnesota Power, Ottertail Power and the wholesale coops have abandoned coal in favor of wind and solar."

Then, out of the blue, Jeronimus exploded.

"What the fuck were we thinking, Liz? Agreeing to pay that skanky bitch millions in exchange for her silence. First, as much as I liked and respected your dad and want to protect his memory, I know the truth is going to come out sooner or later. And when it does, it will look to the world like we paid off the victim to protect the perpetrators. Second, we partnered with a family that represents everything we want to change in this country to protect the reputation of an arrogant dipshit who's at least partially responsible for Bill's death. Third, I don't—"

"That's enough, Alex, you sanctimonious prick," Liz said, refilling her glass and scowling at Jeronimus. "I will do whatever I think will protect my family and my dad's memory. If that little bitch, as you call her, or any of her sorority friends utters a word about their mindless escapades up north, they'll regret it, not to mention that it would be embarrassing and stupid."

Jeronimus didn't say a word. He stood, went into the kitchen, and rinsed out his mug before placing it in the dishwasher. Then he opened the sliding glass door to the back patio and walked out into the twenty-degree weather wearing nothing but jeans and a US Army hooded sweatshirt.

"I'd better go," said Jenny, who couldn't have asked for a better ending to the evening. "I just ordered a Lyft."

"I really don't know what got into him, Jen."

Jenny retrieved her jacket from a hall closet and walked to the front door, expecting her ride within minutes. Liz followed and helped her with the jacket.

"Thanks for all your help, as usual," she said. "I don't know what I'd do without you." Liz gripped Jenny's shoulders and drew her close, kissing her tenderly on the lips. "I really mean that," she said. "Good night."

"Good night," said Jenny. And after the door closed, "I love you." An even better ending to the evening.

CHAPTER 34

February 10, 2020
Minneapolis Field Office
Federal Bureau of Investigation

GEORGE REDMAN HATED EARLY-morning meetings, especially on Mondays when drivers were hungover from the weekend and unprepared for congested highways and black ice. He wasted an hour in bumper-to-bumper traffic on Interstate 94, driving west from St. Paul, past the downtown Minneapolis skyline to the first ring suburb of Brooklyn Center. He'd received a late-night text from Lance Whitney requesting a 7:30 meeting, just the two of them at the Bureau's field office. He parked the Jeep in a visitor's space and reflected for a minute on his decision not to tell Hinton and Whitney about the mysterious ice walker on Lake Superior.

Whitney met him at the reception desk, gave him a visitor's badge, and led him through a maze of cubicles on the second floor to his nine-by-nine workplace domain. As usual, Whitney was dressed in a three-piece gray wool suit, white dress shirt with silver cufflinks, and navy and red–striped tie. As usual, Redman wore khakis and a long-sleeve polo shirt. They sat at a round modular table near the entrance to Whitney's cubicle.

"I thought Michelle might join us," said Redman, still stinging from Hinton's rejection but wise enough to let her make the next move.

"Agent Hinton is in DC," said Whitney. "That's one of the reasons for this meeting. She and the deputy director are meeting with the NTSB today. Apparently, the cockpit voice recorder and flight data recorder have elicited some information that might be useful to our investigation. We should know more after that meeting. But more germane to today's agenda, I had to move my meeting with Mrs. Severinson and the UHG execs from this afternoon. She's a very nice lady."

"Why?"

"Why is she a nice lady?"

"No. Why did you have to move the meeting?"

"Because one of the wolf-study teams on Isle Royale accidently discovered a body at the bottom of an inland lake on the island. I'll be flying to Duluth after our meeting and then on to Isle Royale to be part of the recovery team. By process of elimination, the Park Service and local law enforcement believe it's David Hesse, the third passenger."

"I wouldn't be so sure," Redman said.

Whitney opened a nylon file folder, removed a typed memorandum, and handed it to Redman.

"As I was saying, Jane Severinson was more than accommodating. She offered to move the meeting from the UHG offices today to her home on Lake Minnetonka yesterday afternoon. The place is like a luxury resort. There's a twenty-seat theater and an exercise room that is better equipped than my health club. We met in Larry's office on the second floor overlooking Lake Minnetonka. He has a conference table that seats a dozen. It was me, Mrs. Severinson, and her oldest son, Bart, UHG's chief counsel, and the family's lawyer, a fossil from

Dingleberry & Morris. I thought they'd have more staff, but Larry was kind of a Boy Scout. Good marriage, nice family, filthy rich, but maybe he earned all those stock options. One thing is certain; the execs at UHG aren't worried that Larry's untimely death will expose any corporate secrets or wrongdoing.

"As you know, the principal reason Hinton and I set up the interview was to learn more about the relationship between the three CEOs. When and under what circumstances did they meet? Were they involved together in any investments or other business transactions? The only one at the table who was remotely helpful was Jane. She and Larry discussed everything, including all his business dealings. As you'll read in my report, she claims Larry met both Hesse and Dittrich at a chamber of commerce dinner at the Minneapolis Convention Center about ten days before the fateful night. She recalled possibly meeting the Dittrichs at a fundraiser a few years ago, but wasn't sure about that.

"In any event, the three of them sat at the same table along with a few other chamber members. She said Larry was going to the Super Bowl regardless, but he was flattered that Dittrich would invite him on a 'guys' weekend."

This wasn't news to Redman, but he wanted to know the identity of anyone else at this table. "So, he didn't know either Hesse or Dittrich before this tight-ass chamber of commerce dinner? Do we know who else was at their table that night?"

"As I indicate in my memo, Mrs. Severinson said Larry had never attended a Minnesota Chamber event before even though UHG has been a member for decades. He generally leaves state chamber relationships to his public affairs team. Chip Knapp, the president of the chamber, is younger than Larry but was in the same fraternity at Gustavus. He made a personal plea to Larry to help recruit a couple of new corporate members.

"This dinner is the annual kickoff to the legislative session. The governor is the headliner, and a panel of legislative leaders debate which party is loaded with bigger pricks. Not surprising, the topic getting the most attention from everyone was health care. Chip knew Larry would be a popular addition to any table. He promised to sit at his table and protect him from any unfriendly questions."

"You mean this Chip guy sat at the same table as our three amigos?"

"According to Jane Severinson, he did. She thought there were two or three others at the table, but Larry never mentioned their names. The chamber office won't give out any information about guests without a subpoena. I was going to schedule a quick interview with Knapp, but I don't know when I'll get back, and Hinton won't be back until tomorrow or Wednesday. Frankly, Redman, I think this is a dead end, but I thought I'd give you the opportunity to check it out."

"You're probably right about the dead end, but I've got nothing better to do this morning, so maybe I'll just show up at the chamber offices. Let me get this straight—I spent an hour fighting traffic to get here this morning to learn that the CEO of one of the biggest companies in the world has a mansion on Lake Minnetonka. I already knew about the chamber dinner. We could have covered this over the phone last night. You got anything else?"

"Yeah. The primary reason I asked you to come here. It's about your employer."

"You mean Fagos?"

"You can call them whatever you want. According to the CIA, their holdings through various subsidiaries, shell, and offshore companies and clandestine networks are much more extensive than anyone in our government imagined. Although the original ownership group was comprised of two Chilean families, the organization has expanded from mining interests throughout the Western Hemisphere to gold mining in South Africa, oil exploration and drilling in partnership with the Russians in the North Sea, and commercial real estate holdings throughout the world that dwarf those owned by the current occupant of the White House. Yesterday, Hinton attended a special meeting, a joint CIA/FBI task force charged with keeping tabs on this behemoth that CIA financial analysts estimate generates worldwide revenues in excess of a trillion dollars."

"Holy shit, Whitney. Is all this crap in your fucking memo?"

"It's not. This is highly classified. I'm only sharing it so you get a more accurate picture of your client. You see, Hinton learned yesterday that a rogue biochemist who's a visiting professor at the University of Minnesota was on a team of research scientists studying the effectiveness of an experimental vaccine on the most virulent strain of Ebola. As deadly as the virus is, no one has successfully used it for bioterrorism. Although it spreads quickly through personal contact with the bodily fluids of an infected person, unless a terrorist group or misguided nation grew the virus in a controlled environment, infected a large group of people, and then sent the infected ones into the general population, there isn't an effective way to control the release and outbreak.

"This biochemist was once a respected scientist from Poland who'd experimented with ways to reduce the infectious impact of the virus at the CDC and St. Regis College of Medicine, among other places. Apparently, while working at the U he figured out a way to modify the virus genetically to make it infectious through the air. In other words, he's created an aerosol spray or mist containing highly contagious, deadly Ebola. One of the graduate assistants working on the vaccine observed unusual activity in his lab and alerted authorities a day after the rogue biochemist met with Marcus Dittrich and slipped him a flash drive containing a formula and a small aerosol dispenser filled with a mutated form of Ebola. In exchange, the scientist received a login ID and password for a Swiss bank account holding twenty-five million. We now believe your employer retrieved this dispenser from a small compartment in the nose of the downed King Air."

Redman didn't like where this conversation was going. Here he thought he was getting close to solving a mystery, and now he had a dull ache in the pit of this stomach.

"I get why these people want to mine copper in Minnesota and gold in South Africa, but what are they going to do with a biological weapon? Are you saying they want to commit acts of terrorism around the world? To what end?"

Whitney chose his words carefully. "We don't think the organization would use them to threaten a government or a competitor. Instead, Homeland Security and the CIA believe the Saudis are the ultimate buyers. Iran has become a rival for hegemony in the Middle East. Yemen and Syria are hot spots, and the Saudis are fed up. Just like on 9/11, the crown princes and royal family in Riyadh are not out front on this deal, but they're complicit. There are government agents behind the scenes who have masterminded a deal to acquire what might be the most lethal biological weapon ever developed. We don't know if, when, or how they intend to use it, but think about the leverage it could provide.

"They never would have been able to get close to a professor at the U of M without arousing suspicion. Your employer was simply a courier. In exchange for delivering the vial and formula to a Saudi emissary in Miami, Fagos would have gained access to some of Aramco's richest oil deposits in the Persian Gulf. The most incredible part of all this is, but for that graduate student, we never would have known about this deal. Just like we didn't know that eighteen Saudi terrorists were planning to commandeer four planes in the summer of 2001."

"Has this deal been consummated?" asked Redman.

"We don't know. All we know is the vial and formula are missing."

"So, what do you want me to do? Terminate my contract? Walk away?"

"If you want. We'd prefer if you'd continue to stay in contact, continue the investigation. Of course, we'd certainly appreciate whatever intelligence you can gather without putting yourself in danger."

"Right. I'll get back to you as soon as I have any intelligence."
With that, Redman stood, slipped on his jacket, and stared down
at Whitney, who was in a daze of self-infatuation, slow to recognize
Redman was leaving despite all the fascinating stuff he'd disclosed.
"I'm off to the Minnesota Chamber offices to track down a killer."

"Really?" asked Whitney, finally standing to escort Redman out
of the building. "I doubt you'll find one there."

Redman wasn't sure if Special Agent Whitney was a genius
or an imbecile savant but concluded it didn't matter. "Say hi to
Michelle whenever she gets back," he said, offering Whitney a
perfunctory handshake and walking out the door and into the
midwinter sunshine.

•••••••••••••••

Driving from Brooklyn Center to downtown St. Paul, Redman
mulled the revelations from Special Agent Whitney. Before accepting
the Fagos job, he'd done research on the Chilean conglomerate. He
knew their empire was worldwide and their methods could be illegal
and immoral, but how was that different from any US multinational
corporation? But trading in bioterrorism for profit? That crossed a
line. The ache in his gut was intensifying.

The chief security officer for the St. Paul Airport, also known
as Holman Field, was Reginald Baker, a former homicide detective,
current St. Paul Saints and Minnesota Timberwolves fan, and
occasional drinking buddy of Redman's. Parking in a metered space
on Robert Street, Redman called Baker during his two-block walk to
the Minnesota Chamber offices on the fifteenth floor of the Securian
Life Tower.

"Red, how's it goin' old man? I haven't heard from you since you
retired from the BCA. You got some tickets for me?"

"Retirement made me edgy, Reggie, especially after Rita left, so
I started my own private gig. I thought maybe you could help me tie
up a loose end or two."

"Sorry to hear about Rita, man. That was some bad shit in my opinion. How can I help you, brother?"

"No doubt you've heard about the plane crash at the Split Rock Lighthouse up the North Shore last week."

"Of course. That plane originated right here in my backyard, Red. I didn't know any of the big shots, but I knew the pilot, Trevor, Trevor Drake. He spent a lot of time in the hangar CopperPlus shared with a few other corporate owners. I also ran into him at Holman's Table, our restaurant. He was a helluva nice kid."

"Were you at the airport that night—Friday, January 31, between, say, four and seven o'clock?"

"I worked that day but left around three because there was so little activity. We were anticipating a blizzard that night, and we got one. I think we only had two departures after three o'clock, the CopperPlus King Air and a 3M jet flying to Miami. The FAA and NTSB have interviewed the controller on duty that night and have all our records and data. What are you looking for?"

"What kind of video or closed-circuit TV system does Holman have?"

"Not as elaborate as MSP International, but our three runways, the parking lots, terminal, control tower. Really, everywhere but the restrooms and private hangars are equipped with a video surveillance system that's 24/7. We have a retention policy for maintaining and destroying the digital video in each area."

"Has anyone asked to see video from the night of the crash?"

"Not yet. Usually the NTSB is more interested in what happened on the aircraft during the flight. I don't know what the video of the runway or parking lot would add."

Redman was surprised Whitney hadn't beaten him to the punch. *Idiot savant.* "I'd like to see the video from the parking lots and area around the CopperPlus hangar for three hours prior to the King Air's departure, if that's possible."

"You buy lunch at Holman's Table this afternoon, and I'll show you a movie."

"I'll be tied up for the next hour or so, but how about I meet you at the restaurant at noon?"

"Deal."

• • • • • • • • • • • • • • •

Redman had never been to the Minnesota Chamber of Commerce offices, so when the elevator door opened on the fifteenth floor of the Securian Tower he expected to see a lobby area and hallways leading to several offices. Instead, he walked directly into the reception area of the only tenant on the fifteenth floor, the Minnesota Chamber. A twenty-something male sat behind a raised, curved glass-top desk. The freckle-faced young man with black-rimmed glasses teetering precariously near the end of a button nose was enjoying an animated phone conversation, which he ended abruptly upon seeing Redman approach.

"Good morning, sir, how may I help you?" he asked, making eye contact above rather than through his glasses.

"My name is Redman. I'm here on behalf of one of your members, CopperPlus Metals. I'd like to speak with Mr. Knapp, if he's in. It won't take long."

"Could I tell Mr. Knapp what this is about?"

"Sure. You can tell him it's about the untimely death of three CEOs from three of his larger members."

"Excuse me for a moment, sir," the receptionist said, nervously fumbling with an expensive ballpoint pen. Rather than call Knapp on the phone, he got up and walked back to his office, returning less than a minute later accompanied by Chip Knapp.

"Mr. Redman, good to meet you, despite the circumstances of your visit," Knapp said, towering over the diminutive detective and giving him an extra-firm handshake and insincere smile. "Let's sit in our main conference room overlooking downtown."

The clean-shaven Knapp was a few years past fifty but looked ten years younger. There were few gray strands in his thick, wavy brown locks. He'd left his suit coat in his office, which made him appear even taller and lankier in a fitted Brooks Brothers button-down white and blue–striped oxford cloth shirt with a blue silk tie adorned with tiny American flags.

Born into third-generation wealth from a family that had owned a lucrative seat on the Grain Exchange for a hundred years, Knapp had been educated at a New England prep school before returning to Minnesota to attend Gustavus Adolphus College and then to augment the family's success in business with a career in public affairs and politics. He'd worked his way up from intern to analyst to vice president and, after the sudden and unexpected death of his predecessor two years earlier, to CEO of one of the most influential organizations in the state, with more than 2,000 member businesses and a political action committee that contributed millions to pro-business candidates.

Redman got comfortable in a high-back leather chair and accepted Knapp's offer of coffee. Knapp poured a cup for himself and topped it off with a generous shot of cream, which made Redman flinch while he opened a spiral notebook and silently reviewed a list of questions in his head.

"I didn't know Marcus well, but no one worked harder to achieve an objective than he and his team at CopperPlus to get regulatory approval for copper and nickel mining in northern Minnesota. We continue to send Lona and the family our thoughts and prayers. I attended his service, and the chamber stands ready to—"

"I don't give a shit about any of that, Mr. Knapp," Redman interrupted. "I'm trying to ascertain whether anyone sabotaged my client's plane. I'm also interested in determining whether any crimes were committed on that plane, and if so, by whom. Period. Your outfit sponsored a dinner at the Convention Center two weeks ago. Apparently, the three executives who died on that plane were sitting together at a table at that dinner. Can you confirm that?"

"I can because I was there, sitting with Micky Lydon, our director of marketing, Larry, Marcus and David, and Alex Jeronimus, the CEO of Generosity Energy up in Duluth."

"Jeronimus? The guy running for Congress?"

"That's the guy. His company recently joined the chamber. I think to show the business community that their renewable energy play is becoming mainstream, but we're happy to have them whatever the reason. Anyway, the chamber's theme on the eve of the legislative session was health care in Minnesota and how we're leading the nation in many respects. That's why I put Larry with three guys from the mining and energy industries. Instead of talking about the rising cost of medical care and aging baby boomers, Hesse and Dittrich attacked Alex, saying wind and solar weren't sustainable, were too expensive, that they would never account for more than twenty percent of America's energy consumption."

"I don't get it," Redman said. "I thought rich guys at a chamber deal would be stroking each other and comparing sports cars and yachts."

"It was highly unusual, but I think Alex kind of brought it on himself. It's no secret that he has a disdain for the fossil fuel industry. He's sitting at a table with two men whose livelihood depends on it, and he has this air of quiet confidence and superiority. I don't think either Marcus or David alone would have gone after Alex like that, but they literally ganged up on him. Micky was so uncomfortable with their behavior that she excused herself, saying she had to attend some school function for her kids. She doesn't have kids.

"Remarkably, Alex kept his composure and made some good points with facts and figures, but these two guys completely ignored his arguments and talked over him. Alex mentioned Isle Royale as an example of how climate change had wiped out the wolf population in an otherwise controlled environment. Hesse and Dittrich scoffed, claiming we're all better off without worthless, murdering wolves, that nobody who counts cares about Isle Royale or the wolves.

"Fortunately, the governor started his speech on time, so they had to stop the attack. Then came the biggest surprise of the night. After ignoring Larry and attacking Alex, Marcus completely changed his tune. He became gracious and generous and invited the three CEOs to join him on the company plane for a trip to a PGA event in Arizona and then to the Super Bowl in Miami. His company would cover everything . . . literally everything. I know that didn't mean much to someone like Larry Severinson, but I don't think the other two are in Larry's league."

"So, did they all accept this invitation?" asked Redman, intrigued by the introduction of a fourth musketeer.

"Hesse was an immediate yes, and Larry said he was interested but had to check on some scheduling. He said he thought he was set to attend the Super Bowl in some senator's suite. But he's a golf nut, so the idea of watching the pros at the TPC in Scottsdale and playing Doral on the same weekend probably pushed him over the edge."

"What about the other guy . . . Jeronimus?"

"He was a polite no. In fact, he said he had some important meetings in Duluth over Super Bowl weekend and then wished everyone well and left. He must have been pissed as hell at the way those two guys belittled his business and the future of renewable energy. They were obnoxious and relentless."

"Didn't he announce his candidacy on the Monday after the Super Bowl?" Redman was sure he was right about that.

"That sounds right. Unfortunately, the chamber is solidly behind the incumbent in that race, though Alex has put up some incredible polling numbers in the unpredictable eighth, and his girlfriend can pretty much fund a competitive campaign without help from a PAC or other major contributors."

"Are you aware of any connection between Elizabeth Vandenberg and any of the so-called eco-terrorists?"

"The chamber keeps a close eye on activist groups because they can wreak havoc with our members. Liz Vandenberg is highly intelligent and extremely motivated, but I wouldn't go so far as to connect her with eco-terrorists."

"What about the owners behind CopperPlus? What does the chamber know about them?"

Knapp looked dumbfounded. "I assume you're working for them," he said.

"That doesn't mean I know shit about them," said Redman. "They're richer than God and more secretive than the Freemasons. I just hope they're not more evil than the devil."

"To be honest, I know a few of the folks at CopperPlus, but Marcus was as high on the org chart as I got. I've heard stories about a worldwide network and the Chilean mafia, but that's what they are—stories."

"Okay," said Redman, not surprised but disappointed. "What can you tell me about David Hesse, the Northern Black Gold guy?"

"I didn't know him well, but there's no question he was super intense and driven. Someone told me he worked out twice a day at five in the morning and nine at night and worked at Northern in between those times. He always seemed frustrated and impatient to me. One other thing—he didn't care much about politics, but he was an ardent supporter of President Drummond, who, as everyone knows, is a good friend of the fossil fuel industry."

"What about you? Are you a fan of the president?" Redman thought Drummond was an idiot and anyone who supported him, regardless of the reason, was too.

"I'm a fan of a strong economy and low unemployment, so maybe I am."

"My research shows that both Dittrich and Hesse had been certified to fly small aircraft, but neither was instrument rated and, as far as I can tell, neither had flown a plane in at least five years. Do you know anything about more recent piloting experience for either of them?"

Redman had already checked local airport records and asked

this question to family members and company risk managers, but he was developing a hypothesis and needed to confirm a few facts before pursuing it further or abandoning it.

"I have no idea about that. I don't think Mr. Hesse's company owned a plane; they struggled to grow and make a profit."

"Thanks for your time, Mr. Knapp. I really appreciate your meeting with me without any prior notice, and I apologize for that. I have one last question; of the four CEOs at that table, which one would you say is most capable of murder?"

Turning to gaze out at the downtown skyline, Knapp contemplated this question for close to a minute before replying.

"Mr. Redman, my great-grandfather on my mother's side was a Lutheran minister in Kimball, Minnesota, near St. Cloud. His parishioners adored him, his three kids worshipped him, and his wife said he was the finest man she ever knew. In 1932 he witnessed a homeless teenager steal a bottle of milk and a ring of bologna from the corner grocery store. He grabbed the young man as he was running out of the store and told him either to pay for the items or put them back.

"The boy threw the bologna in his face and yelled, 'Then you feed my fucking family, asshole!' My great-grandfather went into a rage and beat the young man to death. He spent most of the rest of his life in the state penitentiary. Under the right circumstances, anyone is capable of murder, Mr. Redman. But most capable? If looks could kill, Jeronimus would have murdered both Hesse and Dittrich at the dinner that night."

CHAPTER 35

February 10, 2020
Duluth, Minnesota

AFTER SPENDING MOST OF Monday canvassing auto body shops in Duluth, Detective Gail Klewacki didn't expect the breakthrough in her case to come from a voicemail from her boss. Only two of the shops she'd visited had repaired front-end damage on electric cars within the past week. One involved a Nissan Leaf that had spun out of control on London Road and struck a tree, and the other, more suspicious incident involved the Tesla owned by Elizabeth Vandenberg.

According to the owner of Twin Ports Collision, a woman named Jenny brought the car in on Tuesday morning and picked it up on Friday. She didn't want to make an insurance claim and simply paid the $18,000 bill with a corporate credit card. The woman said she'd hit a deer somewhere in northern Minnesota. The shop owner showed Klewacki before and after photos of the heavily damaged front grill and noted that brown and white fur was lodged in the grill and even under the hood.

Klewacki stopped at the campaign office in Lakeside to ask Jenny a few follow-up questions about the accident. Jenny and an elderly female volunteer were the only ones there. The candidate and his principal benefactor were campaigning in Hinckley and Pine City. Jenny was happy to have company and shared foamy hot chocolate and sugar cookies with a weary and grateful detective.

When questioned about the accident, Jenny recounted where she was the night she struck the deer and why. She'd gone to see Walter Amundsen to ask for a meaningful contribution to the Vandenberg Foundation. Amundsen was a seventy-five-year-old recluse who'd inherited millions from his family's window-manufacturing business in Iowa. A biologist by training and dedicated environmentalist, he had written three books and hundreds of articles about the impact of global warming on animal and plant life. He lived alone in a small cabin on Birch Lake near Babbitt. Two years earlier, Liz had visited Amundsen to make a pitch for a donation. After they paddled a canoe on Birch for several hours and hiked in the BWCA, he served her homemade moonshine and started taking off his clothes, assuming Liz would oblige with a *quid pro quo* in exchange for a million-dollar donation. She wouldn't and didn't. She thanked him for the canoe ride and hospitality and left.

Without telling Liz, Jenny started emailing him, this time on behalf of Alex Jeronimus. The old man was enthusiastic about Jeronimus's candidacy and told Jenny he would make a sizable contribution if she'd spend a day with him. She did and he did, but on the way home, she hit a big doe on County Highway 70 about ten miles from Babbitt. She was glad that the deer seemed to bounce off the Tesla and bound into the woods. Though she was embarrassed to return the car to Liz with a big dent in the grill, her success with Amundsen more than made up for it.

Klewacki enjoyed the story, believing most of it to be true. She also appreciated Jenny's spunkiness and wicked sense of irony. Even though the investigation was going nowhere, she'd eliminated two minor leads.

As she climbed into her Explorer to return to Two Harbors, Klewacki wondered whether Greg Thomassoni's recollection of a silent vehicle was leading her on a wild goose chase. He said he'd consumed a few beers that night, but of course Klewacki had to check for herself. Over three hours, he had one martini, three sixteen-ounce Grain Belt tap beers, and a cognac—not that much for an experienced drinker like Thomassoni. Even so, he could have been distracted by the wind, by an airplane or even by his own thoughts. While puzzling this, she listened to a recent voicemail message from her boss on her Bluetooth:

"Hey, Gail, it's Mac. Just got the strangest call from Denny Logstrom over at Denny's Auto Body on Third Avenue. Denny lives in the same apartment complex as Greg and heard about his accident. Yesterday, a woman brings in a '67 Volkswagen Squareback with a huge crease in the hood. I guess the engine is in the back of those things.

"Anyway, she claims her eighty-eight-year-old father was driving home from Pier's End Tavern after midnight about a week ago, probably drunker than a fiddler's bitch, and hit a large animal on Sixth Street. According to her, he's maintained the old buggy for fifty years and now the front end is so misaligned it's not drivable. She's visiting from the Cities for a few days and wants to fix it for him. Denny says it was the same night on the same street as Greg's hit and run. I told him my best detective would be by to see him. He's open until six tonight. Thanks."

Hmmm, thought Klewacki, *drunker than a fiddler's bitch? Where did he pick that up?*

CHAPTER 36

AFTER SWAPPING A FEW stories about their escapades as St. Paul homicide detectives over spicy black bean soup and chicken salad sandwiches, Redman and Reggie Baker sat in the airport's security control center watching four large smart TVs play digital videos from the late afternoon and early evening of January 31, 2020. The cameras shot video from the east and west sides of the parking lot, the two runways in use that night, and the common area around four hangars. For the most part there was no human activity except for airport employees. Blowing snow made visibility less than ideal.

At about 4:30, a tall man wearing a Vikings cap and an open down jacket was dropped off in front of the airport terminal. He was carrying a large duffel bag with a shoulder strap.

"That's Trevor Drake," said Baker. "He'll spend some time in the terminal before going out to the hangar. If the three passengers have golf clubs, they'll get dropped off closer to the CopperPlus hangar."

Baker was right about that. The three men, none of them dressed for winter, were all dropped off with various suitcases, golf clubs and briefcases. Severinson's driver carried all his bags aboard the King Air. Dittrich's clubs must have been delivered earlier. He carried only a small duffel and a laptop case.

"Well," said Baker, "the pilot and three passengers have been accounted for and are on the aircraft. Is that about it?"

"The plane doesn't take off for another forty minutes," said Redman. "Do you mind if I keep watching for a while?"

"You go right ahead, Red. I've got to make my rounds and make a few calls. I'll be back in thirty minutes or so. There's soda and water in that mini-fridge in the corner."

"Thanks, Reggie. I promise not to steal anything."

Fifteen minutes later, Redman's patience and perseverance were rewarded.

"Jesus fucking Christ!" he said. "I knew it; I fucking knew it!" He stopped the video at various stages and snapped photos with his cell phone. Then he made notes of what he saw and what he thought it meant. He watched the screens until the King Air was swallowed up by the dark wintry sky.

Baker returned to the room about an hour later. Redman was gone, but he'd left a note.

Thanks for your help, Reg. Please retain the video, and, if possible, email a copy of the last hour to me. I'll be in touch. Red

CHAPTER 37

February 10, 2020
Isle Royale National Park

THERE WAS SOME GOOD news and bad news for Carl Gruber after Kelly Ann Kinnear braved the frigid waters of Lake Desor to save him. He was alive, but had developed chills and a low-grade fever Sunday night, and there was no way to get him appropriate medical care until Monday. Paul Jusczak gave him Tylenol for the fever, and Kelly gave him soup and hot tea to maintain hydration and comfort him. A thorough examination would have to wait, including an EMG and psychometric testing to determine whether he'd suffered any permanent damage from being underwater for eight to ten minutes. After his fever subsided, Kelly removed his clothes and then hers and crawled in next to him in a double sleeping bag, skin on skin, hoping to create a healing symbiosis. That may or may not have occurred, but they slept like hibernating bears for nearly ten hours.

Shortly before noon on Monday, a helicopter from St. Mark's landed on Lake Desor, carrying a paramedic and two experienced divers from the Coast Guard station in Duluth. Two NPS park rangers who'd been tagging moose and making repairs to the visitor's center at Windigo arrived about an hour later with Lance Whitney. He'd chartered a plane out of Two Harbors and, after a drafty and bumpy ride, renewed his vow that after this assignment he'd never fly in a small plane again.

The recovery effort started at one and was over three hours later. The well-preserved body of David Hesse, cold but otherwise remarkably lifelike, was encapsulated in a heavy plastic body bag and placed on a stretcher for transport to the helicopter and ultimately to the morgue at St. Mark's. Similar to the other fallen CEOs, Hesse was wearing shorts and a golf shirt, but his had the NBG logo, a black grizzly bear with a gold oil rig in his palm, prominently displayed over his heart.

Gruber wasn't thrilled at the prospect of sharing a ride on the copter with a corpse, but Kelly and the paramedic convinced him that he needed to get checked out in Duluth. He was more disappointed by Kelly's polite, noncommittal response to his marriage proposal.

"I never marry men whose lives I've saved," she teased while helping him with an overnight bag she'd packed for his trip to St. Mark's. "I'll find a way to get to Duluth and be your Valentine next weekend, I promise." He embraced her like a man who'd gained a new appreciation for life and love and maybe lust.

Whitney was hoping to hitch a ride with the helicopter, but adding Hesse's body and Gruber took up all the available space. He'd head to Windigo with Kelly and her team, who decided to continue their trek to the west side of the island. On the plus side, Whitney was happy to spend more time with Jusczak, with whom he'd become infatuated. One of the divers had recovered Gruber's snowshoes from the Lake. Whitney had struggled with cross-country skis on the trip from Windigo, so he was grateful when Jusczak suggested the switch and found a pair of extra-long poles for the tall special agent.

The group of six had a three-to-four-hour hike along Minong Ridge to their destination. Interested in learning more about the big investigation, Kelly stayed close to Whitney.

"Was it my imagination, or was there a bullet hole in the back of that guy's head, near his right ear?" Kelly asked Whitney, who wasn't prepared for the question.

"I'm not sure. An autopsy will determine how he died."

"But what do you think?" she pressed. "I read where the pilot and the other two passengers had been shot. Now, if this guy has a bullet in his head, that means that one of the four men on that plane took his own life, probably after shooting the other three. Right?"

"You must have majored in deductive reasoning at ranger school." Whitney smirked. "I'll guarantee you the FBI will figure out what happened on that plane, and soon."

"You must have majored in being a dick," said Kelly, as she accelerated her pace and left Whitney, not quite filling Gruber's snowshoes, slogging like an amateur in the deep snow.

CHAPTER 38

RECURRING NIGHTMARES REPLAYED HORRIFIC events from his past. For years they were confined to the Humvee ride in Afghanistan, when in an instant an IED obliterated his best friend's head, and to other traumatic episodes from the summer of 2009, when, as part of a parachute regiment, he led a platoon of infantry paratroopers in bloody skirmishes with Taliban guerrillas over control of a strategically crucial area southeast of Kandahar in the Arghandab Valley, an area aptly called the devil's playground. He had lost half his men and, in the darkest days, any concern for his own welfare. Part coping mechanism and part survival instinct, an inner, demonic rage transformed him into a killing machine in the sweltering heat that often reached 120 degrees. He single-handedly killed more than a hundred Taliban fighters, often in hand-to-hand combat, slaughtering more Taliban with a knife and his bare hands than with his M4 carbine. He survived when he was certain he wouldn't.

More than ten years after that summer, a summer he'd been trying to forget with a new life and renewed purpose after an honorable discharge from the service, the intensity of the nightmares returned, but the scene was no longer the sweltering desert of Afghanistan; the scene was a blizzard on a frozen sea, where more danger lurked than in any Middle Eastern hellhole.

The rage he'd suppressed, kept below a simmer for a decade, boiled over at a business dinner in Minneapolis. The state chamber of commerce had been courting Generosity for years. A liberal Democrat, he didn't embrace many of the business group's priorities or vote for politicians their PAC supported, but if his mission included persuading the wider business community of the dire emergency presented by the climate and the urgent need for an about-face away from fossil fuels and toward sustainable renewables, then he needed to infiltrate the opposition and convert them one by one. So, Generosity joined the chamber, and he accepted Chip Knapp's invitation to attend the chamber's annual Legislative Session Priorities Dinner and to sit at Knapp's table alongside Dittrich, Hesse, and Larry Severinson. He even said he'd consider joining the board of directors.

Hesse and Dittrich attacked him and Generosity from the outset, downplaying the impact human activity had on atmospheric changes and questioning the ability of wind and solar power to meet America's growing energy needs. What he didn't know was that both men had been drinking heavily since arriving at the Convention Center three hours before the dinner.

Hesse was an incredible prick, telling him that the prior administration had propped up his little company with subsidies and advantages and that renewables would never account for more than a pittance of total consumption. Then, when he mentioned the plight of the wolf population on Isle Royale, Dittrich laughed in his face.

"Those fuckin' predators do nothing good in the world. We'd be better off if they became extinct, and the weather has nothing to do with it. Not a fucking thing to do with it."

He knew rage was destructive, but it overwhelmed his judgment. And then when Dittrich had the audacity to invite him on a boys' weekend, a fucking boondoggle, after spending the evening belittling his life's work and denying the undeniable scientific evidence, he politely declined the invitation and left but, before reaching the parking ramp, began plotting his revenge. For a moment he reflected on the fact that he'd be announcing a run for Congress in less than a week, but that didn't quell the rage or dampen his resolve. He was making a terrible mistake, an irreversible, terrible mistake.

•••••••••••••••

Jeronimus had flown Cessnas and Pipers and even a Citation but never a King Air. He'd studied the instrument panel and avionics in a simulator at the Duluth airport and in a used owner's manual he'd ordered on Amazon. He was amazed at how easy it was to maneuver and program. Planning had always been his strong suit. Devising a detailed, ambitious plan and then executing. Once he committed, it was do or die, literally. It was one of the reasons he became the CEO of the most successful renewable energy firm in the country at thirty-six and participated in three or four Ironman triathlons every year.

His mother spent January and most of February in a rented condo in Tucson, so he used her garage in Eden Prairie to collect and store the equipment for his trip. He studied maps and weather patterns and the reported route of the wolves who traveled from Isle Royale to the mainland on an ice bridge. Realistically, he had no better than a 50/50 chance of survival, but that didn't deter him, not in the least.

The easiest part of the execution took place on the plane. The three men were clearly shocked and confused when he walked up the steps and into the cabin of the King Air about fifteen minutes before takeoff. As suggested by their host, Severinson and Hesse were dressed in casual summer attire. He wore lined nylon stretch pants and a waterproof Gore-Tex down-insulated jacket. He carried a small duffel bag and a backpack.

"I changed my mind about the trip, guys, if that's okay," he'd said apologetically. Dittrich was completely taken aback and pissed but tried not to show it. Instead, he merely questioned the attire of his unexpected guest.

"It was eighty-five today in Scottsdale, pal. I think you might be overdressed."

He kept his cool and explained that he planned to take a side trip to Sedona for some hiking and hang-gliding. All of them were invited to join him. Dittrich didn't really give a shit and hoped he'd get lost in Arizona and miss the trip to Miami.

When Trevor walked back to check on the group before takeoff, he was also caught off guard by the fourth passenger in the cold-weather getup.

"Good evening, sir. I'm Trevor Drake, CopperPlus's pilot. I was told we'd have three passengers today. I guess we've got four. Is that right, Mr. Dittrich?"

"That's right, Trevor. Is there a problem with that?"

"No sir. I've closed the cargo hold, so if our new passenger has any excess luggage that needs to be stowed, it might delay us a few minutes."

"I'll keep everything in the cabin if that's okay with you."

"That's fine, sir." Trevor cleared his throat to get everyone's attention. "Gentlemen. The flight might be a little bumpy until we get down into central Iowa. Prevailing northeast winds will be helping, so we might get into Phoenix early. Refreshments are in the fridge and on the table in the back. Enjoy the flight."

After some small talk before takeoff, he buried his head in a magazine, *The Economist*, while Dittrich and Hesse had an animated conversation and Severinson read a golf magazine and took a nap. He didn't say another word until the plane was fifty miles past Omaha.

Dittrich had bragged at the chamber dinner about his Ruger LC9, saying he always packed it and was always ready to use it.

"Hey, Marcus. You didn't bring that fancy pistol on this trip, did you?"

Within ten seconds Dittrich handed him a compact gray-and-baby-blue Ruger with a full magazine. He quickly inspected the weapon and during the next ninety seconds fired four shots. An eerie silence followed, but nobody noticed. There was blood everywhere; it continued to ooze onto the floor of the cabin for the next hour. The lone survivor methodically turned the King Air 180 degrees and lowered its cruising altitude, utilizing touch-screen flight planning and guidance technology to reprogram the destination and avoid common flight patterns of commercial carriers. Given the weather along the route, he wasn't worried about encountering other small aircraft at 8,000 feet.

Flying over rural Wisconsin, he started preparing for an exit, opening his duffel bag and backpack and removing everything. He added Crampon ice-cleat traction grips to his lightweight hiking boots and made sure he had a windproof ski mask and Arc'teryx Alpha gloves stuffed in his jacket pockets along with an amphibian compass. Wearing a dry suit under his winter gear, he was already sweating, so he dropped the temperature inside the King Air to sixty. He placed two water bottles, two lighters, two Black Diamond storm headlamps and one change of clothes in his duffel bag along with two collapsible carbon-fiber trekking poles.

The plane was over Lake Superior and flying at 3,500 feet. He had anticipated dumping a quarter tank of fuel, but blistering headwinds had impacted consumption, which was a good thing. Once over the lake, he encountered stronger, swirling winds that made it difficult to stay on course. He took full control about thirty miles from the initial destination. Based on the plane's electronic maps, charts and readings, he believed it was flying due west down the center of Isle Royale. The island was over forty miles long but only five to ten miles wide. He locked in his course and maneuvered the three dead passengers next to the exit in the back of the cabin. With zero visibility and blizzard conditions, this would be total guesswork. Tethering himself to one of the front seats with a utility cord he found in the cockpit, he opened the door and used his feet to kick the men out one at a time. He counted on the wind to distribute them somewhere on or near the island. Not what he had intended, but what conditions allowed.

Stretched out as far as the utility cord would go, he used all the strength in his arms and shoulders to close the door to stabilize the plane for the final minutes. He discharged the remaining fuel and checked the plane's course and alignment. He was running out of island. His plan had the plane crashing into the lake about five miles southeast of Tofte and, optimally, breaking through the ice with only the pilot on board, but all bets were off with the weather. He adjusted the harnesses of one of two lightweight, low-profile egress parachutes he'd purchased. He tied the small duffel to his waist, reopened the cabin door and jumped.

• • • • • • • • • • • • • • • •

According to the National Oceanic and Atmospheric Administration's Great Lakes Environmental Research Laboratory, extreme cold temperatures during the winter of 2020 contributed to an ice cover of nearly 90 percent of Lake Superior during the week of January 27 to February 2, whereas the historical average ice cover during this period was about 50 percent. Some homesick wolves took advantage of these conditions but probably picked a better day to do it.

Jeronimus had minimal ability to steer the parachute to avoid landing in trees. He'd planned to use lights from the closed Windigo Visitor Center to guide his landing onto the rocky shore of Washington Harbor on the far-west edge of Isle Royale. He never saw a light of any kind from the air, only dancing snowflakes and darkness. He felt the wind alter his course, so he steered against its effects and braced for a hard landing in the trees, on ice, or worse.

He made a hard landing on the ice a few hundred yards west of the main island, near the shore of Washington Island. At first, he thought his left leg might be broken, but the sharp pain below his knee subsided quickly in the cold. A hairline fracture would be the least of his challenges.

He checked the placement and condition of his gear and clothing and took a headlamp, the compass and ski poles out of the duffel. Orienting his position, he identified Washington Island and the Rock of Ages Lighthouse west of his landing point. His ultimate destination was Hat Point near Voyageurs' Marina, but anywhere close to the Grand Portage Indian Reservation would be a minor miracle.

There was no open water in sight, but even with the headlamp, visibility was severely limited. The temperature was below zero, and with wind gusts pelting him with snow, he'd be fortunate to cover two miles in an hour. He used a compact hunting knife hidden in one of his boots to slice the parachute into small pieces and let the wind take care of dispersal.

Jeronimus wasn't sure he could distinguish between ice, heaving ice and open water, especially at first. He figured he might survive falling into the deep water once but not a second time. The first ten miles of his twenty-mile trek would be the most difficult. At that point, lights from the mainland might come into view, and the predawn sun would subtly illuminate the variable whites and grays of the frigid seascape.

He tried to develop a repeatable pattern—consult the compass and then, using a ski pole like a blind man with a cane, tap the ice five to seven feet ahead of him and take steps in the wake of his pole. He'd count out a hundred steps and then check the compass again. His toes became numb within the first thirty minutes, his fingers within the first hour. The cleats worked well on the ice, but the ice was rarely smooth. There were small mounds of heaved ice, shards, and piles of ice, one that he tripped over and cut his chin. In some places the snow was two or three feet deep with random drifts and ridges.

It was the most haunting experience of his extraordinary life. He wanted desperately to run but knew that to have any chance of surviving he had to follow the pattern. Rarely did he let his concentration drift from the task at hand; this had always been his forte, but even he couldn't suppress random, flickering thoughts—about his mother, the only truly good person in his life, about Liz, the woman who was using him while he reciprocated, about the carnage aboard the King Air. No remorse. Severinson was a rich pig but didn't deserve to die, and neither did the young pilot. Collateral damage.

Two hours into the trek, he was two steps away from certain death. Instead of snow or ice stinging his face, he was sprayed with freezing water. Massive ice floes had broken off, creating treacherous crevices of open water directly in his path to Grand Portage. The howling northeast gale had spit in his face but probably saved his life. He was forced to change course and travel southwest of the desired route. He could hear chunks of ice falling into the open water, which, unbeknownst to him, was a mind-boggling quarter mile deep beneath his feet. He literally ran away from the floes, knowing he might be running straight into open water in the other direction. But only for a minute or two. He was too disciplined not to stop and assess where he was and what he needed to do.

Returning to the pattern, he started gaining traction, moving faster as the storm subsided, especially when he could see lights from Hovland and Grand Portage. Still eight miles to go at 6:00 a.m., he would make better time in the daylight. He suffered severe frostbite at the extremities and on his ears, but the emotional high that coincided with improving prospects of completing the mission made him oblivious to pain. He decided to swing northeast, away from the sparsely populated shoreline and closer to the reservation and the Canadian border, where no one would notice his triumphant footprints on the frozen shore.

At noon he'd be taking a hot shower in the room he'd reserved at the Outpost Motel in Covill, a forgotten transient town between Grand Marais and Grand Portage named after a forgotten Civil War hero, William J. Covill Jr. No one knew or cared about what he was doing in Covill. Besides, he'd been hiking and winter camping on Eagle Mountain and would meet Liz for dinner at the Crooked Spoon in Grand Marais. *Is all this real, or is it a lie or a dream?* Sometimes it was difficult to distinguish. As far as he knew, only one other living person knew that he hadn't been hiking on Eagle Mountain, the same person who dropped him off at Holman field— the person who'd been driving the Humvee that day.

CHAPTER 39

February 10, 2020
Two Harbors, Minnesota

AFTER INTERVIEWING DENNY LOGSTROM and inspecting the Squareback, Gail Klewacki was convinced the old Volkswagen had been the instrument of Greg Thomassoni's near destruction. She also believed the driver had no idea he'd hit a fellow human. He'd been laser-focused on getting home and, at one o'clock in the morning, thought he hit an animal. That didn't mean that there shouldn't be consequences—that he shouldn't be prosecuted or that he should ever drive again. However, after a day of chasing dead-end leads, she and her boss agreed it was time to pass the baton to him.

Carl Heinrich "Henry" Rieke was born in Dusseldorf, Germany, in 1932. His father ran a successful farm-implement shop, and his mother was a bookkeeper for the family business. When he was seven, his parents got into a violent dispute with the regional director of the Reich Ministry for Weapons, Munitions and Armaments, who wanted to turn their farm-equipment building into a warehouse for tanks and other war machinery. The director was a Nazi, literally. The local authorities explained to young Henry that his parents had been killed in an accident. Even at seven, he knew that was a lie.

Henry was an only child without a living grandparent. A French aunt smuggled the boy out of Germany by way of Sweden and sent him to live with his mother's oldest brother and his American wife, in Two Harbors. Like his German uncle, Henry became an electrician and worked for the Duluth, Missabe and Iron Range Railway, and later Burlington Northern for forty years. He and his wife, Hilda, an antique-furniture dealer, had two daughters and six grandchildren. Henry loved German cars—Mercedes, BMWs and Volkswagens— and took meticulous care of the '67 Squareback, his car, and a 1970 Mercedes-Benz 280SE, Hilda's car. After Hilda died in 2015, Henry sold the Mercedes because he cried every time he drove it. He'd been retired from Burlington since 1996, helping Hilda with her restoration business and visiting his grandchildren in the Twin Cities. He'd never been much of a drinker until Hilda passed. But in recent years, he'd been drinking himself to death

MacDonald got the name and phone number of Henry's daughter from Klewacki and arranged a meeting with her and the old man for the early evening. She asked if it would be all right for her to prep her dad about the accident and potential consequences. MacDonald said he'd be surprised if she didn't.

· · · · · · · · · · · · · · · ·

MacDonald had driven by the tidy, mid-century bungalow with an attached two-car garage hundreds of times but had never really noticed it. He parked the Explorer halfway up a driveway that had been cleared of snow and ice down to the pavement. Walking up the concrete steps to a small porch with a red-and-black *Willkommen* mat, he assumed Henry had constructed the white flower boxes perfectly hung beneath matching picture windows on the front of the house. Seeing no doorbell, he tapped a brass knocker that had the name *Rieke* engraved across the top. The door opened before the second tap.

"Hello there, you must be Suzanne."

"Yes. Hi, Sheriff MacDonald, so good to meet you," said a petite woman in her early sixties who looked him squarely in the eyes while offering a delicate, bony hand with a firm grip. "Come in and let me take your coat. Dad's in the kitchen having a piece of pecan pie and vanilla ice cream with his after-dinner coffee. I've cut you a piece as well."

She hung his jacket on a hall tree in the foyer and led him through the living room and into an eclectic kitchen with modern appliances and antique furnishings, including a Swiss cuckoo clock from the nineteenth century on the wall and a tiger-oak pedestal table with four Amish press-back chairs, one of which was occupied by Henry.

"I should probably pass on the pie, but since you've already cut it, I'm sure it's too delicious to ignore."

Hearing MacDonald's voice before seeing him enter the room, Henry shot out of his chair and stood at attention like a twenty-year-old soldier. Always slender, the bald little man in a checked flannel shirt and jeans had lost an inch or three from his six-foot frame but still had a twinkle in his bright-blue eyes and a deep, resonant voice.

"I'm ready to do the time, Sheriff. I thought it was a raccoon that I hit, but Suzanne says it was the county attorney of all the damn luck. I'm so sorry, so sorry, Sheriff. Since Hilda's been gone, I'm not the same. I'm just an old fool."

MacDonald gently cupped Henry's right shoulder with his extra-large paw.

"Why don't we sit down and talk about this over pie and coffee, Mr. Rieke?"

Suzanne had already poured the sheriff a cup of Folger's, Henry's favorite brew. It was twice as strong as she liked, but her dad insisted she use two tablespoons of grounds per cup instead of the one that normal folks used.

"It's really strong, Sheriff, so I can get you cream and sugar if you'd like."

"It can't be too strong for me," said MacDonald, waiting for the old man to get comfortable in his chair before sitting and taking a sip of hot coffee. He and Henry had at least one thing in common.

"Mr. Rieke, you won't be going to jail, but I'd like to know what you remember about last Monday night."

"Yeah, sure, okay, Sheriff. Around eight or nine o'clock I went to the Pier for my usual dinner there, the special pork chop sandwich with a fried egg on top. It's not as good as Hilda's mustard pork chops with hash browns, but it tastes pretty good with a beer. They have my favorite German wheat beer in bottles. I had a few beers with my dinner and then read my book while most other people watched sports or played pool. I don't like to watch television, but I like watching and hearing people having fun in the bar. I get so lonely here. Anyway, I had a few glasses of whiskey after that and left the bar about midnight."

"That's very good, sir," said MacDonald. He could relate to Henry's loneliness after the loss of his spouse. "What do you remember about the ride home?"

"I've been having some trouble with the VW. It starts up all the time, but stalls on me, especially in the cold in third and fourth gear. When that happens, I shift down to second or even first sometimes to get it to turn over. That's what happened that night. I was driving down Sixth a few blocks from home and she stalled on me. I looked down at the stick to downshift into second and *boom*, I hit something just as the engine kicked in. I thought it was a raccoon or a small deer that ran off because when I looked in my rearview mirror I didn't see anything but white. Now that I think of it, maybe I didn't look in the rearview mirror. Maybe when the engine started up I just assumed it was an animal and wanted to get home."

"That makes sense to me, Henry. Mr. Thomassoni claims he didn't hear the car that hit him. Sixth Street slopes a bit down to the lake, so your Volkswagen could have covered a few blocks with a stalled engine. When did you discover the damage to your car?"

"I was too darn tired to deal with anything but my bed when I got home. I went out for groceries the next day; that's when I noticed the big crease in the front bumper and hood. She made a metal-on-metal screeching sound when I backed out of the garage, so I knew the front end was damaged. I can still fix a lot of things, but I don't have the equipment or parts to do that kind of work. I decided not to mess with the damn thing, to quit driving, but when I told Suzanne, she drove up here and took it to the shop."

"That's right, Dad," said Suzanne, enveloping his right hand with both of hers. "That was before I knew about what happened to Mr. Thomassoni."

"And I plead guilty to that," said Henry, shaking his head and tearing up.

"I've discussed your case with the new county attorney," said MacDonald. "She pointed out that we don't have enough evidence of your intoxication on the night of the accident to charge you with driving under the influence. If she believes you didn't know you hit someone, the most she could charge you with would be careless driving. She has offered not to charge you with a crime, Henry, but you must agree to do two things."

"Okay, Sheriff. What do I need to do?"

"First, you have to give up driving, surrender your license. Suzanne and I have talked about getting you a regular Uber or Lyft driver to take you wherever you need to go. Second, you need to visit Mr. Thomassoni in the hospital and tell him the same story you just told me. You can apologize for running into him if you want, but I guarantee that both of you will feel better if you meet."

"Yes, yes, I'll do it, Sheriff, but how will I get all the way to Duluth? Suzanne's leaving tomorrow morning. I can't afford to pay a taxi."

"Someone from my office will set up the visit and drive you to the hospital. Now let's finish this terrific pie before I have to go back to work."

Knowing he was doing the right thing didn't diminish

MacDonald's regret at ending the old man's driving days. Henry would be reluctant to call an Uber, so his isolation would only get worse. Maybe he could introduce Henry to Eva, but octogenarian matchmaking wasn't in his job description.

CHAPTER 40

AFTER TAKING FRED ON a chilly two-mile walk to the cathedral and back before dawn, George Redman spent the morning in his apartment studying digital video courtesy of Reggie Baker. He wanted to unmask the mystery passenger on the King Air flight to oblivion. Because he was covered in winter gear with a ski mask and backpack, Redman wouldn't be able to identify him based on the video footage, but if he could decipher the license plate number on the black Tahoe that dropped him off, he'd be in business.

Sipping from his fourth cup of French roast, he couldn't detect a sign or logo on the Tahoe for Uber, Lyft or any other taxi or ridesharing company. Most of the security footage showed only the passenger side of the SUV. There was no clear shot of the front or back of the vehicle until its final turn to exit the lot. Using the maximum zoom on his computer screen, he wrote down six fuzzy figures from the rear Minnesota plate on the Tahoe: *038 BXR.*

The fastest way to track down the owner was to call one of his friends in the research department at his former employer. There were other ways, but to ensure the most current and accurate information, the Bureau of Criminal Apprehension was the gold standard. He left a message for Chad Wikelius, confident he'd get a return call with the requested information before noon.

His research was interrupted; Michele Hinton was on the caller ID.

"Must be big news if you're calling me from DC," he said sarcastically, still down from Saturday's polite but definite rejection.

"It might be big news, but I'm calling from the Minneapolis airport. My flight out of Reagan got in twenty minutes early. I need to talk to you and be in my office by 1:30. How about meeting me for lunch at the J.W. Marriott at the Mall of America? There's never anyone in a hotel bar this time of day, so meet me there at 11:30."

"Are you asking me or telling me?"

"I'd like to be telling you, but I'm asking you. Don't be an asshole. It's in your best interest to hear what I learned in Washington, and I'll even buy."

"I'm leaving now. Bye." He wondered what her big news could be and if she knew about the fourth passenger. If not, he wasn't inclined to tell her, not yet.

• • • • • • • • • • • • • • • •

As Hinton predicted, the Lobby Lounge at the J.W. Marriott was nearly empty when Redman spotted her seated at a cocktail table for two. She wore a tailored black suit with a pencil skirt and pink blouse. She looked the part of the professional woman she was, not the type who'd have lunch with a sixty-something hack wearing worn khakis and a pilly crew neck sweater under a bomber jacket that was older than their server. It occurred to him that she had good reason to back out of their second date, but she looked and smelled so good he preferred to think there was still hope. She rose to greet him, lightly gripping his shoulder while giving him a cold peck on the cheek.

"It was fifty degrees warmer in DC, but I still had to wear a winter coat," she said, sitting down and opening a white nylon case. She removed a mini iPad and spiral notebook and sipped on a Diet Coke. "I don't have much time, so I ordered you a Diet Coke with a lime and got us each a chopped chicken salad. I hope that's okay."

"A couple of shots of rum in the Diet Coke would have been nice, but I know you're on duty, Special Agent."

"Funny. Except for writing the report, I think the FBI is close to completing our investigation of this totally fucked-up case. I say fucked up because none of it makes sense."

"Then how can your investigation be close to completion?" asked Redman, shocked by her statement. Now he was sure she was unaware of crucial facts.

"I attended two briefings in Washington. One by the NTSB and one by the CIA. The flight data recorder on the King Air shows that the plane basically did a one-eighty west of Omaha, dropped to a lower altitude and flew northeast through Iowa and Wisconsin before making a left turn over Lake Superior near Isle Royale. Though the plane was nearly out of fuel, the data recorder noted a fuel dump somewhere in the vicinity of the island. And for the most part, the cabin door is open for the final thirty minutes of the flight.

"On the other hand, the cockpit voice recorder is a piece of junk. The pilot's conversations with Holman Field and air traffic control are clear enough and routine, but voices in the cabin are just garbled noise. A word here and there, but nothing discernable or helpful until the gunshots. There are five distinct gunshots. The first three occur in rapid succession in the middle of the flight, near Omaha. The fourth is maybe thirty seconds later and is preceded by someone yelling 'Hey, what the—' and then *pop* and silence. Silence for the next ninety minutes or so and then a final gunshot. That's it. Someone shot people on that King Air and then flew it to Isle Royale, tossed three bodies off, and shot himself. That's what the evidence shows."

"You're sure three bodies were tossed out? You've only recovered two." Redman knew where this was going.

"David Hesse was fished out of a lake on Isle Royale yesterday afternoon. He's resting comfortably at St. Mark's in Duluth. He's been positively identified and has a bullet hole behind his left ear. Hesse was the only passenger with a current pilot's license, but he wasn't instrument rated and hadn't flown in over two years. If he turned that plane around and flew it to Isle Royale, I've got a big yellow dick."

"And I'd like to see it," Redman said, toasting her with his water glass.

"Didn't Whitney tell you he was going to Isle Royale to lead the recovery effort?"

"Sure he did, but at the time he didn't know the identity of the submerged body. So, now that all three are accounted for, tell me what you and the FBI have concluded."

"There can be only one conclusion. Trevor Drake was having an affair with Dittrich's wife. Dittrich may have discovered the affair and confronted him. Ballistics reports confirm Dittrich's Ruger was used on Marcus, Severinson and Drake. And Drake was shot in the temple, not the back of the head. We also know he had significant credit card debt and was delinquent in paying support to the mother of his child. There are a number of factors that could have led to mental instability and one important discovery of which I don't think you're aware. Drake's tox screen revealed he had cocaine in his system, just like several of the perps in other suicide-by-pilot cases."

"Are you shitting me, Michele? If it were suicide by pilot, why go to the trouble of flying to Isle Royale of all places and dumping the bodies? Why not fly into one of the Rocky Mountains on the way to Phoenix? Your theory makes no sense."

"That's because you're trying to attribute rational thoughts and motives to a desperate, irrational man. We'll never really know what happened on that plane, but there's simply nowhere else to go with this, and there's another aspect of the investigation that's highly confidential but you should know."

"Are you talking about the Ebola thing?"

"Yes. I know Lance told you about the research scientist and the vial or cannister that your employer retrieved from the plane and may have already delivered to the Saudis, but there's more and it's all classified at the highest level." Even though no one else was in the bar, Hinton was constantly scanning the room and talking in a hushed voice as she leaned in, grabbed Redman's sweater and pulled until his face was within a few inches of her lips.

"Just between you and me, I don't think the CIA director has informed the White House that we know about this. The president has been critical of both the Bureau and the CIA, especially since the impeachment acquittal. Both directors know if he's reelected, they're toast. This is a big, big deal, Red, and the only reason I'm telling you is because of your involvement with Fagos. That research scientist was here on a restricted visa, and he'll never see the light of day, except from the modest confines of a minimum-security facility in the middle of nowhere. Think Guantanamo. He's classified as a terrorist and an enemy combatant. We also know that a key Fagos operative in this hemisphere, a brutal assassin known only as Ramon, was spotted in northern Minnesota earlier this week and has recently left the country.

"But here's the most incredible part. The CIA has evidence that the president and certain family members are in on the deal, both politically and financially, but at this point the evidence is weak and the consequences of going public or even going to Congress and being wrong would be catastrophic. On the other hand, it's probably not a coincidence that the Drummond Organization has just broken ground on a massive $300 million hotel near the Kingdom Tower in the center of Riyadh, 100 percent financed by Bank Al Jazira. There's no way the idiot son negotiated a deal like that with the Saudis. In the end, the Saudis gain leverage, the Drummonds expand the empire, and Fagos gets access to one of the richest oil fields in the world. What's the matter, Red? You look like you've swallowed a turd."

"Nothing this president would do would surprise me, but are you saying that Fagos doesn't care about mining copper in northern Minnesota?"

"Of course they do. But they can find someone to replace Dittrich, and perhaps they'll get some goodwill sympathy out of his unfortunate demise."

"What, if anything, are you and the Agency and the Bureau asking me to do about this ugly mess, which is getting uglier and messier by the day?"

"Nothing more than what you'd do if we weren't involved, mainly because I know that's what you'll do anyway. I only ask that if you learn anything that would affect our national security or involve anyone other than the men who died on that plane, you'll share it with me."

"At least Fagos is paying me for being used." Redman had finished his salad and decided it still wasn't the right time to tell her about the fourth passenger. "Is that about it?"

"One last thing," she said, raising her hand to get their idle server's attention. "I'm sorry about Saturday night. I like you, Red, and I'd like to spend more time with you away from my work, but until this case is totally closed for both of us, I won't risk my career over it. I hope you'll understand and be patient." She gave the server a credit card as Red slipped his jacket on and rose to leave.

"I guess that means you won't be my Valentine on Friday," he said, preparing to shake her hand.

Hinton stood and gave him a gentle hug. She was surprised when he pulled her close and kissed her on the mouth.

"Sorry," he said, red faced. "I don't know what made me do that, but at least no one saw."

"That's okay," she said with a wry smile. "Good to know you still carry a pistol in your pocket."

• • • • • • • • • • • • • •

Redman was about halfway home when the caller ID on his cell flashed a foreign number with a 56 country code. It was Chile—someone with Fagos.

"Redman here."

"Hello, Mr. Redman. It's Julian Bande from Fagos. We saw the press release that was issued this afternoon about Mr. Hesse and wondered how your investigation was proceeding."

"It's going well. I hope to have something to report to you by the end of the week." *Assuming you don't spray me with Ebola virus before then,* he thought, smirking to himself.

"As you know, we are most concerned with evidence of terrorism or attempts to sabotage our plane by some person or group, environmental or foreign, outside of the four men who were on the plane, unless of course one of those men was acting in concert with such a group."

"I don't think anyone has found evidence of the involvement of a foreign person, group or country unless you'd include your organization, Mr. Bande. I have a few potential leads to follow up on in the next few days, and then I might be ready to issue at least a preliminary report."

"What about your girlfriend at the FBI? Will she agree with your report?"

"I don't know what you're talking about."

"We look forward to reading your report, Mr. Redman. Just remember this—we know everything you know. Everything." *Click.*

"What the fuck was that all about?" Redman said out loud. He didn't have time to reflect on that question because Wikelius was calling from the BCA.

"Chad, I knew you'd come through," said Redman. "How's my favorite criminal data man?"

"Flattery will get you a returned call, Red, especially when the assignment is so easy. Your Tahoe is a 2018 registered to a Russell Colgin of 925 Grandview Avenue in Duluth."

"That's great, Chad," said Redman, knowing there'd be more.

"He's got quite an impressive resume. Forty-seven-year-old decorated war hero in Iraq and Afghanistan, he was honorably discharged from the Army with a rank of sergeant major in 2012 after twenty years of service. He grew up in Bakersfield and enlisted after one year of community college. He returned to California after his discharge and utilized the GI bill to earn a degree in risk management. I think Russ had a little trouble getting reacclimated to civilian life. He was married and divorced in 2014 and lost three jobs in four years. He's deaf in one ear as a result of an IED explosion and has been diagnosed with PTSD. He got a big break in early 2016 when Generosity Energy hired him as VP of Facilities, Safety and Security. Based on my review, I'd say he and Alex Jeronimus, the Generosity CEO, served together. Jeronimus hired him and probably protects him."

"Is that all you got in ninety minutes?"

"No, but I know you can only process so much sitting in that old Jeep. What did this guy do, and why does an old retiree like you care?"

"I'm doing a few odd jobs for hire, Chad. Nothing big. I think Russell may have given a suspect of mine a ride to the scene of a crime, though I don't think he's got any culpability. As usual, buddy, you've given me all I need. I owe you a lot more than a burger and a beer, but I know that's a currency you'll accept."

"I got my dad's seats at Williams behind the visitors' bench for the Gophers game against Michigan. You buy the pizza and beer at the Gopher Lounge and we're square."

"I'll meet you there at six."

CHAPTER 41

February 11, 2020
Manchester, New Hampshire

PRESIDENT DRUMMOND EKED OUT a win in the New Hampshire primary. There were about a dozen Republicans on the ballot, but no serious challengers to the imperious president, who garnered 90 percent of the vote against a bunch of no-names. The turnout on the Republican side was the lightest in over forty years, though Drummond tweeted that it was the biggest margin of victory in the history of the New Hampshire primary.

On the Democratic side, the turnout was in fact the largest ever. There were over a dozen candidates on the ballot, ranging from the level-headed, straight-talking gay mayor of a college town to a socialist US senator waging war against large corporations and the richest one percent. No one polled more than a quarter of the votes, but they all had one thing in common; they all fervently believed their number one objective was to defeat Drummond.

The president needed another term to stay in power, stay in the limelight and stay out of prison. To succeed, he needed to maintain his polling strength in the heartland swing states of Ohio, Michigan and Wisconsin and, if possible, to take a state that hadn't voted Republican in a presidential election since 1972. Even Reagan, who won every other state in 1984, couldn't capture Minnesota's ten electoral votes against favorite son Walter Mondale. It was the kind of accomplishment that would mean a lot to President Drummond. It was one of several reasons he would be holding a rally at the DECC over the weekend, followed by a $2,500-a-plate fundraising dinner for more than 300 of his most ardent and well-heeled supporters in the Palisade Room of Overlook Lodge on the North Shore of Lake Superior.

Drummond's aides had informed him that the Republican incumbent in Minnesota's Eighth Congressional District, a loyal supporter of the president, was in deep trouble against a charismatic war hero who was convincing too many voters that subduing climate change and preserving the area's wilderness against global mining concerns was the paramount issue not just of the election, but of their lives. If those reasons weren't sufficient to capture the president's attention, the Holdens had invited him and his organization to northern Minnesota to do what the president loved more than anything else—*to make a deal.*

CHAPTER 42

February 12, 2020
Two Harbors, Minnesota

IT HAD BEEN NEARLY five years since MacDonald resigned as assistant director of the Secret Service's Office of Protective Operations, where, among other duties, he coordinated the operations of the Presidential Protective Division, keeping two presidents and their families safe. It was a challenging and gratifying experience, but reflecting on it with his successor on the 210th anniversary of the birth of Abraham Lincoln, he was content to be sheriff of Lake County, Minnesota.

"I enjoyed my time on that stage, Jay, but I love my job and living in this part of the country. The awesome power and serenity of Lake Superior and the wildlife, natural beauty and recreation in the parks and forests are unsurpassed in my biased view. And the people are friendly but reserved in a good way. And they're wiser and more diverse than you'd think. I've got a small, close-knit group of professionals, and we'll assist your team in any way we can. I don't envy your job of trying to protect President Drummond."

"You don't know the half of it, Mac, and it's even tougher when the First Lady isn't with him. I wouldn't have this conversation with anyone outside the Service but you, but President Drummond is the most difficult, most authoritarian leader I've encountered in thirty years in government service."

Rising to the rank of lieutenant colonel before leaving the army for the Service, Jayson Harris had served multiple tours of duty in Iraq and Afghanistan and had been awarded a Distinguished Service Cross for rescuing two wounded soldiers under heavy fire in the mountains between Afghanistan and Pakistan. He was only the second African American to reach the level of assistant director at the Service, and, like MacDonald, he was going to give it all up, and return to Columbia, which was less than fifty miles from his boyhood home in South Carolina.

"Working for this man has changed me, Mac. Made me cynical and less hopeful for a better world for my children. Last week I accepted a position as director of security for the governor's office in South Carolina. I feel bad for my team, but I can't lead them if I'm constantly being countermanded and second-guessed from above."

"I totally get it, Jay. By the way, how'd it go with my colleagues in Duluth this morning? That's the big show, right? He might be spending the night up here, but it's much more manageable."

Harris had spent the morning in Duluth, meeting with local law enforcement that would assist the Secret Service in protecting the president. The DECC's seating capacity for concerts was 8,500. Drummond's campaign staff wanted to accommodate 10,000 in the arena and another 5,000 waiting and watching outside in temperatures that were expected to plunge below minus twenty over the weekend.

"The state patrol commander, the Duluth police chief, and the St. Louis County sheriff were all helpful and prepared. The woman mayor down there is nice enough, but she wouldn't shut up about how the Drummond campaign and the White House were going to pay for the beefed-up security for his visit. I felt like saying, 'Good luck trying to collect on that one.' Drummond has a way of outlasting his opposition by being more audacious, more obnoxious and more outrageous than anyone else can even imagine."

"How many protesters are you anticipating at the DECC?" asked MacDonald. "If the weather were better, you might have more protesters than supporters. Anti-mining, anti-gun, pro-impeachment, anti-Drummond."

"Let's hope you're wrong about that. Originally, we were thinking four or five hundred, but that was before this political newcomer, Alex Jeronimus, ignited some kind of revolution up here. Now we're planning on twenty-five hundred. The fundraiser at the Overlook shouldn't be a problem. The Holdens are closing the resort to the public Saturday at noon. It's private property, so any protesters won't be able to get close to the lodge where the festivities will occur. Since your folks are more apt to know any troublemakers, I'd like to place a few of them at the main entrance with two of my best guys. My agent in charge will be conducting the final briefing with your team on Saturday morning."

"Where will you be on Saturday?"

"In DC helping my wife pack. We leave on Monday for South Carolina. As you know, the AD rarely comes out to a site like this, but I wanted to see you and give you a heads-up on what to expect. I think the cocktail reception and dinner will be fine. Drummond will be staying alone at what I'm told is the most luxurious cabin on the property, a three-story, two-bedroom log home with every amenity known to wealthy men. He's recently invoked what he calls a blackout period, meaning none of my agents can be in or around his room or cabin or other living space. And no eyes, meaning no video cameras or other means of surveillance, on the president or anyone in his party."

"Why?"

"Again, Mac, this is sensitive. Homeland Security has decided to protect POTUS on this, and it's not within my purview to do anything but follow orders."

"And that's one of the reasons you're leaving?" MacDonald had a good idea what might follow.

"No comment, except there are a number of reasons. When the president is traveling without the First Lady he sometimes has late-night female visitors. They generally arrive in expensive Mercedes sedans, stay two to three hours, and then get picked up between one and three in the morning. We know that these women are being supplied by a worldwide service owned by a Saudi prince. There's no transactional record of what the president or anyone on his behalf is paying for this service. We don't think one exists; it's a gift of sorts from the Saudis to POTUS in exchange for the administration's support for certain energy and geopolitical initiatives in the Middle East and who knows what else."

"So, it's not really a gift, then," said MacDonald sarcastically. "How does the protection team know if this blackout is in effect?"

"My agent in charge gets a confidential text from the White House sometime during the day."

"That's crazy," said MacDonald. "You're damned if you do and damned if you don't, especially with this guy."

"Tell me about it."

• • • • • • • • • • • • • • •

Redman was more upset with himself than with Fagos. He spent most of Wednesday afternoon and evening scouring every square inch of his apartment with a radio frequency signal detector and a high-powered flashlight. He found two hidden CCTV cameras cleverly attached to the smoke detectors in his bedroom and living room. While he was studying video footage from the St. Paul airport, Fagos was watching video footage of him studying the footage.

"We know what you know."

When and how did they plant the devices? That was easy, and Redman knew it. He never locked his apartment during early-morning walks with Fred. He also never locked his old Jeep that was usually parked on the street. There had to be a listening device somewhere in there as well, but he couldn't find it. Regardless, Bande wouldn't have made the threatening statement had he not wanted Redman to know he was being surveilled.

Redman wasn't used to being a pawn, but it felt like both Fagos and the feds were using him to do what they'd have difficulty doing directly. The timing of his next moves would be critical. He was satisfied that he'd earned the $50,000 down payment and would transfer all of it to the boys' college fund. His final payment would probably not be in the form of spendable currency.

CHAPTER 43

February 13, 2020
Brooklyn Center, Minnesota

"HINTON." THAT'S HOW SHE answered her office line if she didn't recognize the number on the caller ID.

"Special Agent Hinton, this is Sheriff Sam MacDonald up in Lake County. We met at the CopperPlus plane crash site up at Split Rock earlier this month."

"Good morning, Sheriff. I hope you're not calling me about that case. I'm writing up a preliminary report for my AD. It's a brutal, senseless scenario but not a complicated one. You're not going to complicate my life, are you, Sheriff?"

"I just got off the phone with George Redman. Unfortunately, I think I've got a duty to complicate your life. Besides the fact that I don't think George appreciates what he's up against, or maybe he doesn't care."

"Okay, Sheriff, now I'm curious." She was more than curious; she was worried.

MacDonald recounted his meeting with Eva and her description and photos of the ice walker in the blizzard. He said he only shared the encounter and photos with George because he assumed Redman and Hinton were working together on the investigation.

"Wait a fricking minute, Sheriff. You're telling me that there could be a fourth, unaccounted-for passenger on that plane who walked over twenty miles on that frozen ocean during a blizzard? That's preposterous. What other evidence do you have besides some old woman's delusions and photos that could have been doctored?"

"Maybe I should call someone in DC," MacDonald said, clearly agitated by her response. "You didn't interview Eva. I did. George was skeptical, but given the other evidence he and the feds uncovered, he was having a hard time accepting the conventional murder/suicide scenarios. I assume you know that the three CEOs on that plane met for the first time at a business dinner three weeks ago."

"Sure. I think Whitney mentioned that. So what?"

"So, the head of the state chamber of commerce was at the table," MacDonald continued. "George interviewed him and learned that Marcus Dittrich had invited three CEOs on that trip—Larry Severinson, David Hesse and Alex Jeronimus."

"What? You mean the guy who's running for Congress?"

"He's the guy running for Congress, yes," said MacDonald. "He was the CEO of Generosity Energy. According to the witness, Jeronimus declined the invitation. The witness also said Jeronimus got into a heated argument with Hesse and Dittrich."

"Okay. So, how do we get from there to a fourth passenger?" Hinton knew there'd be more, and her day and weekend would be fucked.

"George obtained digital surveillance video from Holman field."

"How'd he get the video?"

"From the head of security, a friend and former colleague with the St. Paul PD. George emailed the video file to me. If you recall, there were winter storms throughout Minnesota and Wisconsin on the night these guys were flying to Phoenix. Conditions were worse up here, but there was blowing snow in the Twin Cities. Only two flights took off from Holman that night—the King Air and a Hawker jet owned by 3M. Fifteen minutes before the King Air departed, a black Tahoe dropped off someone wearing winter hiking gear and a large backpack. He walked straight towards the CopperPlus hangar and away from 3M's. From the size alone, George and I think it's a man, but it's not possible to identify the person from the video. However, George was able to get a license plate number off the Tahoe."

"Sure he was."

"It's registered to a Russ Colgin. He's an Army veteran, a noncom who served as the sergeant major in Jeronimus's units in Iraq and Afghanistan. He was struggling after leaving the service, and Jeronimus hired him as the head of security at Generosity."

"Is that it?"

"Probably not, but it's all I got for now. Jeronimus is campaigning on the Iron Range today and tomorrow. I know he's scheduled to be home on Saturday because my detective is meeting with Liz Vandenberg at his campaign headquarters on a different matter."

"Let me get this straight. You're suggesting that a corporate executive who's running for Congress hitched a last-minute ride on Dittrich's jet, used his host's gun to kill everyone on board, flew the plane over five hundred miles, threw the other passengers overboard and then parachuted to safety. But wait. He had to parachute onto an uninhabited island or a frozen lake in below-zero temperatures during a blizzard and then find a way to get to the mainland. Did I forget anything?"

"He left the pilot on board with a bullet in the temple and the murder weapon at his feet to make it easy for you to write your report. This guy is a trained killer and a triathlete. He succeeds at whatever he does, and he was once instrument-rated as a pilot. He was also aware that wolves had traveled from Isle Royale to the mainland across an ice bridge on more than one occasion over the past two winters."

"You've done your homework."

"Redman did his homework. I'm just reading from notes I took during our call and filling in blanks with what I know from living up here."

"This is crazy, Sheriff. Why didn't Red tell me all this shit? I gave him everything I had on his scary client."

"Because he felt you'd react as you have. He wanted to connect all the dots and then give you an airtight case before reporting to his client. That's one of the reasons I called you. The Chileans bugged his apartment and probably his car. I'm worried that once they think they know who sabotaged their plane they'll act swiftly and decisively, and I don't want George to get caught in the crossfire."

"They really surveilled their own guy?" She said it rhetorically. Now she wasn't sure what to do. "Okay, MacDonald, tell me what you need. I'm still going to finish my report and essentially conclude that the evidence points to the pilot as the culpable party. Even if your incredible hypothesis is correct, I don't know how we prove it."

"At this point, I don't care about proving anything. I thought you could have a few sharpshooting US marshals on standby if George gets into trouble. He intends to interview Jeronimus on Saturday. If his theory turns out to be true, the candidate might not react well. The Chileans may also be in play."

"Based on the latest from the CIA, I thought those evil bastards were laying low for a while. I don't know, Sheriff. POTUS is in Duluth on Saturday, so most able law enforcement bodies will be involved in the protection effort. You know the drill."

She thought MacDonald would respond to that, but when he didn't she continued.

"Once I finish my report, I'm headed to Denver for a leadership conference. I don't want to be within five hundred miles of that asshole Drummond. Lance was delayed on Isle Royale after Hesse was recovered. I think he may have fallen in love someone up there, which is his business. In any event, he can be in Duluth on Saturday.

I'll give you Lance's cell number, and I'll make sure he has a team of two or three shooters at the ready. I'm not going to contact George, but I will check in with my CIA contact about Fagos." She had a hunch Redman would contact her in some way on Valentine's Day, but MacDonald didn't need to know about that.

"I appreciate it, Special Agent Hinton."

"Now that you've talked my ear off, Sheriff, you can call me Michele."

• • • • • • • • • • • • • • •

MacDonald sat back in his chair and closed his eyes. The call hadn't gone as well as he'd hoped, but one of the reasons was something he should have recognized but was too invested in Redman to consider. Hinton made him step back and reevaluate. While each phase of Redman's theory of the case *could* have occurred, combining all the unlikely phases into a plausible scenario was downright unbelievable. What if Alex Jeronimus had been at the St. Paul airport that night for a different reason, for a reason other than to get on an airplane? To use a simulator, perhaps. What if his ugly interactions with Dittrich and Hesse were simply a coincidence? What if Eva's photos were of an ice fisherman taken on a different night? What if the findings and conclusions that would appear in Hinton's FBI report were true— that Trevor Drake went berserk? That explanation was certainly more plausible than Redman's. *Maybe,* thought MacDonald, *but I don't believe any of it.* MacDonald was confident Redman would ultimately get to the truth, even if it killed him.

The sheriff opened the top drawer of his desk and pulled out a rectangular box that contained a present for Hallie. It was a white-lacquer, platinum-plated Montblanc ballpoint pen with the words *Lake County Attorney* laser-engraved on the metal forepart. He regretted not accepting the jeweler's offer to gift-wrap the shiny silver box, but knew his wife would appreciate his messy, well-intentioned effort much, much more.

CHAPTER 44

Valentine's Day, 2020
Lake Elmo, Minnesota

REDMAN SPENT THE DAY shopping for a new SUV. Though he never found the listening device in his Jeep, he knew it was there, and besides, he'd put over 200,000 miles on the old Wrangler that was well used when he bought it.

He drove out to Lake Elmo where a retired cop he knew operated a mostly legitimate used car business and hobby farm about a mile off Highway 36. Phil "Shiteater" Mower, a seventy-something former vice squad detective, loved to grow vegetables and tinker with cars, so in 2002 he bought his very own slice of heaven, forty acres of raw land zoned for both commercial and agricultural uses. He traveled throughout the Midwest attending auto auctions and buying used cars that other dealers couldn't move. One of his lieutenants in vice started calling him Shiteater because of the crooked scowl that seemed permanently affixed to his face. Unfortunately for Mower, the name stuck, and, fortunately, he came to like it, though he chose *Mower Motors* as the name of the dealership.

Mower sat at a gray metal desk that occupied over half of the ten-by-ten windowless office in the back of a one-story concrete block fortress that housed his sales force, consisting of the Shiteater himself, Sandy, a fifty-year-old receptionist/finance specialist/ex-prostitute, and Shiteater's thirty-two-year-old son-in-law, Mitch. The showroom was an outdoor lot with roughly thirty used vehicles, the best ten in the front two rows, cleared of ice and snow. Redman sat on a folding wooden chair on the other side of the metal desk, drinking vending machine cocoa from a paper cup. He told Mower what he was driving and what he wanted.

"Red, I've got a 2014 Jeep Wrangler 4 x 4 with all the goodies and only eighty-two thousand actual miles. Take it for a test drive, and if you like it, it's yours for fifteen grand and that piece of shit you're driving."

Redman took his checkbook out of the inside pocket of his bomber jacket. "It's below zero out there, Phil. How about I write a check for twelve and we're done."

"Okay, Red. We gotta deal."

After thirty minutes of paperwork, Redman was driving his less-used Jeep back to St. Paul. His call to Hinton went directly to voicemail.

"Michele, it's Red. I know you're in Denver, but I wish you were here. Happy Valentine's Day. I hope you meant it when you said you'd like to see me when this is over."

Forty-five minutes later, while he and Fred watched the 76ers hammer the Wolves from the comfort of the overstuffed couch in his living room, Redman got a text from Hinton.

WTF, Red! Fourth passenger?

Redman looked down at Fred.

"MacDonald," is all he said.

• • • • • • • • • • • • • • •

Carl Gruber was sleeping in his hospital bed at St. Mark's. Flown there for tests after his near-death experience on Isle Royale, he'd contracted bacterial pneumonia in his weakened condition. Wearing a surgical mask, Kelly sat on a padded chair next to his bed, waiting patiently for his eyes to open. She'd taken a few days off from the study and hitched a ride on Whitney's chartered flight to Two Harbors. He'd arranged to have an agent from the Duluth office drop her off at the hospital. She planned to rent a car and drive to her parents for the weekend after spending some time with Gruber. A coughing fit forced him to sit upright and open his eyes. Kelly moved to the edge of his bed and wrapped both her hands around his big right paw.

"I was worried you'd never wake up, handsome," she said, thankful he couldn't see how he really looked after his ordeal and several days without a shower.

It took a few moments for him to get his bearings and clear his throat enough to talk. Kelly handed him a cup of water. He drank it down, set the cup on a side table and, feeling weak, slid back onto the three pillows behind him.

"I didn't think you'd really come," he said. "How'd you get here?"

"Courtesy of the FBI. How are you feeling? I should have told you that hospitals are the worst place to be when you're sick."

"It's a little late for that. I had a fever and felt horrible yesterday, but the antibiotics and fluids have helped. I really appreciate the visit; isn't it Valentine's Day?"

"They said you might be delirious, but at least you know what day it is." She repositioned the surgical mask around her neck so Carl could see her face. "You might not be in a frame of mind to hear this, but I didn't just come to visit a sick friend in the hospital. I've been thinking a lot about the proposal you made when you probably weren't thinking straight, and when you're better I'd like to talk about accepting it."

Gruber had closed his eyes right before she moved the mask and now was definitely asleep, breathing rhythmically, with a smile on his face. That's what she focused on, as she gently stroked his cheek with her fingers and waited.

• • • • • • • • • • • • • • •

"I think it's time for you to move out, Alex. It doesn't change a thing about the campaign, but we're through as a couple and you know it."

Liz Vandenberg was at the wheel of the silver Tesla sedan, driving south on US 53 after a day of speeches, handshakes and meetings in Eveleth and Virginia. Jeronimus was reading the electronic edition of the *New York Times* on his iPad and wasn't the least bit surprised or upset by what she was saying.

"Of course, I know it, Liz. I'll move my stuff back to the condo over the weekend." It was the same condo where a rejuvenated Megan Holappa had been meeting him for recovery sex after her release from the hospital. "I need to spend the day tomorrow preparing for a meeting with the hospital association on Monday. I'll be out by Sunday at noon."

"That's fine," said Vandenberg, unaware of his relationship with the object of her scorn. "I'll be out all day tomorrow. I assumed you'd be laying low while Drummond is in town."

"I'd like to be there," he said. "But I don't trust myself not to do something I'd regret."

Liz didn't respond. She knew how true that was.

• • • • • • • • • • • • • • •

MacDonald knew Hallie would be working late, so he left work at five and stopped at SuperOne for the ingredients he'd need to make dinner. He'd already picked up a case of her favorite wine in Duluth. After a few days of unseasonably mild weather, a polar vortex would put Minnesota back in a deep freeze over the weekend, so additional firewood from the cord of birch and oak he'd stockpiled behind the cabin would be an essential ingredient for a perfect winter night with his Valentine.

When Hallie walked through the door at 7:30, she was greeted by the sounds of crackling logs in the fireplace and Ray Charles singing "Georgia" with his jazz trio through the cabin's strategically placed Bose speakers. Her husband's famous lasagna with chorizo, mushrooms and spinach filled her nostrils with a familiar aroma. He was sitting on the loveseat, pretending to read the latest issue of *The New Republic* while nursing a glass of Pine Ridge Estate's 2017 select cabernet, one of her favorites.

She dumped her coat and boots and sidled up to her man, who kissed her lightly on the lips and handed her a generous pour of the cab.

"This is all a wonderful surprise, sweetheart, but I'm going to have to pass on the wine."

"Why?" asked MacDonald, suddenly off stride. "Are you feeling ill?"

"Oh, no," she quickly replied, placing a hand on his chest. "You're not going to believe this, and I need to confirm it next week at the clinic, but I'm ninety-nine percent sure I'm pregnant."

MacDonald let the words sink in slowly and reverberate in his brain amid images of the beautiful wife and precious little girl he'd lost forever in an instant. Hallie had said she and Ricky Holden had tried for three years and then resorted to fertility clinics and tests, and accusations and frustration. And then Ricky knocked up a server at his country club after a night of partying and it was over. At thirty-nine, Hallie had abandoned hope. They might adopt some day, but having children naturally wasn't a possibility, until maybe it was.

A tear and then two appeared on his cheeks. He wrapped his arms around her waist and buried his head in her breasts.

"Hey, I'm hungry," she said, caressing the back of his head with her fingers.

"You just sit here," he said. "I'll be your server tonight."

"Okay," she said, "but you need to promise me two things. First, that you'll keep your excitement meter on low until we get official confirmation and have given this some time, and second, please be careful out there, Sheriff."

MacDonald wasn't sure which promise would be harder to keep.

CHAPTER 45

February 15, 2020
Duluth, Minnesota

THE MAKESHIFT CAMPAIGN OFFICE was buzzing with activity. More than thirty people, from high school students to senior citizens, sat at desks and around two conference tables using contact information from twenty-five different environmental and conservation groups, including Friends of the Boundary Waters, Environmental Initiatives, Nature Conservancy and the Northstar Chapter of the Sierra Club, not to ask for money, but to gather the faithful for a rally and protest against President Drummond at the DECC. The campaign had purchased a thousand pairs of wool mittens and the same number of stocking caps to distribute to ill-prepared protesters. If they could produce a few thousand hardy souls to brave the frigid conditions, they'd be making a meaningful statement.

Jenny met Klewacki at the second-floor entrance and walked her back to one of two enclosed offices in the rear of the space. Seated at her father's antique partner's desk, Vandenberg rose to greet her visitor.

"Good to see you again, Detective," she said. "Please have a seat. Jenny brought in an extra chai tea latte if you'd like it."

"Thank you," said Klewacki, "That sounds perfect."

Jenny handed her a white mug and a cocktail napkin and then, to Klewacki's surprise, closed the office door and sat down next to her.

"I need to speak to you about a private matter," she said, hoping Jenny would get the hint and leave.

"I thought you were giving us an update on the Thomassoni investigation," said Liz, "and I was hoping you might have some information on Rick Holden as well. The Duluth police seem to be at a dead end. I don't see why Jenny can't stay for that."

Klewacki decided not to press the issue for the moment. She turned her chair to facilitate eye contact with both women and told them about old Henry and the runaway Volkswagen Squareback. Jenny was expressionless during the story, while Liz smiled wistfully and shook her head.

"I would never have guessed that scenario," she said. "Now I suppose you'll tell me that Mother Theresa returned from the grave to give Ricky Holden the kiss of death."

"That's not our case, but like you, I've heard there's nothing new. I'm convinced he knew his killer, but Ricky got around; it could be any one of hundreds of potential suspects."

"Including me, I guess," said Liz.

"Including all of us," said Klewacki. "Listen, I hate to be a bitch, but I've got a highly confidential and sensitive matter to discuss with you, Elizabeth."

"Sure. Of course. Jenny, dear, why don't you check on our numbers for the big event? I'll join you, shortly."

Without saying a word, Jenny walked out of the room, closing the door firmly enough to make a statement.

"She's okay," said Vandenberg. "Just overprotective."

"You're about the last person I'd think needs protecting," said Klewacki.

"So, what's the big secret? Something or somebody else my dad was into?"

"No," said Klewacki, taking a deep breath before testing uncharted waters. "It's about Alex."

"Really? What about him?"

"Do you remember where he was on the night of January 31, the night of the plane crash at Split Rock?"

"I wasn't with him, if that's what you're asking. He went up to Eagle Mountain, up by Grand Marais. That's crazy, I know, but he's into winter camping and hiking. Apparently, Eagle Mountain is the highest point in the state, so he planned to climb to the top, camp out in his tent and hike down. Given the terrible weather, I was surprised he decided to go, but, hey, my dad was snowmobiling that night. Anyway, I drove up to Grand Marais and had dinner with him on Saturday night and then we came home."

"How did he get up there? Did you drop him off?"

"No. His best friend, a guy from his company, drove him up there on Friday afternoon."

"Could this guy have been a Russ or Russell Colgin?"

"How did you know that? What happened up there? Have you talked to Alex about this?"

"No, and I'm going to ask you not to mention anything about this conversation to Alex or anyone else until at least Monday. Can you agree to that?"

"I will if you'll promise not to tell anyone what I'm about to tell you until it's public knowledge."

"I will if it doesn't endanger anyone."

"Alex is moving out of my place this weekend. It's likely I won't see him until Monday. I'm still a thousand percent behind his candidacy, but we're no longer a couple. We'll make an announcement sometime next week, but I didn't want it to interfere with today's activities."

"I'm sorry to hear that," said Klewacki, wondering what precipitated the breakup but not intending to ask. "That's your personal business, so I won't be repeating it." *Unless for some reason I have to,* she told herself.

"I appreciate that. I don't have any other information about Alex's activities that weekend except for his injuries."

"His injuries?"

"I told him if he wanted to be in Congress, he had to stop breaking bones and losing digits. After that night, he was diagnosed with a hairline fracture of his right tibia and he lost two toes on this left foot to frostbite. All that from climbing more of a hill than a mountain."

"Do you know whether he'll be involved in the president's visit today?"

"That's an interesting way to put it, Detective. The campaign decided it's best for him to stay out of sight during Drummond's visit. Jenny and I will attend the protest. How about you?"

"I'm heading home after this meeting, but I'll be on duty tonight. That's all I can say. Is there anything else you can tell me about Alex? Any unusual behavior or activities."

"It's difficult to answer that question when I don't know why you're asking. Alex is one of the smartest, most driven people I've ever met. I think he'll be an incredibly effective congressman. I consider myself to be driven, but compared to Alex, I'm a load. That's one of the reasons we're no longer together."

Klewacki wondered if the word "dangerous" could be inserted for "driven" in the description of Jeronimus. She stood and slipped on her jacket. "I wish I could tell you more, but I really appreciate your candor as well as the delicious latte."

Vandenberg led her through the crowded bustle of the main room to the second-floor hallway. "I hope we can count on your vote in the primary and in November," she said with a manufactured smile.

"Thanks again," said Klewacki, ignoring the political talk while on duty. "I'm sure we'll talk soon."

Jenny spied the two women leaving Liz's office and followed from a distance. When Vandenberg opened the door to the headquarters, she was waiting.

"She knows," said Vandenberg.

"Good," said Jenny. "You're a better candidate."

CHAPTER 46

February 15, 2020
Duluth, Minnesota

REDMAN LOVED SOLVING RIDDLES and brainteasers, possibly because he was good at it, but definitely because of his dogged, tireless, ridiculous persistence. He and Fred left St. Paul in the less-used Jeep at sunrise. They stopped in Hinckley for gas, a snack and to respond to nature's calling and arrived at the crest of Thomson Hill on Interstate 35. From there, he had a bird's-eye view of the Aerial Lift Bridge, Duluth Harbor, and most of the port city that somebody called the "San Francisco of the Midwest."

Though it would be nice to collect the rest of his fee for the boys, Redman knew Fagos didn't care about his report. They "knew what he knew," after all, so why was he still pursuing this case? Sheriff MacDonald had already called him twice with the same suggestion. "George, let the FBI take it from here," he'd said. On the other hand, MacDonald also said he'd be in Duluth all morning and to contact him if he needed backup. That was during the first call. Then he called to remind Redman to wear a Kevlar vest and to apologize for telling Hinton, though because he did the FBI might be in position to come to his aid.

Russ Colgin lived in a two-bedroom bungalow built in the 1930s, with a detached one-car garage, a quarter-acre lot and a relatively spacious front porch where he liked to have a beer, smoke a joint and watch the world go by from the comfort of a swing he'd installed shortly after he bought the place. Twice divorced with a teenage son who lived with his mother in California, Colgin's only roommate was a well-trained German shepherd named Otto. His house on Grandview was less than five minutes from both Chester Bowl, a winter recreation area with ski jumps and sledding hills, and UMD, neither of which places he'd ever visited.

Redman took a calculated risk. He didn't contact Colgin before parking a block from his house, hoping he'd be spending some part of Saturday morning at home. Locking Fred in the Jeep and adjusting the uncomfortable vest under his bomber jacket, Redman wondered if Colgin would be packing. He had to assume so. Sometimes it seemed as if everyone was carrying these days. Everyone but Redman.

A black, late-model Tahoe was parked on the street directly in front of Colgin's house, and the plate number was a match, so Redman might be in luck. Walking the block from his Jeep to Colgin's reminded him how cold it was and what a fool he was for not wearing his Vikings wool cap and gloves. He hadn't reached the middle porch step when the front door swung open and a bull of a man stepped out.

"See the sign, mister. No soliciting, for anything or any cause. You have a nice day." In his mid-forties, Colgin was about six feet tall and 250 pounds, most of it in his massive chest and shoulders. His intimidating physique was on full display, sculpted in a black, mock turtleneck with tight Levi's worn over Timberland winter boots. He briefly turned to his left to return a wave to his neighbors, a young couple who'd just returned home from walking their shih tzu. When he did, Redman observed the handle of a Beretta M9 sticking out of the back of his jeans. He should be afraid of this ugly oaf, but he wasn't.

"I'm not selling or soliciting anything, Mr. Colgin. My name is George Redman. I'm investigating multiple homicides that originated out of the Downtown St. Paul airport, and your black Tahoe over there dropped someone off on Friday, January 31, between 6:30 and 7:00. I'd like to know the name of your passenger."

"I don't know what the fuck you're talking about. You want to show me some identification?"

"Sure." Redman anticipated the request, handing his expired BCA badge and identification card to Colgin. *It's a crime to misrepresent yourself as a peace officer, except when justice requires.* That was Redman's rationale for a lot of his best work that wasn't exactly by the book.

"Well, Agent Redman, I still don't know what you're talking about. I haven't been to the Twin Cities since before Christmas."

Redman took out his iPhone, found the still of the back of Colgin's Tahoe and handed the phone to him. "That isn't your license plate? Sure looks like it to me."

"It must be a duplicate. I wasn't there. I worked that Friday until six. Check the sign-out sheets in the security and risk management department at Generosity Energy. You can't drive from Duluth to St. Paul in an hour."

They were at an impasse, so Redman decided to change the tenor of the dialogue. Besides, he was freezing to death, so why not? "You're right, but you can manipulate your employer's work records. I think you're full of shit, Russ. I think you drove Alex Jeronimus from Duluth to Holman Field on that Friday night. Depending on what you knew and what you know now, that might not even be a crime. You can come clean with me and tell me why he went to the St. Paul airport that night, or you can continue to bullshit me and deal with the FBI. I don't really give a shit."

"Get the fuck off my porch before I kick your ass, little man. I've got nothing to hide, so I'll take my chances with the feds. You just get out of my sight."

"Thanks for all your help," said Redman, shoving his phone in his jacket.

Worried about leaving his dog in the car in the frigid conditions, he actually ran back to the Jeep. Fred was sleeping under a wool blanket in the back seat. Redman started the engine, gave Fred a puppy treat and patted his head. "You're a good boy, Freddy."

He drove into an alley behind Chester Park Drive, a block west of Colgin's house with a clear sightline to his Tahoe. "If I know this meathead, Fred, he'll be leaving to visit our fourth passenger within the next thirty minutes."

Five minutes later the Tahoe started up and moved out. Redman and Fred followed but at a professional distance.

• • • • • • • • • • • • • • •

One of the reasons Sam MacDonald loved the North Shore was the ease with which he could find solitude. He was an avid reader and professional daydreamer, and he often combined both activities for hours at a time on his three-season porch, in the Two Harbors library, or in one of the northland's bookstores.

He'd slipped out of bed at dawn and dressed quietly so Hallie would sleep late. After logging three miles on the treadmill, he ate a banana with a couple slices of peanut butter toast and made a pot of Italian roast which he poured into a thermos. Not knowing what the day would bring, except that it would be cold, he dressed in layers of county-issued winter garb, topped by a long navy parka with the word *SHERIFF* boldly printed in white on the back. His Glock 19 and an extra clip fit into an inside pocket. A Kevlar vest was in the back seat of the Explorer if needed. Ergodyne thermal utility gloves and a black cap with fleece ear flaps completed his contingency outfit.

The drive to Duluth took about an hour. Hopping onto I-35 at Twenty-Sixth Avenue East, he took the freeway to Central Avenue in West Duluth and a minute later parked a block away from his destination. Leaving his parka in the driver's seat, he walked into the Zenith Bookstore at ten minutes after ten with his thermos and the *News-Tribune.*

MacDonald voraciously consumed Minnesota-based mysteries and thrillers. Dr. Higgins had recommended Vidar Sunstol's Minnesota trilogy. The weekend store manager confirmed the three volumes were in stock, so he bought them all and got comfortable in an overstuffed armchair and ottoman in the back of the store. About thirty pages into *Land of Dreams,* he took a call from Klewacki.

"How'd it go with the heiress?" he asked. "Anything new?"

"Very, very strange," said Klewacki. "I admit I've been skeptical about anyone being able to kill everyone on that plane and survive. Plus, I really like Alex Jeronimus and believe he'd be a great congressman. According to Vandenberg, Jeronimus broke his leg and lost some toes to frostbite hiking up Eagle Mountain on that Friday night."

"I've been on Eagle Mountain," said MacDonald. "It's not much of a climb, but it was cold that night. How'd he break his leg?"

"She didn't know. But the weirdest thing is she could have protected him but didn't. She didn't have to tell me about the frostbite or broken leg. And she could have said she didn't know who gave him a ride to Grand Marais that night, but she said it was his best friend, Russ Colgin."

"It's looking more and more like Jeronimus did it. It reminds me of an episode of *Mission Impossible*, only less believable."

"One more thing, boss. There's something going on between Vandenberg and her right-hand person, Jenny Pierce. I'm not sure if it crosses the line between professional and personal, but it wouldn't surprise me if they're deliberately sacrificing Jeronimus."

"Let me think about that. Are you on your way home?"

"Two o'clock basketball game in Cloquet and then I'll assist the feds with screening guests for the dinner up at Overlook. I should be home before midnight."

"I forgot about the boys' game. Good luck. Drummond's plane

lands within the hour, so travel in Duluth is about to become challenging. Just got a text from Red. Talk later."

MacDonald packed up his thermos and books and hustled out to the Explorer, nodding to the store manager on his way out the door. Redman's text was short:

Colgin belligerent, armed, heading to Park Point. Will follow. Bridge closing in 10.

He tried calling Redman but got his voicemail, so he left a message and then sent the same text. *Red, I'm on my way; don't do anything till I get there!!!*

A text from Hinton followed on the heels of Redman's.

Sheriff—heard from CIA, Ramon and others may be back in states. Redman not picking up. Michele.

Then he called Whitney's cell and went straight to voicemail. He hoped his voice conveyed the urgency of his message:

"Lance, it's Sheriff MacDonald. I need you and your team to get to Liz Vandenberg's place on Park Point ASAP. I think Redman's in danger."

The Duluth International Airport was north of town, so MacDonald figured traffic on the freeway from West Duluth to the Aerial Bridge would be moving freely. He was wrong. It was 11:40; Drummond's rally at the DECC was scheduled to begin at 1:00, but traffic was bumper to bumper and crawling at 5 mph. Not wanting to use the siren, he activated his emergency lights and drove as fast as he could, about 50 mph, on the right shoulder, exiting onto Lake Avenue, where he encountered another backup. The Aerial Bridge was closed, meaning reinforced electronic gates prevented vehicles from driving over the ship canal to and from Park Point. It would be closed until three in the afternoon. Even so, a line of thirty-some cars stretched from the entrance to the bridge down Lake Avenue. Most of the vehicles were vacant, their occupants taking advantage of "free" parking during the three-hour closing to hit the restaurants and shops in Canal Park or to attend the rally.

The oncoming lane was empty, so MacDonald took it. He activated his siren and hit the gas. He would crash through the gate if the bridge operator, ensconced in a heated control room over the bridge, didn't lift it to let him through. Luckily for him and his SUV, she did, and by the time MacDonald crossed the 500-foot span, he'd flipped off the siren and emergency lights. He tried Redman's cell again. No answer.

Three blocks from Liz Vandenberg's house, he noticed a newer black sprinter van with tinted windows and Illinois plates parked in the empty lot of a closed elementary school. *Fagos is here*, he thought and hoped that Redman would have noticed. He passed a parked white Jeep a block down the street and figured it was Redman's new car. Fred's head popped up from the back seat.

Liz's lakefront modern was barely visible from Minnesota Avenue. MacDonald turned left onto a curved, stamped concrete driveway. He assumed the black Tahoe parked halfway down the right side was Colgin's. Looking up at the front porch, he felt a surge of raw emotion. He parked, opened the door, grabbed his parka but not the Kevlar, and ran full bore towards a stone-and-concrete porch centered by brushed-copper wrought iron railings and glass double doors. The glass had been shattered into thousands of tiny pieces, and a small, gray-haired man wearing a brown bomber jacket was lying in a pool of blood.

"God damn it, Red! God damn it! Why don't you listen, God damn it!"

MacDonald checked Redman's wrist and neck for a pulse. There was none. None was expected. He'd been shot at close range by a high-powered rifle that exploded in his cranium. He raced back to the Explorer to retrieve the wool emergency blanket in the back seat and called 911 to report a homicide. Whitney should be here by now, he thought, and then gunshots rang out from the backyard.

He covered Redman with the blanket, took out his Glock and kicked in the shattered front door. Entering the open, spacious house, he assumed the thick fellow in tight jeans facedown in the middle of the foyer was Colgin. His throat had been slashed so viciously that his windpipe was visible from the back. He wasn't the only casualty. A bearded man in a black suede jacket was slumped over the kitchen sink, as if he'd been shot in the back while filling a glass with water.

There was a muted humming sound in the place, a post-murder drone that was disrupted by the distinctive *Pop! Pop! Pop!* of an AK-47 semi-automatic rifle. The sliding glass door from the kitchen to a wraparound deck was open. Looking out the wall of windows, MacDonald saw the backs of two tall men, one wearing a black leather jacket and black wool ski cap, the other a black wool winter coat with gray leather gloves, a long, machete-like instrument in his right hand. MacDonald pegged him as Ramon. They were leaning against an elm tree, using it for cover. The other guy was aiming the AK-47 at an open garage or boathouse in a neighbor's backyard.

Jeronimus must be pinned in there, thought MacDonald. The candidate fired two quick rounds from somewhere near the northwest corner of the building. He might be a killer, but he wasn't getting out of this trap without some help. MacDonald surmised that Ramon and his two henchmen had surprised Alex and intended to execute him in the house and then dispose of his body. Colgin showed up and Ramon skewered him on arrival while the other two covered Jeronimus. When Red knocked on the door and Mr. AK-47 greeted him, Jeronimus made his move, shooting Ramon's other thug with his own gun and running out the back.

MacDonald knew he couldn't wait any longer for Whitney. He had to act. *What the hell,* he thought, *maybe they'll all surrender.* He stepped out onto the deck, pointed the Glock at Ramon's head and yelled in his most commanding voice, "*This is the sheriff. Drop your weapons, and raise your arms so I can see your hands.*"

He wasn't sure about the other two, but he knew AK-47 wouldn't comply, so as soon as he saw him pivot rather than drop the gun, he shot him in the face, twice. It was the perfect opportunity for

Jeronimus to come barreling out of the garage driving his neighbor's silver snowmobile. Wearing a borrowed snocross helmet and neoprene gloves, he raced by Ramon, kicking up ice and snow in his face, and then, skidding hard as he turned ninety degrees, he gunned the engine and headed for the lake. Furious, Ramon attempted to pursue him on foot but soon realized the futility of the effort and started swearing in Spanish or Portuguese. As if possessed by demons, he did an abrupt about-face and charged MacDonald, brandishing the machete.

Knowing Ramon would be valuable to the feds, MacDonald tried to shoot the machete out of his hand. Incredibly, he actually hit the blade, but Ramon hung on and tackled him before he could squeeze off another shot. MacDonald was six four, 230 pounds; Ramon, a few inches taller and ten pounds lighter. He hit the sheriff like a blitzing linebacker, landing astride of his midsection and quickly shifting his weight to gain leverage to decapitate his prey. MacDonald's Glock was pinned under Ramon's left knee. Sensing doom, he maneuvered the nose of the gun a few centimeters and then fired a round that tore through the Chilean's balls and right thigh, causing him to cry out in pain but not lose focus. Raising the machete over his head, Ramon never saw the marshal or heard the sound of his STI Staccato emitting a round that pierced his skull between the right ear and temple. He felt a momentary hot flash and then nothing, collapsing like the dead weight that he was on top of MacDonald, the machete falling uselessly onto the snow. Before the shocked and relieved sheriff could react, two federal marshals tossed Ramon's body about twenty feet into the firepit while Whitney helped MacDonald to his feet.

"Where the fuck have you been?" asked MacDonald, rubbing his neck for good measure and brushing snow off his pants.

"A 'thank you' might be in order," Whitney replied, surveying the backyard scene. "Where's Jeronimus?"

"He should be dead instead of George, but he took advantage of my arrival to escape on his neighbor's snowmobile."

"Where could he go? The bridge is closed, and now there are cars parked in both directions. Lake Avenue is a parking lot."

"He's out on the lake. Drove straight south towards Wisconsin. I'll call in an APB and alert the Coast Guard, though we still don't have solid evidence that he committed a crime."

"You think he's innocent?" asked Whitney.

"That's not what I said. Hey, I called this in when I found Redman out front. Where's Duluth on this?"

"Sheriff, we came on foot across the bridge. There's no way to get a vehicle across right now. It's ten below, and there could be thirty or forty thousand people surrounding the convention center. The crowds have spilled over onto Canal Park and downtown. It's absolutely nuts."

CHAPTER 47

February 15, 2020
Duluth Entertainment and Convention Center

A BOISTEROUS CROWD FILLED the seats of the Duluth arena. A larger crowd shivered, paced and marched outside, carrying signs protesting everything from the president's foreign policy to his failure to release his tax returns. Jenny held one that read: *It's not too late for a President who cares about climate!* Liz was handing out earmuffs and hot chocolate. The protests were loud but mostly law-abiding; it was too cold to fight, and anti-Drummond protesters outnumbered supporters ten to one. Whitney had exaggerated the size of the crowd. The liberal mayor had predicted five thousand, not appreciating the strength of the movement. The police chief, a closet Drummond supporter, said no more than three thousand. The truth was more like fifteen.

Inside the arena, truth was elusive. Drummond was in the middle of a rambling speech intended to whip his admirers into a frenzy of hate and idolatry. He'd already said *there are many, many more folks inside cheering than outside jeering.* In fact, he claimed the attendance inside had set a record for the largest crowd ever assembled in the history of Duluth. And he said it with such confidence and conviction. He was just getting started.

"You, what do you call people from up here, Iron Rangers? Duluthians? Let's just say the great people of northern Minnesota are lucky to have a most wonderful man, a really great, great man representing you in Washington. One of the best we've got. Maybe the best. And now Climate Man comes along and tries to scare everyone into thinking the world will come to an end. Take it from me, folks, the great things we're doing together are not going to end; they're just beginning. Look at the schmucks outside with their global warming chants and signs. They're freezing their asses off on one of the coldest days in the history of the world. The climate gets warmer some years and colder other years. That's it. Intelligent people know man-made climate change is a hoax perpetrated by the far left and leftwing media. Climate Man is just a pied piper. Don't let him fool you. On the one hand, he's trying to con the masses into believing the oil, gas and coal that have made this country great are destroying it; on the other hand, he's got windmills and solar panels to sell them. I've seen it all before, folks. Don't let Climate Man fool you.

"Climate Man is crazy, but not as crazy as the pilot who went nuts and killed three of the finest Minnesota guys ever and, by the way, three very, very good friends of mine. We should do a moment of silence for Marcus, David and Larry." (Five second pause) "There, is that long enough? You know they call it a moment of silence, but then some people let it go on and on for minutes—that's not a moment, folks.

"A few more words about these American heroes. David was a pioneer in the oil and gas exploration business. His company is producing more crude in North Dakota than Iran and Iraq combined. And my good buddy Marcus was creating thousands of good paying jobs mining copper up here, where I guess you people have the richest copper deposits in the world. The secret is out, folks, and you're going to benefit greatly, hugely. Thank you, Marcus.

"And you all know Larry, the king of health care. Nobody knew health care better than Larry, and his company is working behind the scenes with my administration to bring you something that will deliver cheaper and better health care than anything ever imagined under the terrible failure of Obamacare. We love you, Larry.

"I also want to thank the FBI for their quick work in cracking this case and getting it right. We know they haven't always gotten it right, but they nailed it this time, so thank you."

He was still just getting started.

• • • • • • • • • • • • • • • •

MacDonald didn't get across the Lift Bridge until well after four. By that time POTUS and his entourage were on their way to Overlook Lodge and the crowds had dispersed without serious incident or injury, other than some frostbite.

Engaging the services of a tow truck, emergency responders found a way to drive across the bridge about thirty minutes after Whitney and the marshals made it on foot. The Duluth homicide crew arrived in their wake. They gathered evidence and took hundreds of photos as MacDonald and Whitney provided graphic details after stealing a bottle of expensive bourbon from the bar in Liz Vandenberg's kitchen.

Liz and Jenny returned to campaign headquarters after the rally. They would remain unaware that Liz's home had become a crime scene for at least the next twenty-four hours.

MacDonald felt a gnawing in his midsection that wouldn't subside for a long time. It intensified as he watched EMTs put Redman's tarp-covered body on a stretcher. He'd removed his friend's wallet and keys and rescued his dog from the less-used Jeep.

With Fred in the front passenger seat, MacDonald drove up Lake Avenue to Superior Street, turned onto London Road at Leif Erickson Park and then up Highway 61 to the North Shore. He called

Hallie and broke down several times while recounting his day. She was sad, worried and relieved all at the same time, telling Sam she loved him and beseeching him to come home.

Next, he called Hinton. Whitney had already shared the terrible news about Redman.

"Why, Sheriff? Why did he go there alone?" she asked in a halting, sobbing, choked-up voice.

"Because that's who he was. He worked alone. You're aware he lost a partner in the line of duty, a terrific guy who was more like a son."

"Yeah, I knew. I just feel so goddamn bad."

"Me too. Red had incredible instincts, but I don't think he anticipated Fagos would be there. Not so soon. I told him to wait for me, but he didn't appreciate the danger."

"Did he have any family?"

"No wife, kids or siblings. His parents have been dead for years. I think everything he's got will go to his partner's wife and two boys."

"That's nice. Was he right, Sheriff?

"Right?"

"About the fourth passenger. About Alex Jeronimus, wherever he is."

"I think he was, but the feds will have to prove it."

"I can't think about that now. I'm in a total funk about Red. I'll call you tomorrow. I'm coming home. Thanks for calling, Mac. I appreciate it."

Driving through Two Harbors, MacDonald decided not to check in at the office. Instead, he called Klewacki.

"I'm glad you called," she said. "Hallie already told me about George and your close call. It's horrible, Mac. She's worried about you. We both are. I loved that strange little man, and I know you did, too."

"We all did," said MacDonald, tearing up again. "How were the ball games?"

"Way to change the subject, boss. The games were great; we finally won a couple. I'm meeting Ryan and the Secret Service AIC at Overlook at five thirty, so I need to push it. I'm ten miles south of Two Harbors now."

"I'm going home. I've got George's dog with me. We've had it. Listen, Gail, I don't care what anyone with the Service or state patrol says, I want everyone from Lake County out of there by nine o'clock tonight. No exceptions. If there's a problem with that, you call me right away, okay?"

"Yes, sir. After the huge turnout at the DECC today, I'll be shocked if more than a handful of whack jobs show up on a night it could get to twenty below. Besides, there's literally nowhere for anyone to protest, unless they want to stand out on 61."

"You're right about that, but be careful and let the feds do the heavy lifting."

"Okay, Mac, I'll keep you posted." Klewacki wondered about Jeronimus, but decided MacDonald didn't need to relive the afternoon to satisfy her curiosity.

• • • • • • • • • • • • • • •

Alex Jeronimus's campaign for Congress was over, but nobody knew it, yet. He called Megan Holappa while bouncing across the southwest corner of Lake Superior on a borrowed Yamaha snowmobile. He asked her to drive across the Blatnik Bridge to Wisconsin and to take US Highway 2 to East Superior. He'd call her again when he made it to the neighborhood.

He never called. Five hours later, she called the police. A day later a Coast Guard cutter embarked on a search and rescue mission looking for Jeronimus.

The captain's report said the snowmobile must have hit open water and sunk to the bottom of the lake. Jeronimus was able to jump out and swim to an ice floe, but within thirty minutes he froze to death, literally in mid stride. When the cutter crew spied him, he was upright and frozen solid into the ice, resembling a human popsicle. He never knew the president had dubbed him Climate Man, and only a handful of people ever suspected him of being the ice walker, the fourth passenger and a murderer. In fact, the CIA and FBI issued a joint press release indicating that Jeronimus and Colgin, both renewable energy advocates, had been attacked and murdered by foreign terrorists working for international oil interests.

Hinton never changed her report, but who could blame her? Events of greater importance ensued.

CHAPTER 48

February 15, 2020

Overlook Lodge and Conference Center on Shovel Point

THE PRESIDENT WAS FAVORABLY impressed with the Overlook properties and staff. An advance team from the Drummond Organization had spent most of Saturday inspecting the resort and reviewing its financials. In the end, the Organization wasn't interested in making an offer to buy Overlook; instead, they submitted a letter of intent to the Holdens to make the resort a Drummond property, which meant the name and, more importantly, the brand would be changed to Overlook Lodge, *a Drummond International Resort Property*. The Drummond Organization would manage the resort in exchange for licensing and management fees of a modest $5 million per year and a percentage of the operating profits. Richard Holden laughed out loud when he read the letter. "Fuckers," is all he said.

The Secret Service set up a command center in a conference room near the lobby of the lodge. Two agents and a Lake County deputy stood at each of the two entrances to crosscheck IDs against a master list of 350 guests and to screen each vehicle for weapons and explosive devices. There was a second, electronic screening at the lodge. Part of the protective security detail would also patrol the woods between the resort and Highway 61. Others armed with high-powered binoculars and rifles positioned themselves as inconspicuously as possible on the roof of the lodge and on verandas and patios throughout the property.

Though he only drank Diet Coke with a lime, Drummond arrived early for the evening cocktail hour and was clearly in his element, pressing and grabbing flesh, pointing at people he didn't know as if they were long-lost friends, and ogling female servers. Dressed in a black tuxedo, he genuinely believed he was the best-looking man in the room, but when your ass is broader than your shoulders, you're going to look like Baby Huey no matter what you're wearing.

The man craved attention, and this crowd, equal parts male and female, was primed to give it to him. They even wrote big checks to stroke and be stroked by *The Man*. Yes, 350 of the president's most ardent supporters, mostly over sixty and wealthy, some pretentious and some pretenders, from Minnesota, the Dakotas and Wisconsin, sat ten to a table in the magnificent Palisade Dining Room with crystal chandeliers and floor-to-ceiling windows overlooking a lighted skating rink and Lake Superior in all its frozen splendor.

As usual, the dinner had to include a number of Drummond's favorite foods—porterhouse steaks from northwest Iowa (well-done for POTUS) along with crab legs and jumbo shrimp, French fries imported from McDonald's in Canada, and chocolate cream pie topped with vanilla bean ice cream. The post-dinner entertainment was provided by a country music legend, who ended his program by saying the biggest problem facing the nation during this election year was the fact that President Drummond was term limited—that they'd lose him in 2024. The crowd erupted with deafening applause, catcalls and a standing ovation. Some staffers brought out boxes of red baseball caps with *Drummond for Life* stitched in gold lettering on the front. The president started flinging them around the room, and everyone went nuts. Then he made a few remarks, thanking everyone for coming, railing against his potential Democratic opponents, and concluding by stating, "After today, Climate Man is through, folks. Good night, Minnesota. We love you."

• • • • • • • • • • • • • • •

By eleven all the invited guests were gone. Holden sat at the main bar in the lodge sipping on Fanny Fougerat Cognac with a few close friends and family members. Drummond and his entourage were safely in their rooms, suites, condos and, in Drummond's case, luxury townhome. Following orders, Klewacki dismissed all Lake County personnel at 8:30. She stayed until the agent in charge assured her that everyone but overnight guests had left. At 10:45, she texted MacDonald that all went well and that she was heading home. He never told her or anyone else about the blackout period.

The president's late-night visitors usually arrived before midnight in a black Mercedes S500 sedan and left two to three hours later. The driver never waited at the drop-off site. At ten minutes after eleven, someone appeared on the porch of the president's three-story townhome. An agent on the lodge roof called the AIC on his wireless two-way communication set.

"Unknown near the Eagle's nest, sir. No visible means of transportation. Permission to intervene."

"Not during blackout. Continue surveillance but be prepared to move."

The AIC was the only one who could contact the president. He made the call even though it could cost him his job. Drummond ignored it, but he didn't ignore the insistent knocking at the front door.

Expecting a female visitor, the president opened the heavy wooden door.

"Well, well, hello there," he said, wearing a blood-red silk robe with fur-lined black slippers and boxer shorts. He didn't know that a sharpshooter had his telescopic sight trained on the blonde head of his visitor.

Standing before Drummond was a tall woman with waist-length, platinum-blonde hair, covered on top by a red baseball cap with *MAGA* stitched in white across the front. She was wearing a black, full-length, fleece-lined puffer coat with black boots and black leather gloves. The subtle yet seductive scent of her perfume drew the president closer. Then she opened the coat to reveal a sleek, athletic body with large, bare breasts and with nothing covering it but a red-lace bikini bottom.

"May I come in, Mr. President?" she asked, her pleading, raspy voice not much louder than a whisper.

Drummond backed up without saying a word; she stepped forward, following his lead. He swung the door shut as they embraced and kissed.

• • • • • • • • • • • • • • •

At 11:45, a black Mercedes S500 appeared at the main entrance to Overlook. The driver flashed his brights and then got out of the car.

"President Drummond is expecting us," said the bald man in a navy wool coat.

"Get back in the car and wait a minute," said the agent at the front gate.

The AIC was perplexed. He hadn't been on the president's detail for long, but this—multiple visitors—had never happened before, and he didn't like it. He jogged from the lodge to the front gate. He saw a young lady sitting in the back seat of the Mercedes wearing a mink jacket over a white sequin party dress.

"I'll be accompanying the lady to the president's residence," he told the driver while opening the passenger door and sliding into the front seat of the luxury car.

Jenny's lungs burned while her cheeks and forehead ached in the cold. She crouched down to avoid detection and ran as fast as she could. A tiny LED tactical pen light she'd "borrowed" from Alex's office helped her navigate in the moonless night. The crampons attached to her boots provided traction on the ice and snow, as she retraced her route through a half-mile of dense forest. She'd cut her leg on a pine branch while climbing out of a back bedroom window and worried that the wound was dripping blood.

The AIC knocked on the president's unlocked door three times and waited a full minute before opening it and stepping in ahead of the woman in the mink. Everyone at the resort, even Holden and his guests, heard her screams.

The silver Tesla hugged the woods just off the shoulder of Highway 61. Jenny opened the front door and fell into the white leather seat, ripping off her cap and wig and gasping to catch her breath. Liz didn't wait for her to close the door, turning onto the highway and driving north to Cascade Mountain Lodge, where she'd rented a condo to hide in plain sight and reassess the future.